The Second Target

by

Howard P. Giordano

International Standard Book Number 13: 978-1-60452-115-3
International Standard Book Number 10: 1-60452-116-0
Library of Congress Control Number: 2016935427

BluewaterPress LLC
52 Tuscan Way Ste 202-309
Saint Augustine FL 32092
http://bluewaterpress.com

This book may be purchased online at -

http://www.bluewaterpress.com/2target

Please note that address information is subject to change. At the time of printing, the address was correct, but may have changed since. Please check our website for the latest address information for BluewaterPress LLC.

ACKNOWLEDGMENTS

I owe a big thanks to Linda Renick, my alpha reader and sounding board;

Mike Dingello, NYPD retired, for his guidance concerning police procedures;

Jim Robison, novelist, short story writer, for his inspiration and encouragement;

Carole Greene, my editor and agent, for her keen eye and editorial touch;

and my wife, Rita, for her patience and support during the writing process.

Chapter 1

He saw her as a stylish woman in dress and form, someone of class. Twenty years ago, she might have interested him, perhaps convinced him to forget she was the bastard daughter of one of the men he wanted to kill—after he killed her.

Werner Schmitt fought to steady the barrel of the Walther PPK balanced on the window edge of his rented van.

The raw, late-October weather had brought a chill to his arthritic hands. From his curled position across the front seat, he watched Amy Chatsworth open the door of her Jaguar sedan, step out and brush back loose strands of her shoulder-length hair. In a moment of rare sentimentality, he imagined the clean smell of her shampoo.

She stood by the car door checking her watch, waiting for her husband, Lord Avery Chatsworth. He would soon emerge from the heavily secured St. Stephen's Tower of the Palace of Westminster and walk the three streets to where she had found a legal parking space.

Schmitt had followed her routine every afternoon for the past week. Chatsworth, a member of the House of Lords, had been attending committee meetings preparing for the 2000 State Opening of Parliament. He knew Amy Chatsworth's routine would be no different today.

Nearby, Big Ben chimed its familiar notes before striking three. The light traffic on the thoroughfare gave him a clean line to the Jag. He would wait until the woman's husband approached and she moved forward to greet him. Once she cleared the vehicle's front end he would take his shot. His aim had to be accurate. There would be no time for a second opportunity. Five years ago, pulling the trigger and hitting his target would have been as easy as breathing. Now he shook.

His flight to the U.S. would leave Heathrow Airport at seven-thirty. He had already posted the cryptic message to the Chatsworths' home. Once he disposed of Amy Chatsworth, he would have completed his purpose for being in London. Killing her was an elected bonus in his vendetta. His two primary targets were somewhere in America.

Schmitt spotted the burly man nearing the Jaguar. Hatless, with a full head of neat gray-white hair, he wore a dark-blue, pinstriped suit, the plaid wool scarf tossed around his neck in typical English-casual fashion making him appear indifferent to the weather's iciness. The Member of Parliament approached the woman walking as though he were eager to leave behind the weight of government service.

Amy Chatsworth moved toward her husband. Before she cleared the front end of the Jaguar, Schmitt felt the ache in his arthritic trigger finger. Ignoring it, he squeezed back and the round discharged. The silencer muffled the sound. The bullet ricocheted off the top of the Jaguar's bonnet, passing close to the woman's shoulder. The pinging noise startled her. She spun around, lost her balance and toppled to the pavement. Lord Avery Chatsworth rushed forward and threw himself over his wife's facedown body.

With no time for another shot, he slid back under the van's steering wheel and pulled out behind a passing tourist bus. Before leaving London for the airport, the former East German Stasi agent made one stop. Unobserved, he deposited the Walther PPK in the dark waters of the River Thames.

* * *

Felix Decker's heartbeat quickened.

"Oh...oh my, Werner. Where are you?"

The call had caught him off guard. Werner Schmitt's pending arrival had slipped his mind even though he had paid for the man's airline ticket as part of the deal.

"I am here, Felix," he announced. "At the LaGuardia Airport in New York. I arrived last evening and spent the night in a motel. Why do you sound surprised? You have not changed your mind?"

The man's voice triggered the ambivalence Decker initially felt when Schmitt first proposed the idea. In a phone call from London last month, he realized, ambivalent or not, he could not turn away the ex-Stasi's offer. He held the key to a great deal of money. They would split the prize if Decker would finance the operation.

"No, no," Decker said. "I knew you were coming soon, but you gave me no specific date."

"Well, I am here now. I board my connecting flight to Pittsburgh in forty-five minutes. I will call you from there once the detective arrives."

"Very well. Have a good flight," Decker said.

Schmitt hung up without responding.

Decker knew all about the man and his villainous background, a problem he would live with. Thankful Mildred was up in Atlanta visiting with their daughter, he would not have to explain the calls from Schmitt.

Decker walked out to his lanai and watched a snowy egret wade through the tall grass toward the lake at the rear of his villa. Its long graceful neck formed an S, and the tubular shape bobbed in rhythm with each stride as though under the control of a puppeteer. The bird was his favorite among the species that domiciled on the southwest coast of Florida.

Twenty years of the "Sunshine State" had not dulled his appreciation for the surrounding wildlife. He remembered all those frigid winters of his youth in upstate New York, where the birds he admired were Canadian geese flying south every fall. Now, living on the edge of the Florida Everglades, he found that watching the great blue heron and soaring osprey gave him a sense of pleasure and serenity, even at his advanced age of seventy-five. He wanted his lifestyle to continue.

Decker's pension from the U.S. Justice Department provided a small portion of his retirement. The long-gone rewards of his father's good fortune at the beginning of World War II had enhanced his lot growing up. It provided him with a first class Princeton education, and later, that connection opened the door to a staff translator position within the Justice Department.

On his deathbed in 1980, Decker's father had revealed the source of the family's windfall: In 1942, the German high command had placed under his stewardship a $2.5 million-dollar fund earmarked to finance an eight-man team of Nazi saboteurs, but never used—except for a half million his father expropriated. The whereabouts of the balance remained a mystery. That is, until the former Stasi, Werner Schmitt, contacted him.

* * *

Luke Rizzo's left hand rested on the end of the armrest. He eyeballed the leggy brunette flight attendant leaning across to retrieve a serving tray from the sleeping passenger in the window seat. Her short, royal blue uniform jacket hiked up, revealing a white nylon blouse and the curving definition of a well-formed right breast. Rizzo inhaled her fresh perfumed fragrance, conscious that her pressing thigh lingered longer than necessary against his fingers on the armrest. He looked up and squeezed out his best Dean Martin smile. Any other day, he would have taken a run at her. Not this morning. His P.I. assignment, well defined, allowed him limited time. No room for play.

She disappeared into the plane's galley, leaving Rizzo with teasing images of what-could-have-been. In times past, Rizzo would leap at these opportunities in a heartbeat, drunk or sober. Often the outcome would be intriguing and sometimes downright bizarre, especially after a few shooters.

For example, that waitress from the cocktail lounge near his hotel in Indianapolis a few months back. She admitted to having a weakness for Italians, those with thick, black hair and sparkling white teeth. He remembered her remarkable collection of 1940s Sulka silk ties, treasures she used in ways the famous haberdasher never had in mind. Instead of wearing them, she liked to employ these ultimate fashion statements—with a certain snobbish pleasure—as gentle restraints on her spread-eagled bed partners.

Rizzo leaned into the headrest and let go a sigh, remembering it was those antics that got him in trouble with Terri and put their marriage in jeopardy. That and his drinking.

An old saw popped into his head. He couldn't recall where he'd first heard it: Italian men drank before having illicit sex to numb their Catholic conscience. It offended his ego. Hey, this Italian had been a free spirit in matters of drinking and lechery all his life. He felt the words forming, but no sound came out—a silent protest. Good thing. He doubted the person next to him catching a few zzz's would be amused.

Terri was never amused either, which explained the arrival of the court's notice six months ago. It jolted Rizzo when he opened the envelope. There, staring at him, was the assigned date, the indisputable date, the date that the court would declare their fifteen-year marriage history. Not that he didn't expect the notice, simply that the reality of seeing a date-certain for the hearing printed on that official-looking document in big black letters and numbers, had rocked him off balance. He remembered thinking, *If only I was still boozing…well...*

Rizzo recalled how Terri would complain, "You never finish anything you start." She was right. He would leave incomplete projects around the house with empty promises to finish them later. She accused him of lacking the drive needed to succeed, always accepting whatever level of achievement he could get away with; that his alcoholism was a manifestation of how little he thought of himself, and drinking and cheating were his way of handling it. Joining AA was his first step in changing all that. Too little, too late for Terri. She could never absolve him of the cheating.

A chime rang in his head. The captain had turned on the seatbelt sign. The valley-girl voice of the flight attendant announcing their approach to the Greater Pittsburgh International Airport echoed throughout the aircraft.

Rizzo shuffled together the loose papers on his tray: the summary of Amy Chatsworth's 10-year search for her father—the letter datedJune 27, 1987 from the State Department, kissing her off—her letter to Frank Bard of New Brighton, Pennsylvania—the unsigned reply saying her father died and was buried at Sylvania Hills, a cemetery in nearby Rochester. He slid all of them into the document folder.

The pitch of the 747's engine changed. He felt the plane bank into its final approach, followed by the sound of the lowered wheels locking in place. The landing was smooth and as they bumped along toward their arrival gate, Rizzo questioned if his trip would end up being a waste of time. On the other hand, maybe he would get lucky. Make a positive difference in someone's life. That would be novel.

* * *

She introduced herself as Flo and began filling in spaces on the computer screen, asking a litany of questions he had heard a thousand times. Rizzo peppered his answers with double entendres. Flo, the rent-a-car angel, took no offense. When she completed a printout of the contract, she looked up.

"Well, darlin', that should do it. Sign where the X is, and initial the space signifying you refuse the liability insurance, you defyin' little dawg, you."

He smiled at her sense of humor. Her accent was pure Kentucky. Salty women, Rizzo recalled from his Army days as an MP stationed at Fort Knox. He scratched in his signature and twisted the form around.

"Now, you goin' to need directions?" Flo asked, sounding like a concerned parent sending her first-born off to school. She flipped open a small folded map with *AVIS, We Try Harder* printed across the top. With the map turned upside down, he focused on the long painted nail of her index finger as she asked, "Where you headin', darlin'?" The shaped tip of her red talon rested on The Greater Pittsburgh International Airport, poised to etch a route over the multi-colored maze of roadways.

She was around forty-five with frosted-blond hair that glittered in the reflected glow of the overhead neon tubes. The red uniform blazer snuggled at her waist, giving her an hourglass silhouette. She was firm, for sure, with lots of good mileage left. He guessed they were not far apart in age, yet he found her mothering a turn-on.

"I'm going to a town called Rochester...to a cemetery... Sylvania Hills Memorial Park. Any idea how far?"

"Oh, dear, a funeral," Flo said, lowering her voice and eyelids. "Somebody close?"

"No, not like that. Trying to find out if a guy I'm looking for is buried there." Her vacant stare made him think she was going to ask more questions. She did not.

"Well, it's not that far," she said, "maybe twenty, thirty miles north of here. Shouldn't take all that long, except—" Flo leaned back and called to a woman at the far end of the counter. "Velma, honey, they still doin' road work up at the north end of 60? Isn't that the way you go home?"

"Yeah, but the detour signs are pretty plain," the co-worker replied without turning her head. "You can't get lost."

Flo's pointy red nail traced the route to Rochester.

When she lifted her chin, Rizzo gave her a playful smile. "You know something, Flo?"

She returned his smile with a mischievous one of her own. "What's that, darlin'?"

"You do."

"I do? Do what, hon?" Her eyelashes fluttered, performing a great butterfly imitation.

"Try harder," he answered. He chuckled, flipped up the end of her silk scarf, took up the rental contract and car keys and turned in the direction of the terminal exit and the Avis parking lot. "Hey, maybe I'll catch up with you when I get back. Ya think?" he called over his shoulder. No harm in leaving her with a small sign of hope.

* * *

Cradling the phone between his shoulder and chin, Werner Schmitt massaged the pain in his lower spine while he watched the detective. Thanks to a night on an uncomfortable bed at the LaGuardia Inn, he had awakened that morning with an aching back. He had a handful of coins stacked on the shelf beneath the public phone. His right foot rested on top of his American Tourister suitcase while he waited for the long-distance operator to return.

Upon his arrival earlier from New York, he had purchased a Colt .45 in a gun shop on the outskirts of the Pittsburgh Airport. When the shopkeeper asked for ID, the ex-Stasi produced the false U.S. driver's license he carried across the Atlantic, keeping his passport out of sight. The clerk completed the sale without asking further questions. Schmitt slid the weapon under the seat of his rental and drove back to the airport. Luke Rizzo's plane was due to arrive a half hour later.

Schmitt admired Rizzo's penchant for detail, making it easy to follow him. During Rizzo's last phone conversation with Amy Chatsworth the week before his departure, the detective had provided his client with the specifics of his travel. Schmitt had tapped into the call, courtesy of a former Stasi communication expert now in the employment of Edison Telephone of London. He quickly booked his own flights, managing to arrive ahead of Rizzo.

The operator's voice buzzed through the line. "Please deposit three dollars and forty-five cents for the first three minutes." He fed the coins into the slot and listened to the pulsing ring of the phone at the other end. He counted seven before Felix Decker answered.

"Hello."

"Schmitt. I am at the Pittsburgh airport ready to move."

"And the detective?"

"I am watching him now," he said, rummaging his fingertips through his graying mustache. He scooped up the leftover change from the ledge and put the coins into his pocket. His eyes remain fixed on the man at the Avis counter.

"Werner, listen. I've been giving this a lot of thought."

Schmitt's brow tightened. The apologetic sound in the man's voice was not what he wanted to hear. He reminded himself not to be curt. Decker was financing the operation. The wired twenty-five thousand committed him to the partnership. Moreover, they agreed to share equally when he found the two million.

"About what?"

"It's about killing them. After all, Vogel is the one who holds the key to the money's location. And once you have it—"

"Why are you asking? You know my reason…my family's honor…my promise to my mother before she died."

Schmitt's stare never left the detective at the counter. Was Decker going to renege on this part of their agreement? His neck grew warm. The need to find the two men had burned deep for many years. Find Luedecke and Vogel. Kill them. Avenge their betrayal of his father. He blew out several quick breaths, mindful of his coronary artery disease, a condition that subjected him to angina attacks. He needed to be careful.

"Yes, yes, I remember your promise. I'm concerned that something bad may come of it, something that would prevent you from completing the mission. The police could—"

"You should not worry about that," Schmitt blurted. "I have removed many enemies before. Nothing will get in the way." He drew a breath and looked toward the Avis counter. The errant shot in London crossed his mind. He was certain his attempt on Amy Chatsworth's life had raised Scotland Yard's interest. However, he would not admit that to the voice at the other end.

"I have to go. The detective is leaving for his car. I will call you when I get back to New York City." He pulled his nitroglycerin spray from his pocket, removed the plastic cap and opened his mouth.

Chapter 2

R izzo tossed the folder onto the passenger-side seat and slipped behind the wheel of the Ford Taurus. He waited at the exit of the Avis parking lot, watching the traffic flow on the airport's main road. A black Civic had moved from the rear of the lot and came up from behind. "Damn! We're going to get stacked up here if I don't catch a break," he said aloud, as though issuing a warning to the driver behind him. When he finally found his opening, he moved the Taurus out into traffic.

Rizzo cruised to sixty-five heading north on State Highway 60. The last traces of an Indian summer hung tough in the late-October morning. Perfect weather. He hoped it was the same back in New York for the fourth game of the 2000 World Series at Shea Stadium between the Yankees and the Mets. The Yanks took the first three games. If they won today's matchup, they would have achieved a four-game sweep. He would miss watching the game on television, but Amy Chatsworth's generous retainer more than made up for it.

Instead of cranking up the A/C, Rizzo kept the windows rolled down. His bent left elbow formed an effective airfoil; the push of warm air caressed his neck. Before long, perspiration blotted his blue denim shirt, reminding him of those early years on the Job, a time when he argued with partners over using the A/C instead of driving with open windows. These contests continued that way during the years he rode in patrol cars, even after he made detective, although most of that time, he worked alone.

Rizzo's dislike for air conditioning came close to making Terri a young widow. He got lucky. The bullet careened downward after hitting the window post of his Mustang Cobra and found the fatty muscle of his ass. The shot forced him into a three-quarters disability retirement after a dozen years with the NYPD. His slight limp and a minute slug fragment were the leftover memories of his near miss.

Someone had blown his cover on that stake out, set him up, sold him out. On top of it, he received a ton of shit from his squad commander about sitting in the Cobra with open windows. He told Rizzo that if his windows had been up, the drug dealer would have had to shoot through glass and maybe that would have diverted the bullet elsewhere. "Yeah, like into my head or chest," Rizzo had answered back. "Who the hell knows? It's all bullshit speculation anyway."

He approached the Rochester exit, tapped the brake pedal to cancel out the cruise control and mumbled something about life being more exciting in those days. Running his private-eye business had not been that difficult. He was good at it. He had been a good detective, too.

In little time, he had built his client list through personal referrals. Today's assignment, for example, came all the way from London, the happy by-product referral from a former case. His new client wanted him to find a father she never knew. She had only one lead, and the information indicated the father might be long gone.

Rizzo found Sylvania Hills and entered the cemetery office. Several desks were set up with computers. Behind the front counter, a row of metal file cabinets flanked a small mainframe, looking impressive and efficient.

A short, plump woman with a pleasant oval face, in her mid-twenties, worked the keyboard of one of the computers. She appeared to be alone. Rizzo glanced at his watch, guessing he had arrived at lunchtime. He hoped she could provide the information he needed so he wouldn't have to hang around until the boneyard boss returned. Maybe he could catch an earlier return flight than the one he had booked.

"Good morning, miss," he said, almost in a whisper. He removed a business card from his shirt pocket. "My name is Lucas Rizzo. Wonder if you can help me."

* * *

Rizzo was right. The impressive and efficient computer confirmed that Frank Bard was buried there, as the unsigned letter to Amy Chatsworth had stated. The whole story, right up there on the screen: date of death, burial date, plot number and location, wife's name. After employing a wee bit of his Roman charm, he managed to wheedle from the woman the name of the funeral parlor in Beaver Falls that handled the arrangements. Frank Bard was sixty-three when he died. That was twenty-seven years ago, which confirmed for Rizzo that he was not Amy Chatsworth's father. The person he was looking for was around that age—now.

No matter how much flattery he laid on, he could not talk her into providing names of the rest of the family. When he probed, she became protective. He hoped the Palumbo Funeral Home would have the information.

Rizzo headed north on Route 51. After several miles, he spotted the sign: WELCOME TO BEAVER FALLS. He remembered Beaver Falls as the hometown of Joe Namath. He grinned recalling the Jet's GM, Weeb Eubank, and his contract signing of Joe in 1965, and all the overblown media hype about the new Jet's birthplace, as though the town were some sanctified Brigadoon of pro football, the Nazareth of all great quarterbacks.

Rizzo's stomach rumbled as he pulled into a fast-food restaurant on the main drag, a timeworn McDonald's that had seen brighter days.

Seated in a window booth, he gazed out from behind a hoisted French fry dripping ketchup. The barren appearance of the area struck him as a place long deserted. Beaver Falls' citizens had to have enjoyed a more prosperous lifestyle while the former Jet star grew up here, when the location thrived as a busy steel-mill town, long before the mills closed down. Now Beaver Falls looked empty, as if everyone, besides Willie Joe, had left to find a better place.

Rizzo was sure his son, Matt, would get a kick out of having lunch at a McDonald's in the middle of Joe Namath's hometown. Matt was a Jets fan too, following the team with his youthful passion during a time when their shared closeness existed. He tried to imagine his son sitting next to him. He could hear him saying, "Hey, maybe that old guy over there saw Joe play football in high school," trying to relate in his teenage way. Rizzo stared past his Big Mac, past the old man, out the wide front window. Nothing moved, as though someone had called a time out, and everyone was waiting for the ref's whistle to start the clock.

* * *

The nice woman at Sylvania Hills had given him 3300 Norcross for the Palumbo Funeral Home. Rizzo traversed the length of Main Street, found Norcross and spotted the home from several hundred yards away. The large, two-story, grandiose affair had a splendor that contrasted with the surrounding houses as though under a spotlight. He chuckled. The best-looking house in any small town was always the funeral home.

He had a choice of parking spaces in the lot. A slow day for dying. Except for the green Buick that had pulled to the curb, he saw no other vehicles.

He entered and crossed the carpeted anteroom on tiptoe, stopping at the funeral director's opened door.

"How ya doin'? I'm Lucas Rizzo," he said, handing his card to the youth behind the desk. "Trying to get information about a person. Maybe you can help. The people at Sylvania Hills Cemetery tell me you handled the man's funeral arrangements."

The face was altar boy-cherubic. He reminded Rizzo of Matt. The kid seemed too young to understand death, much less offer compassion and support to grieving family members.

Mr. Palumbo was not on the premises, a fact made apparent by the youthful zeal with which the assistant took charge. Rizzo gave him the name of Frank Bard, and the young man retreated to the row of file cabinets like an Eagle Scout on a nature hunt. Rizzo dropped into the chair next to the desk, winked at the framed photo of Mrs. Palumbo at the corner and waited.

No computers this time. Instead, the assistant produced a large, black ring binder.

"Bard...let's see, that's Frank Bard," the young man said, coaching himself while thumbing over pages. "That would be Frank Senior, right?" he asked, as if he already knew the answer.

* * *

Rizzo reached the Taurus and paused, taking deep breaths to clear his nostrils of the aroma of lily. A black Civic, similar to the one he saw earlier at the airport, zipped by at a pace well above the posted speed limit.

Before he opened the car door, the parked green Buick started up. He watched the car pull away, make a U-turn at the end of Norcross and stop. A lot of activity for a small town. Any other time while conducting an investigation, he would be on alert for a tail. No reason to suspect that today. No one knew he was here.

My, my, heavy traffic in Beaver Falls. No wonder Joe left.

Luke Rizzo's visit to the funeral home and the ready help of the young director-in-training had turned up something interesting. Now he knew why the response to Amy Chatsworth's letter to Frank Bard arrived in London six months ago—unsigned: *The Frank Bard you seek is buried at Sylvania Hills Memorial Park in Rochester, Pennsylvania.* Nevertheless, records at the Palumbo Funeral Home listing the surviving family members revealed a Frank Bard, Jr. also residing in New Brighton. If he was breathing after these twenty-seven years, Junior should be sixty-two or three, about the same vintage as Frank Bard, Sr. when he died.

The young man in the funeral home had described New Brighton as a five-minute drive back in the other direction. Rizzo slid behind the wheel of the Taurus. Next stop, the Tax Collector's Office.

As he drove back to New Brighton, Rizzo recalled the details of Amy Chatsworth's report: how the twenty-year-old American airman met, fell in love with, and knocked up a young English girl from a small town outside of London. He had confessed to being married, but he'd told her his estranged wife had filed for divorce. He was due to return Stateside in two months and had assured his new love he would come back after his divorce was final so they could be married. Her angry family stepped in and prevented the girl from further contact. Seven months later, in 1958, the birth of baby Amy relegated her to the growing corps of English-American bastards.

Recalling this, Rizzo winced, a reaction, he admitted, owed to his ingrained papal conditioning. Hey, face it, he told himself; in 1958, an out-of-wedlock birth was not highly regarded. Today was different. No big deal. Hollywood's morality had made liberals out of most people; except the odds were better than even that old Frank Junior's moral compass remained stuck in 1958.

The State Department letter was the one official acknowledgement Amy had received from the U.S. Government since launching her search ten years ago. The letter confirmed that Frank Bard, Air Force serial number 12400717, had been stationed in England in 1958. *This is all the information we are required to supply. Sorry.* Boy, talk about your basic "tough shit!" message.

She persisted, nevertheless. Rizzo could not help admiring her strength, her tenacity. In fact, he envied her. The need to find the missing piece of her being was so great, so consuming, she dedicated a decade of her life to the search.

A thought occurred to him. He might be a mere few moves away from uniting two people who, until now, had never been certain the other existed. Something gnawed at him. Why didn't he feel a sense of optimism? His old man used to call those feelings *the beguiling promises of paradise*, except in his father's case he was referring to the deceitful lure of his alcoholic demons.

* * *

He reached the address given to him and parked in front of the building. The town's tax collector should be able to confirm whether Junior was living in New Brighton.

"Frank Bard? Oh, certainly. Lives in New Brighton, not more than a half mile from here," the large woman behind the counter said. She sounded happy to have her otherwise dull day interrupted by a New York City private detective with a mission. "Sweet, sweet man. He's retired now." She paused and lowered her voice as though she caught herself being too forthright with information. "Hasn't done anything wrong, has he?"

"No, no, just trying to locate him for a relative. I may not even have the right Frank Bard," Rizzo said, shooting her a toothy smile. "You have a fix on how old he might be?"

"Well, I haven't seen him in quite a time. Used to work for the Post Office. I would say he has to be in the neighborhood of fifty-five, more or less. I'm not sure. His wife used to clean house for my mother, maybe twenty-five years ago."

"Do you know if your Frank Bard served in the Air Force... stationed in Europe?"

The tax collector squeezed her lips together while her cheeks billowed and her brow furrowed. "Gee, Mr. Rizzo, I couldn't say."

Rizzo produced the faded snapshot Amy Chatsworth provided of a young, uniformed airman standing on the side of a road lined with stucco and ivy thatched cottages.

"Here's a picture of the Frank Bard I'm looking for. He was about twenty at the time. You might see a resemblance."

She stood, brought the photo up to her face and studied it, then pushed the picture out at arm's length as if trying to find the proper focus. Finally, she handed back the photo, shaking her head.

"Yeah, there's a resemblance. I couldn't swear, though."

On a hunch he asked, "Does he happen to drive a green Buick Le Sabre?"

Again, she let him down. She shrugged and replied, "Sorry," in a tone that revealed her growing impatience.

He decided to give it one more shot. "Well, is there a VA office in New Brighton?"

"Matter of fact, there is," she answered with raised eyebrows and a grin, as though relieved she could finally provide a bit of useful information. "Downstairs, first floor."

Bingo!

* * *

Office Closed on Wednesday, the note on the door explained. How's that for bad timing? The Air Force serial number was his only evidence to link Frank Bard, Jr. with the father of Amy Chatsworth. Now what? Frustrated, Rizzo leaned back against the wall to consider his next move. He cut his eyes to the other end of the corridor and spotted the door to police headquarters. He had missed seeing it coming in. Town hall buildings in these small towns were great. Render your taxes while you pay off your traffic violations. One-stop shopping.

He entered the small station house. The desk sergeant on duty looked up and smiled as though he already knew the professional identity of his visitor. Rizzo was sure he did. The way he walked, the way he carried himself, all signs that gave him away. Rizzo knew he could always spot a cop in plain clothes. When he handed the officer his card and introduced himself as a retired New York City detective, now a private investigator, the sergeant's smile turned into a knowing chuckle.

At once, Rizzo felt at ease. The familiar setting embraced him like an old girlfriend. He remembered telling a stranger he'd met at a bar one night about this reaction. "I mean, watch any retired cop when he's rapping with an active member of his blue-uniformed brethren. It is like witnessing one of those experiments where they unfreeze a body that has been stored on ice for a hundred years and the stiff picks up right where he left off. No matter how long retired, he's never left the job, never missed a roll call. Like something eerie. Happens all the time."

"Hey, Sarge, I'm tryin' to check out somebody with the VA Today's Wednesday. My bad luck. Looks like they've gone fishing," Rizzo said.

"Yeah, tough duty, a four-day workweek," the sergeant replied. "But hell, the main office for this county is over at the courthouse in Beaver. They must be open."

"Is that right? Damn! I just came from there not a half-hour ago. Thought maybe I'd run into Joe Namath. Guess I missed him."

The sergeant laughed. "That's Beaver Falls. This is Beaver. Different town. It's southwest of here, about six miles. Let me call first, make sure they're open. No sense making the trip for nothing."

"Hey, that'd be great."

The sergeant dialed. He identified himself and told a voice on the other end, "I'm sending someone who needs information on an Air Force veteran. Please help him the best you can. Much obliged."

* * *

The sergeant's phone call made the day. The suspicious frump guarding the VA's records said she was not supposed to give out information such as serial numbers to unauthorized people. However, since Rizzo was there by way of the New Brighton police...well, that would be okay.

"You a relative?" the heavy-bodied woman asked.

Steel-blue, bureaucratic eyes squinted with caution as she clutched Junior's personnel folder to her complementing bureaucratic bosom. Rizzo imagined if she had weighed sixty pounds less, they might look like boobs.

He forced a grin, dismissing the boob image. "I'm a relative of a relative." He hoped she wouldn't ask what a *relative of a relative* meant. "Listen, all I need is to verify a serial number," he told her, trying to ease her angst. "I'm not interested in getting you in hot water, so suppose I read you the number I have. If the number jibes with what you have on record for Frank Bard, Junior of New Brighton, just nod your head. Okay?"

This seemed to agree with her sense of professional ethics, so he recited the eight digits with a slight dramatic flair as though he were on TV reading this week's winning lottery numbers. She nodded and looked at him stone-faced, giving the impression that he had successfully coaxed her out of her virginity. He was tempted to vault the counter and bear hug her. He simply said thanks. He would save his celebration until he reached his car in the municipal lot.

* * *

For a third time since leaving the cemetery, he noticed the '86 metallic green Buick LeSabre parked several spaces away. Its hood and windshield reflected the late afternoon sun. This time Rizzo spotted a man's shape behind the wheel. He heard the engine of the Buick turn over. The sound of screeching tires jarred him alert as the car pulled out and headed toward him. Rizzo leaped up on the fender of the Taurus as the vehicle raced past, clearing him by a few feet. He made note of the license plate before the Buick disappeared onto the street.

Rizzo's exit from the Beaver Courthouse parking lot was unhurried. He had what he came for—positive identity of Amy Chatsworth's father and irrefutable proof as back-up. He could leave for the airport, maybe see if Flo, his little Avis angel, was hanging around. If not, catch the next flight back to LaGuardia, make his report to his client in London and await his fee. Amy Chatsworth did not expect him to make contact, merely to locate her father. Nevertheless, if the man behind the wheel was Junior, the man almost made contact with him—fatal contact. His cop instinct told him to stick around, find out why Frank Bard, Jr. bolted like a scared rabbit.

Rizzo found a public phone at a nearby 7-11 and dialed the number the information operator had given for the New Brighton police station. Courtesy of the desk sergeant, Rizzo learned that the plate number of the Buick—no big surprise—did belong to Junior. He was glad the sergeant failed to ask why he needed the I.D., and he did not volunteer the information. Nor did he mention the brush in the parking lot.

A second call to the information operator provided Bard's home number. Rizzo purchased a bag of chips, munched on them in the store for several minutes before making the call.

A raspy voice answered after several rings. "Hello."

"Mr. Bard, my name is Lucas Rizzo, a private investigator employed by Mrs. Amy Chatsworth of London, England. I believe you know of her."

The steady, raspy breathing assured him the man had not hung up.

After a long pause, the man said, "Ah, I wrote her a letter... told her...ah...don't know any more than what I said in the letter. Please don't call me any—"

"Mr. Bard, you've been following me all afternoon. You almost flattened me in the parking lot of the Beaver Courthouse a while ago. You remember that, don't you? Now, if that hadn't happened, I might be on my way home. But you've piqued my curiosity, enough to convince me to hang in here a while longer."

"What is it you want?"

"Sir, I'd like to discuss the matter of Mrs. Amy Chatsworth with you. Are you okay with that?"

Rizzo could hear Bard take quick gulps of air, the way an asthmatic does.

"Or I can go to the police...report the incident in the parking lot."

He heard the wheeze come from deep within the man's chest. He figured Bard used one of those inhaler things to help him breathe.

"Privately? No one else gonna be there?"

"No, sir, just the two of us. You tell me where."

Chapter 3

Schmitt sat behind the wheel, studying the flow of people entering and leaving the three-story government building. He had nestled the car between two large SUVs in a parking spot fifty yards away, giving him a good angle to the entrance. Ten minutes ago, he had seen the detective leave his car in the parking lot and go inside. What does Rizzo expect to find at this latest stop? The detective's list of checkpoints so far had included a cemetery, a funeral home, then an office building in New Brighton, and now this government building in Beaver.

After the cemetery stop, Schmitt suspected the man he had set out to kill, Frank Bard, was already dead. Rizzo's visit to the funeral home appeared to confirm that. Yet the detective continued to search, chasing clues from one spot to the next.

Rizzo knew what he was looking for. The Chatsworth woman had given the detective an assignment to find the son, Frank Bard, Jr. He had listened in on their telephone conversation when she called him from London. With patience, he would find him. They would both find him. Then Frank Bard, Jr. would serve as a suitable substitute for his father.

Rizzo exited the building through the revolving door and turned toward the parking lot. Schmitt started the Civic and waited. When the detective pulled out onto the street, Schmitt eased the car from his parking space and followed at a distance. Several blocks later, he suddenly pulled to the curb. Rizzo had stopped his car at the side of a 7-11 and got out. He watched the detective come around to the front door, enter and remain inside for several minutes. Growing impatient, he began to think the detective had slipped out unseen.

Rizzo finally appeared at the doorway, returned to his car and drove away in a hurry. Schmitt cautiously tailed him, overcome with a feeling of anticipation. He was closing in, and he could visualize the outline of his prey forming in his gunsight.

* * *

Rizzo found the place Frank Bard, Jr. had described. The tavern was the first he had entered since he went dry. He felt ridiculous drinking Coke in a mug through a straw. The hard wooden booth hurt his hip, but its location allowed him a clear view to the front door. Noisy, sociable beer drinkers filled the establishment, the type who refer to each other as old-timers and sound natural doing it.

A haze of cigarette smoke choked the air and mingled with the aroma of stale beer. A fat Wurlitzer jukebox lit the front end of the long bar with a rotating sequence of colorful hues, dispensing polka tunes that no one heard. Any moment, he expected Bobby Vinton, the Polish Prince, to belt out one of his ethnic melodies. The atmosphere was an odd throwback to the saloons of the past—warm and friendly, missing only the sawdust on the wide-planked floor.

Halfway into his Coke, a tall man entered. He took a quick look around and headed to the bar. Rizzo watched as the man bent across to whisper to the bartender. It had to be Frank Bard; he fit the mental picture Rizzo had formed earlier during their brief telephone conversation. The one surprise was his height. Frank Bard was a skyscraper.

The man's plaid shirt hung on his bony, gaunt frame like a house painter's drop cloth. Rizzo could tell the baggy khaki trousers belted to the man's hips once fit a lot better than they did today. The tall man gave the impression of a one-time athlete, powerful but now used up. His gray, wooly hair stuck out clownishly from beneath both sides of a baseball cap with STEELERS stitched on the peak. Rizzo recognized the shape of an inhaler device in the breast pocket of the man's plaid shirt.

Frank Bard, Jr. approached the booth, shuffling his large feet like a dog-tired mail carrier. He grasped a mug of beer with two hands, taking care not to spill any.

"Lucas Rizzo?"

Up close, Rizzo could see a trace of the young airman from the picture. He had a handsome face despite his roadmap of age lines.

"Yeah. Thanks for coming, Frank."

The man nodded, slid across the bench opposite and swung his long legs under the table. Their knees collided.

"Sorry, these damn things weren't meant for...maybe a table?"

Bard's head turned on his swan-like neck to survey the alternatives. He squinted as though weighing the advantages.

"Yeah...well, if you don't mind."

They headed for a small two-seater along the back wall. Settling in, Bard took note of Rizzo's Coke. He made no comment. His soft, penetrating eyes did the asking.

"I don't drink anymore," Rizzo said, the words rolling out without hesitation. Then, as though Bard expected him to provide further clarification, he added, "Been in AA for over a year." He tried not to sound apologetic.

The man's expression showed understanding.

They sat for a while without speaking. The wheezing sound made by Bard's breathing punctured their silence. It seemed to be keeping time with the polka tempo coming from the Wurlitzer Jukebox. Rizzo realized Bard was waiting for him to begin.

"First, maybe you can explain how you knew I was here. I mean, out of curiosity."

Bard raised his eyebrows and grinned. "That was my daughter you talked to at Sylvania Hills. Called me soon as you left the cemetery, like I told her to if ever someone comes nosin' around about my father."

"She know why I was nosing around?"

"Only that her grandfather left a bit of unfinished business. That there are people tryin' to lay claim to property he owned."

"After all these years?"

"She don't ask a lotta questions, Mr. Rizzo."

This time Rizzo grinned. "It's Luke, and I have a few questions of my own." He tipped back in his chair and folded his arms across his chest. Rizzo figured he might as well start with the sixty-four dollar one. "Are you Amy Chatsworth's father?"

He didn't need to ask. He had the required proof. Maybe he simply wanted to hear Bard say it, like getting final closure.

"Don't really know. The word of a girl I never seen don't make it so, does it?"

"Why would she make it up?"

Frank Bard raised his beer, took a mouthful and stared down into the mug as if he was considering chug-a-lugging the rest. "Sometimes," he said, holding the mug close to his face, "people have reasons that's hard to understand."

"I don't believe that's the case here, Frank. Amy's motive is simple. She'd like to know who her father is, find out something about him, perhaps even meet him, if that's possible. You know, get it behind her, fill in the piece of life's little puzzle that has been missing for forty-two years. Simple as that."

"She's not looking for somethin'...to get somethin' out of—?"

"You mean like money? Hey, Frank, Amy is a wealthy woman. Married quite well. She's not looking for anything but a chance to find out who her father is."

"I was thinkin' more about settlin' a score...somethin' like that."

A burst of raucous laughter carried back from the front of the tavern. Rizzo cut an eye to the cluster of celebrating beer drinkers.

Leaning into the table, he said, "Sorry, I don't follow you."

"She's gotta believe I abandoned her, that it was my doin', my not goin' back."

"Not for a moment. The background report she supplied indicates she knows what happened. She holds no bad feelings. None at all."

"I...I don't understand then...why...why would she spend all this time tryin' to locate me?"

"Frank, I told you why."

Bard's bewildered expression would not disappear.

"How'd she find where I live? My military records?"

"No. All she had was your Air Force serial number. The State Department would not tell her diddly. When she discovered the international network called Birth-Search, she made contact with them. In no time, she had your address in New Brighton."

The man took several deep breaths, picked up the mug and emptied it. When he set the glass down, he asked, "Luke, you married?"

The question pulled Rizzo up short. Bard sounded as though he had run into an old Air Force pal on the street.

"No...well...I mean, no longer. My divorce became final six months ago."

"Kids?"

Rizzo stiffened against the back of his chair. "Boy, fifteen, name's Matthew. Listen, Frank—"

"Live with you?"

"Well, no, with his mother. Listen, Frank," he repeated, "no one I spoke with today knows why I was looking for you, so you've got nothing to worry about."

He was not sure Frank Bard was listening. The man had fixed his attention to the bottom of his emptied mug.

"You don't want Amy to contact you again, that's okay." Rizzo continued, "I know she'll oblige, except personally I feel you—"

"How's he takin' the whole thing?"

"Oh, fine, like I told you, she holds no—"

"Your son."

"Who?"

The question confused Rizzo for a moment. The man's focus had remained locked on Rizzo's own family problems.

"Oh, you mean Matt?"

Rizzo felt a slow-rising anxiety. He was giving away control of the conversation. Then he realized he welcomed the outlet, to be able to talk with someone about Matt, and Frank Bard appeared interested.

"Tell the truth," he began, "not too well. I'd always had a tight relationship with him, but after the separation, Terri managed to shake that."

"How so?"

"Oh, filling him with all sorts of stories...you know... like making me the heavy, blaming me for everything. That I refused to cut back on my drinking...which she knew wasn't a realistic option. That I'm an absentee father and husband. Now I'm worried about losing him."

The words spilled out like an overturned jar of marbles.

"What's your son like?" Bard asked, encouraging the spillage.

"A good kid. Likes sports, plays a pretty good third base. Haven't seen him in close to a year, not since the night I showed up at the house on his fourteenth birthday."

"How come?"

"He was throwing a party. I don't know where Terri was, but damned if I don't find a house full of kids drinking beer."

Bard gave a knowing look. "That's today's kids, I'm afraid. Wantin' to grow up so fast."

"Well, seeing them through my own bourbon-fogged eyes, I must have gone ballistic. Chased everyone home. That did it for him, I suppose. Me too. I joined AA right after that. Haven't tasted a drop since. But until I pass the first real test, I'll hold off telling him."

"Guess he's pretty important to you?" Bard looked toward the bar, waving his long arm like a flagpole in a stiff wind. "Need another of whatever you're drinkin'?"

"No. No, thanks. I'm fine."

"My family's important to me, too," Bard said when the server left. "Always been."

Rizzo wanted to say, Amy is your family too, but he realized that was only a technicality.

"Been married over thirty years. Three children and six grandchildren. You met my youngest daughter today. We're a close family. They all live in this area."

Rizzo visualized a Norman Rockwell Thanksgiving at the Bards.

"Frank, you've no legal obligation to Amy, but you sure as hell went out of your way trying to avoid knowing she exists. Fact is, you damn near ran me down avoiding it."

"I'm real sorry, Luke. The sun glare and all that. Didn't see you comin' until you were right on top of me. Thought you were the other..." He stopped and took a deep breath.

The other what? He saw the man's wheezing, quiet for a time, now intensified.

When he caught his breath, Bard continued. "I regret what happened back then, that Amy's grandparents interfered with her mother's life. I loved her mother. Would have married her. Can't change anythin' now."

Rizzo watched him twist against the back of his chair. For a moment, he thought Bard would stand up.

Bard continued. "Don't blame Amy tryin' to find me, but comin' out in the open ain't gonna serve no real purpose. My family is too important. My wife, my children…don't think they would understand. Luke, you ain't got nothin' if you don't have family. And damned if I'm ready to risk losin' them."

The voice was that of a man under siege. His asthmatic breathing shortened and came in rapid intakes. The table shook beneath the weight of his large, flat palms. Rizzo was convinced Frank Bard and Amy Chatsworth would never meet.

"Frank, I was hired to find Amy's father. Done that. What happens now is up to you two. You have her address, don't you?"

Bard's eyebrows scrunched down over his closed eyelids for several moments. Rizzo could guess what he felt. When the man opened them, his beaten look was gone.

"You got a picture?" he asked in a firm tone.

Rizzo slipped the photograph out of the document folder, looked at the woman in the picture before handing it across the table. He could see Frank Bard's features in Amy Chatsworth's face.

After a brief but detached examination, Bard set the photo down as if the paper had burst into flames. Seconds later, he picked up the photo again, taking a closer look. He shifted his long body to capture maximum light from the wall fixtures at his back, and then he brought the photo up to his face.

Rizzo sat across from Bard, watching him. Over his shoulder, he could see a pair of old timers dancing to the music that drifted back from the Wurlitzer. He could make out the tune over the noise rising from the bar. "…*little things mean a lot*," warbled Pretty Kitty Kallen, the '50s songstress. He recalled that little blast from the past was on his mother-in-law's list of favorites. In the early years, whenever she was at the house baby-sitting, she would sing Matt off to sleep with it.

"Looks a lot like her mother," he heard Bard say. "Of course, it's been a long time."

"She get nothing from you?"

"Maybe my pointy chin...little bit 'round the eyes, but she's mostly her mother. Much as I can remember."

Rizzo stared out through the haze of cigarette smoke that circled overhead. Listening to the man speak had triggered his own reverie, of Terri as a thirteen-year-old girl, the prettiest in his freshman class and the first girl he ever told, *I love you.* Of course, when he said it, he swore her to secrecy. At that age, you don't go around owning up to such feelings, not without risking your macho friends razzing you. Terri had teased him about that a lot.

Rizzo looked across at Bard, remembering he wanted to ask him a question. Something had been nagging him for the past few minutes. "Frank, you ever see Willie Joe Namath play football in high school?"

Bard eyed him with a quizzical look, his absorption with Amy Chatsworth's image interrupted by the query. He placed the photo on the table and pushed it across.

"I have the feeling," Rizzo explained, "as soon as I call my son when I get home and tell him about this trip, he's going to ask me that question."

The old man looked at him with understanding. "I did," he answered, "many times. But Luke," his fingers continuing to rest on the photo, "can I keep the picture?"

* * *

"Come with me," Frank Bard said before exiting the tavern. "I got something I want to give you."

Rizzo followed him out of the rear of the tavern and stood next to him in the parking lot. He watched Bard lean though the open passenger door of his Buick and rummage through papers and maps crammed into the small space of the glove compartment. He pulled items out one at a time, tossing each onto the front seat. When he emptied it, Rizzo could see over the man's bent position that he had something taped to the bottom of the cavity. Bard tore the object free with care and stood holding a small envelope, browned with age.

"I want you to send this to Amy," he said. "Do it soon." His words came out with a sense of urgency. He held out the envelope and added, "I trust you, Luke."

At first, Rizzo thought the envelope might contain a personal note to his daughter, a communiqué written on impulse after Bard had responded to her inquiry last year. Maybe he had second thoughts about reconnecting with her. Nevertheless, why the secrecy?

"What is it?" Rizzo asked, as he took the envelope from Bard's outstretched hand.

The old man stared and pealed out his answer. "It's a photo...a snapshot...my father...Amy's grandfather...and his best friend. I want Amy to have it."

"And you don't want to mail the photo yourself?"

Bard shook his head.

Rizzo was puzzled. Why had Bard taped the envelope to the base of the Buick's glove compartment? Why had he kept the envelope hidden?

"Okay," Rizzo said. "I'll get it off to her when I get back to New York. Want me to say anything about it, like why you're sending her a picture of a grandfather she's never seen?"

Bard continued to stare at the envelope. "Yes, please," he said. "Tell her to keep it somewhere safe, away from prying eyes. Don't let anyone know she has it."

Rizzo's investigative sense was urging him to probe further, but Frank Bard's stern expression said the conversation had ended.

"I'll take care of it, Frank."

* * *

Several rows away, Werner Schmitt watched from behind the steering wheel, listening to the conversation through his ear-bud amplifiers. His informant in the U.S. Justice Department had informed him of the photo's existence, and he was prepared to ransack Bard's house to find it. That changed in the tavern's parking lot. The man had been carrying the photo around in his glove compartment, and had he known, he might have broken into Bard's car earlier.

He heard the exchange between the two men, thereby quashing his opportunity to lay hands on the photo before he disposed of his target. He was angry with himself. If this had been an official Stasi operation back in East Germany of the 1980s, his superiors would have found him negligent, subjecting him to severe punishment. Erich Mielke, the Stasi's feared Minister of State Security, was a rigid and uncompromising leader.

The Buick turned out of the parking lot, and Schmitt moved out behind him. The detective had left moments before, heading in the opposite direction toward Route 60 and the airport. Schmitt had considered pursuing him, but hesitated, fearing Rizzo might be armed. He could not risk a confrontation. His indecisiveness cost him minutes, allowing the detective to disappear into traffic. Take care of Frank Bard first, he decided. He would figure a way to deal with Luke Rizzo and the photo later. He knew where he could find the detective.

Bard edged the Buick through neighboring streets, making it easy for Schmitt to follow. He tailed him to a local shopping plaza where the man entered a supermarket and returned twenty minutes later carrying several plastic shopping bags.

Bard left the parking lot and drove through town to a split-level ranch house in a rural area of New Brighton. The late fall sun slowly disappeared behind the cluster of tall pines that bordered the back of Bard's modest home. Lights of the nearest neighbor farther down the road filtered through a thicket of leafless trees.

Bard stopped the Buick on his driveway incline. Before he could activate the garage opener, Schmitt pulled up behind and jumped out. "Herr Luedecke," he called.

The man sat paralyzed behind the wheel as Schmitt approached.

Chapter 4

A t twenty past four, Rizzo arrived at the Avis counter. Flo, his rent-a-car angel, was not behind her computer. He was too late. Like a smoker trying to quit, he felt relieved. Gone was the temptation of another one-night stand.

Damn! I have to get my life together, starting right now.

Two new attendants in red and white Avis uniforms occupied both ends of the counter, helping travelers with their rentals. He dropped off his keys and looked toward the escalator. Find the Admirals Club, see if there is a flight to LaGuardia in the next few hours.

He spotted her before he stepped onto the escalator. Her snug blazer and tight-wrapped rear end wiggled through the automatic doors opposite. He bolted and reached her at the curb before she entered the crosswalk. "Flo," he called out, his voice full of confidence. He was sure she would remember him. The Avis agent stopped and turned. Rizzo sauntered toward her.

The beginning of a smile tipped the corners of her mouth. "Well, hi there, darlin'. You got back early."

"Early enough to take you to dinner. Okay?"

* * *

The first gray light of dawn slipped over the horizon through red and gold trees already singed with October frost.

Werner Schmitt, ten miles from the Pittsburgh Airport, pulled into the rest area off Route 60. He had spotted the facility yesterday morning while following Luke Rizzo to Beaver Falls. The small lake adjacent to the parking area was a perfect spot to dispose of the Colt .45 before boarding his early flight to New York City.

Schmitt steered his car into the area marked *cars only*. Two other vehicles occupied the white-lined parking spaces. An elderly man and woman stood at the vending machines in the kiosk at the entrance of the building, trying to make up their minds how to spend their quarters. He tucked the .45 into his belt under his zippered windbreaker and passed them, keeping his eyes focused straight ahead.

Entering the men's room, he looked around. Even though the facility was empty, Schmitt went through the motions at the urinal in the event someone came out of one of the stalls. He paused at a mirror and ran a comb through his hair, noting his thinning strands of gray no longer remained in place without the aid of hairspray. It mattered not. Before returning to Germany, he would need to shave his head clean and remove his mustache in order to match the photo on his other passport.

Schmitt left the building and stretched his arms and each leg, creating the appearance of someone tired from a long drive. The cars in the parking lot were gone, and the sun had yet to appear in full above the horizon. He needed to move on.

He approached the small lake, heading toward the two stone benches at the water's edge. A large trash container flanked the bench on the left. Taking a seat, he surveyed the area. For a moment, he considered depositing the .45 in the receptacle next to him, then rejected the idea. The bottom of the lake would be a safer place.

He rose, reached under his jacket for the gun, and glanced again at the trash receptacle on his left. Holding the .45 close against his chest, he decided the lake would do.

Schmitt raised his arm like a baseball pitcher preparing to throw a strike. Without warning, the beams of a vehicle landed on him. He froze; his eyes jumped to the bar lights flashing from the top of a Private Security SUV. The vehicle swung into a parking space to the rear of the benches where he stood. An overweight uniformed man stepped out carrying a Mag-Lite. The private security guard, making his checkpoint rounds, hurried toward him.

Schmitt lowered his arm, the weapon at his side, and waited. Being detained or questioned was not an alternative. They could have discovered the killing of Frank Bard, Jr. by now. He had no way of knowing if this security guard was armed. Had he already received an alert? He could not take the chance. The man closed in on him.

"Excuse me, sir, is that—"

Schmitt raised the .45, pointed and fired, hitting the guard in the chest. The Mag-Lite flew when his hands went to his chest. Shock burst upon his face as the blast forced him backward. The .45 slug pierced his body, tearing away shards of uniform shirt to the right of his security badge. Ten splayed fingers covered the bullet's entry area as he rolled to the ground, landing on his back with his legs tangled under his large torso.

Schmitt looked down at the crumpled body and shook his head. His errant shot in London had spared Amy Chatsworth. That shot was from a distance. He had hit Frank Bard and this security officer up close. With regret, he acknowledged his sharpshooter days were behind him.

He faced the lake. This time he gripped the .45 with one hand, twisted at the waist to build torque and side-armed the weapon out into the water. He heard the .45 splash as he sprinted for the rental car and slipped in behind the wheel.

* * *

The Boeing 747 crossed the Hudson River from New Jersey. Ahead, the glass and steel towers of Wall Street glistened in the afternoon sun. The air was frosty clear. Off to his right, Werner Schmitt could see the heavily populated areas of Brooklyn, where he was born, where his parents lived for a few years in the late 1930s. In the distance, the cold waters of the Atlantic formed a choppy collar of waves along the shoreline of Brooklyn and out toward Long Island. He heard the rising pitch of the engines as the pilot made his final correction, banking back toward Queens. In a few minutes, the jet would touch down and taxi to an arrival gate at LaGuardia Airport, where he would deplane, disappear among the millions of New Yorkers, and wait for the private detective's return.

Schmitt had expected Luke Rizzo to lead him to the first of the two traitors. Despite learning that Frank Bard Senior had already died, he was satisfied. Eliminating the son brought him half way toward vindicating his father, Walter Schmitt. Taking out Amy Chatsworth would have been a bonus. To his great shame, he had bungled the shot.

The second-half of his quest remained somewhere in New York State. Ulster County was all Felix Decker could tell him with any certainty. He hoped Vogel hadn't moved on since 1953. Decker had given him Vogel's cover name, but he couldn't tell him what he looked like today. He had snapped the photo close to fifty years ago when Luedecke and Vogel were still young men. "That was the last time I saw them," Decker told him. "I can barely remember what either man looked like back then."

The photo, while dated, remained the only form of identification Schmitt could go on. When Bard gave the photo to the detective in the parking lot, he had lost that advantage, at least for now. Once the detective returned to New York City, he would get the photo from him even if he had to take the detective's life.

The Boing 747 taxied to the arrival gate at the American Airlines terminal. The moment the engines shut down, the metallic symphony of safety belts clicking free filled the plane's cabin. Passengers eager to deplane rose and stood in the aisle, pulling down their carry-on bags from the overhead bins.

In no hurry, Schmitt remained seated, staring out the window. While he watched the ground crew scurry about on the tarmac, he thought of the difficulty facing him in obtaining a weapon in New York State. Gun laws, he knew, were restrictive. He doubted he could walk into any gun shop, as he had in Pennsylvania, and purchase one by merely producing a driver's license. No, that was not possible. He did have a contact or two from his active Stasi days who had relocated into this area. Perhaps one of them...well, he would worry about that later.

He stood and retrieved his bag after the man seated next to him moved into the aisle. The lineup of people finally inched forward, and Schmitt stepped out to join them.

Inside the terminal, the moving herd of passengers made their way toward the baggage claim area. Schmitt approached the nearest exit on the ground level, following the signs directing him toward the taxi stand.

Before he reached the door, flashing strobe lights atop several New York City Police cruisers caught his attention. He froze. Had the detective been alerted to Luedecke's murder in New Brighton and contacted the authorities in New York City?

Schmitt looked back. Two uniformed police officers rushed in his direction. He stopped, frantic to make a decision. He could feel his heart racing. If he tried to run, he certainly would not escape.

Before he could move, the track of the two police officers split apart when they came abreast of him. They sped past, and he watched with relief when they exited the terminal. What was going on? Teetering on his heels, he fingered the nitroglycerin spray in his pocket.

Schmitt pushed through the exit doors and received his explanation. Outside, traffic was at a standstill. Three police cruisers scattered about, bar lights flashing, added to the congestion. A Yellow Cab parked at the curb in front the terminal was the center of attention. An EMS ambulance crawled toward the taxi, snaking around the double-parked vehicles along the curb. A pair of legs dangled out of the cab's opened passenger door. Schmitt became transfixed on the sight for several seconds. Heart attack, he guessed, and he hurried to the taxi stand.

The bottleneck in front of the terminal took thirty minutes to dissolve before traffic could flow again. Schmitt was fifth in the taxi queue. When his turn came, he slid into the cab's passenger seat and squeezed a stream of air through his compressed lips. "Bushwick, Brooklyn," he told the driver.

* * *

Flo left the bathroom door open while Luke Rizzo watched from her bed. Her small, firm breasts jiggled from the vigorous toweling across her back and shoulders. Her toned upper arms were impressive, and when she raised them to dry her wet hair, Rizzo saw only tight, well-formed biceps. She was a first-class package. Exploring her body last night with hands and mouth had been an extraordinary experience. Images of his head-to-toe performance resurfaced and his erection returned.

"Flo, come back to bed. It's early."

"Darlin', I have to work and you got a plane to catch."

"That's the problem, angel, I don't want to leave. But I have to."

"Well, hon, that's sweet, you know. I mean, you can always come back. You hear?"

Rizzo pulled off the sheet, swung his legs to the floor and sat naked on the edge of the bed. He watched Flo slipping into her panties and bra. Damn! Last night had been—

The beeping of his pager interrupted his revisited erotic experience. His pants with the pager clipped to his belt lay over the back of the chair in the corner. He reached the annoying sound in two strides. The caller number was unfamiliar. Remembering he had left his cell phone in New York, he looked toward the Princess phone on the nightstand.

"You mind?" he said to Flo. "It's local."

"You go ahead, darlin'. I'll finish up dressing in the bathroom."

Rizzo dialed the number on the display.

"New Brighton Police," the voice answered.

"Hello, this is Luke Rizzo."

"Mr. Rizzo, this is Sergeant Maddox. We met yesterday. You came by looking for the Veterans Administration office. Left your pager number with me."

"Oh yeah, that's right, Sarge. What's up?"

"Are you here...that is...I mean...you back in New York?"

"No. Haven't left. I'm...I'm in..." Rizzo looked at Flo standing at the bathroom door.

"Ashton," she mouthed, loud enough for him to hear.

"Uh, ah Ashton... In Ashton. I plan to leave about an hour from now. Why?"

"Well, sir, our captain would like to have a word with you before you head out. That way you wouldn't have to make a special trip all the way back to New Brighton."

Holding the phone to his ear, Rizzo looked down at his flaccid condition then toward Flo. He shook his head in resignation and grinned.

"Can you give me a head's up, why he wants to see me? Maybe we can do this over the phone."

He doubted he had broken a law with his visit to the VA office and the way he got confirmation of Frank Bard's Air Force serial number.

"No, sir, too important," the sergeant said. "That's all I can say right now. If you'd like, we can come by and pick you up."

Rizzo shot a look at Flo. Her face was a blank page, struggling to make sense of his mysterious conversation. He shrugged and said, "Hey, that's all right. If it's that important, hell, I don't want to get in bad with the New Brighton Police Department. Be a couple of hours, okay? I need to grab a shower."

"Around noon, then. Oh, and the captain would like you to bring along anything that would substantiate the official reason for your visit to New Brighton."

What the hell was that about? He didn't think he would have to comply. He figured they would need a court order to force him to reveal privileged information shared between him and his client, such as a doctor and his patient. On second thought, he could be wrong.

"Yeah, I can do that," he answered. "Bye, Sarge."

Chapter 5

Rizzo remained standing in front of the desk, the document folder tucked under his arm, and watched as Sergeant Maddox pushed open the door to the glass-enclosed office of Captain Albee Jarvis. Maddox stuck his head in without entering.

"Mr. Luke Rizzo here to see you, Captain."

"Okay, Andy. Give me a couple of minutes."

"Sure thing," the desk sergeant said. He closed the door and turned to Rizzo, motioning to the bench against the back wall. "Have a seat, Mr. Rizzo. The captain will be right with you. Coffee?"

"That'd be fine, Sarge. Black, no sugar,"

Rizzo sat down, placed the Frank Bard, Jr. document folder next to him and looked around. He sensed none of the warm friendliness that had greeted him yesterday when he first walked into this small, rural police station. Yesterday, Andy Maddox had referred to him by his given name. "Hey, Luke. Great to meet you." Today, it was Mr. Rizzo. Something serious was going down.

Andy Maddox returned and handed Rizzo a mug filled with steaming black coffee. "It's fresh."

"Thanks, Sarge." Luke took the cup with both hands. "Any idea how long this is going to take?"

The desk sergeant looked down with an expression of concern. A red flag went up, signaling something Rizzo was not eager to hear.

"Don't know, Mr. Rizzo. Depends on what you have to tell the captain. Really, that's all I'm at liberty to say."

The captain's door opened. "Come on in, Mr. Rizzo. And bring the coffee with you."

Albee Jarvis, a short man as wide as he was tall, had a dark, bushy growth under his nose creating a contrast with his balding head. The solid body gave him the look of an athlete, while his small wire-framed cheater glasses resting on the bridge of his wide nose conveyed the appearance of a no-nonsense law officer.

An image formed in Rizzo's head. Jarvis was the Keystone State's version of Dennis Franz, the TV actor he remembered from the show "NYPD Blue." Rizzo took note. Be guarded with your answers to the captain's questions, he reminded himself; save the tendency to be New York-flip for another time.

"Have a seat," Jarvis said, motioning to the chair at the side of his desk. The captain swiveled his own chair and fell into it. His expressionless eyes locked onto Rizzo's face. "And thanks a lot for coming," he said after several long seconds. "I appreciate it."

"Well, I'm glad you caught up with me before I left the area," Rizzo said. "Makes it convenient for both of us."

Jarvis nodded. He folded his arms across his barrel chest and leaned back. He squeezed his eyes behind the wire frames as though he was trying to figure out something. He began a smile, but the friendliness disappeared as he spoke.

"And I wonder... Would you mind telling me the reason for your visit to New Brighton?" He posed the question without sounding accusatory.

Rizzo set the coffee mug on the corner of the desk. He opened the document folder balanced on his lap, ready to produce his assignment letter from Amy Chatsworth. After a moment, he changed his mind, closed the folder and looked across to Jarvis.

"Well, you know, of course, I'm a private detective...that I came to New Brighton to check on something for my client."

"Which was what?"

Rizzo hesitated. Was he going to stand behind his right of confidentiality or cooperate?

Before Rizzo could decide, Jarvis spoke again. "Mr. Rizzo, you have every right not to answer that question, but you know if you don't, well, I'll be forced to get a court order, make you return at a future date...and soon."

The emphasis on the word *soon* was a gunshot. Shit! Rizzo moved the mug, making room on the desk for the folder and withdrew Amy Chatsworth's letter.

He placed the letter on the desk within the reach of Jarvis. "Captain, that's not necessary. I'm happy to tell you. Believe me, it's not anything criminal...a personal matter of one of your citizens here."

"Mr. Frank Bard?"

An alarm went off. Albee Jarvis was way ahead of him. No time to blow smoke.

"Yes, sir."

Jarvis remained mute, waiting for Rizzo to continue, glancing at the letter.

"I came here at the request of my client, an English lady... lives in London...to see if I could locate a man she believed to be her father."

"Lost touch, did she?"

"No, not like that. She was...well...illegitimate," Rizzo answered. "Frank Bard was a young airman stationed in England in 1958 when he knocked up her mother. Left England three months later and never came back."

"And that's why you went to the VA?"

"Right. All she had was an Air Force serial number." Rizzo nodded to the letter on the desk. "She located Frank Bard through a birth-search service and wrote to him. He answered saying the man she was looking for was dead and buried in Sylvania Hills Cemetery."

"And you checked that out, too?" Jarvis said.

"Yes, of course. She hired me to verify that the Frank Bard buried there was her father. Turned out to be Frank Bard Senior. I was looking for Frank Bard, Junior."

For the next few minutes, Rizzo repeated the details of his visits to the cemetery, the Palumbo funeral home, the tax collector, the police station, and the Veteran's Administration office in Beaver, where he was able to verify that Frank Bard, Jr. was his client's father.

"Did I break any laws, Captain? Tell me."

Jarvis ignored the question. "What did you do next?"

Rizzo thought about Frank Bard following him around all day, and the brush in the VA parking lot. Should he even mention it? What other reason could he give for contacting Bard and meeting with him at the tavern? None. He had better level with Jarvis.

He explained the way Frank Bard almost hit him fleeing the parking lot, triggering his investigative curiosity to request the license plate check. He took the captain through the tavern scene, repeating much of their conversation.

"That's it," he said. "So, mind telling me what this is about?"

"And what time did you leave the tavern?" Jarvis asked. His oatmeal expression remained cemented on his face.

"Maybe around three-thirty. I got to the airport minutes after four o'clock. I know that because the woman I was meeting...she works at the Avis counter...was getting off work. From there we went to dinner, and then back to her place in Ashton, where Sergeant Maddox reached me this morning."

"Okay," Captain Jarvis replied. "And you can verify your timing?"

"Sure can. I checked in my rental and dropped my keys off around four-thirty. I checked out another car not fifteen minutes later."

Jarvis raised an eyebrow.

"I didn't know I was spending the night when I checked in the first time."

Now Jarvis grinned easily.

"Captain, what's going down?" Rizzo asked. He could feel his throat tightening.

Albee Jarvis sat erect and leaned forward. His face became grim.

"Frank Bard, Junior was murdered last evening. We think you were the last person to see him alive."

Rizzo's eyes jumped wide. "What! Holy Christ! I don't believe it."

"Believe it, Mr. Rizzo," Jarvis said.

Rizzo sat riveted to his chair. An image of a dead Frank Bard's face, gray skin with empty eyes, floated outside his mind's field of view. He shook his head as though trying to deny entry to the spectral figure.

"When...how...I mean, how was he killed?"

"A bullet in his head...up close, yesterday afternoon, on the driveway of his home."

"Good God! Why? Why would someone murder him?"

"Maybe you can tell me," Jarvis answered. "Anything he said or implied during your conversation raise a red flag? Like family problems, trouble with neighbors, anything suspicious that would give us a hint why someone would want to kill him?"

Rizzo sat back and drew in a deep breath. He felt his chest heaving. The soft features of Frank Bard's aged but handsome face came into focus, and the sound of his asthmatic wheeze filled Rizzo's ears. A heavy silence captured the moment. He wiped away the moisture from the corners of his eyes without looking back at Jarvis.

Jarvis waited. Finally, he asked, "Anything?"

"No. Nothing," Rizzo mumbled. "I can't imagine—"

"Was Frank Bard German?"

Rizzo lifted his head. "Who?"

"Her father. Do you know if he was German? "

"No. I don't know. Why do you ask?"

"We found this," Jarvis said, removing a small, clear plastic envelope from the center drawer of his desk. "It was tossed on the seat next to Mr. Bard after he was shot."

Rizzo recognized the container as an evidence envelope: an unfolded piece of notepaper with one line of lettering visible through the transparent plastic. He held up the envelope to eye level and stared at the strange writing.

"It's German," Albee Jarvis said. "That much we know."

"What's it say?"

Jarvis rolled out the words. "*Verräter, die rache gehört mir. WS.* Loosely translated: Traitor, revenge is mine."

"The initials, WS?"

"My guess it's the author of the message," Jarvis said. "This county has a fair share of German families, mostly second and third generation. This could be the result of a long-standing personal dispute. We haven't interviewed members of Mr. Bard's family yet to see what they can tell us."

The telephone intercom buzzed, interrupting Jarvis. He listened and hung up. "Sorry," he said. "Now, Mr. Rizzo, can you think of anything that Mr. Bard said during the time you spent with him, anything that might lead you to think his life was in danger?"

The photo. Should he mention it? Bard had given it to him to send to Amy Chatsworth. He recalled the way he had the envelope taped to the bottom of the glove compartment of his car. He was oddly secretive about it. "*Do it soon, please? I trust you, Luke,*" he said. "*Tell her to keep it somewhere safe...away from prying eyes. Don't let no one know she has it.*"

Rizzo never intended to open the envelope before mailing it to Amy Chatsworth, but Frank Bard's murder changed that. The question was whether to tell Albee Jarvis. *"Don't let no one know she has it."* He remembered Bard's confusion in the VA parking lot. *"I thought you were someone else,"* he had said.

"No, sir. All we talked about was family, his and mine."

Jarvis got to his feet. "We've fixed the time of Frank Bard's death at about four-ten yesterday afternoon."

Surprised they would know that so soon, Rizzo asked, "You did an autopsy?"

Jarvis looked through the glass wall, at his deputy. "Yes. The M.E. completed their report this morning."

"That was quick."

"Deputy Maddox checked with Avis a short while ago. They confirmed you turned in your rental at four twenty-seven. So, Mr. Rizzo, you're free to leave."

Rizzo got to his feet and slipped Amy Chatsworth's assignment letter into the document folder.

"And if anything comes to mind from your conversation with Frank Bard," Jarvis continued, "that might be helpful in our investigation, be sure to give us a call, won't you?" Then pointing to the folder under Rizzo's arm, Albee Jarvis added, "And please give your client our most sincere condolences."

* * *

The terminal at Pittsburgh's airport hummed with activity when Rizzo arrived. Coming through the automatic sliding doors, he caught sight of Flo standing behind the Avis counter, her eyes fixed on the computer screen, attending to a customer. He checked his watch, comparing the time with that shown on the lighted digital display behind the counter. Flo would be quitting soon. He could try to make the five-fifty flight to LaGuardia or hang around with her for another night and leave in the morning. He hesitated, thinking of the promise he had made to himself. He had to win back his son's respect. That meant knocking off his womanizing as well as his drinking. He knew that—wanted that.

Rizzo looked again at Flo. His indecisiveness was painful. Images of last night's tasty lovemaking teased him. She was a vanilla sundae, ice water in the desert. Maybe she is a necessity right now, he rationalized, a distraction from dwelling on the sad fate of Frank Bard.

Flo raised her head and spotted him. He was sure she had picked up his thought-waves. Her warm smile was all he needed to make up his mind.

Rizzo held up his pager and pointed to it, hoping Flo would understand the gesture. She nodded and turned back to her traveler. Before anything else, he needed to call Amy Chatsworth, to let her know what happened to her father. He did a quick calculation of the time difference between Pittsburgh and London. Ten at night, her time, not too late to make the call. He had standing instructions to phone Amy Chatsworth, reversing the charges, at any time.

He glanced around, looking for a public telephone, and remembered his membership in the Admirals Club. He rode the escalator to the second level and settled on a sofa in the club's lounge. Dialing the operator, he gave Amy Chatsworth's number at her London home. Within minutes, a female voice agreed to accept the charges.

"Mrs. Chatsworth," he said. "Mrs. Chatsworth, this is Lucas Rizzo. I hope it's not too late. I'm calling about Frank Bard. I found him in New Brighton, Pennsylvania."

"How wonderful. Tell me about it, please. Did you get to speak with him?"

Before Rizzo could answer, he heard a soft voice over his shoulder asking, "Would you like a cocktail?" He turned to see the club's hostess standing behind him, pantomiming the act of drinking. He shook his head and waved her off.

He sat paralyzed as he wrestled with Amy Chatsworth's question, wondering how to break the news.

"Yes, I met with him for about an hour. I'll cover it in my report to you."

"Splendid."

"But I'm afraid I have bad news, ma'am...no, terrible news, in fact."

She remained silent.

"Mrs. Chatsworth, there's no easy way to say this."

"Tell me. What happened?"

Rizzo could hear apprehension in her question.

"Later, that is, after we met at this local tavern and talked, someone murdered Mr. Bard at his home."

He thought the connection had been broken until he realized she had taken the phone from her ear. He pictured her looking at the instrument in disbelief. Seconds passed before he heard her breathing into the receiver again, struggling to get words out.

"Oh, my...good Lord...how...how, in God's name—"

Rizzo jumped in. "The police are working on it, but they're baffled. Your father was a well-liked man, from what I gathered."

"Why, then...why...why would anyone want to murder him?"

"I don't know. We hope the police will come up with that answer."

"Do you believe it was deliberate?"

The question sounded funny. Murder was always deliberate. "Ma'am, I would think so."

"I mean, it wasn't...ah...what you in your country call a passing...ahh—"

"A drive-by-shooting?"

"Yes, that's it."

Bard took the bullet in the head at close range. Rizzo didn't feel it was an appropriate time to disclose those details.

"No, ma'am. The shooting was definitely a deliberate act." He recalled the strange message in German and added,

"Whoever shot him was looking for revenge. The police found a note on the seat of his car."

"They did? What did it say?"

He glanced at his watch. Flo would end her shift in ten minutes. He hoped she would wait around until he got back down.

"Ma'am, I don't want to keep you on the phone. It's after ten over there. I can call you tomorrow, provide you the details then."

"No, Mr. Rizzo. Tell me. I want to know now." She spoke the words with a force that discouraged a challenge.

"Well, ma'am, the note was in German, which is puzzling. I mean, the police made the translation easy enough, but the question is, why in German?"

"Well, what did it say?"

He knew he would butcher the words if he tried repeating it to her. "The translation," he said, "was 'Traitor, revenge is mine.' The writer signed it with the initials, WS."

She drew a breath and gasped, "Oh, my God...my God in heaven."

"Mrs. Chatsworth?... Ma'am?...What's wrong?"

"Mr. Rizzo, give me a moment."

He heard her put down the phone. He checked his watch and scanned the near-empty lounge. Spotting the club's hostess clearing cocktail glasses from a cluster of tables nearby, he called to her. She assured him she would call down to the Avis counter and give Flo his message.

His phone came alive again.

"Mr. Rizzo, are you there?"

"Yes, ma'am, I'm here."

"Mr. Rizzo, do you recall the German words on the paper your police found?"

Rizzo hesitated. Did she expect him to repeat them back to her? "Well, ma'am, I saw the note, but I don't think I can do justice reciting what it said."

"Then listen to me carefully, Mr. Rizzo. Did the message say, *Verräter, die rache gehört mir?*"

He remembered Albee Jarvis speaking the German words badly. Her pronunciation sounded more authentic. "Sounds right," he said.

"And signed with the initials WS. Correct?"

"Yes, ma'am, that's what I said before."

"Mr. Rizzo, can you call me back in about an hour? I need to confer with Scotland Yard. However, I wish to speak with you further. Is that all right?"

"That'll be fine, ma'am. I'll call you around five-thirty, my time."

"Goodbye, Mr. Rizzo, and thank you."

He replaced the phone and stared down at the instrument. Scotland Yard? What in hell did Scotland Yard have to do with Frank Bard's murder? He rose from the sofa and started toward the door of the club. Making the five-fifty flight was now a non-issue. He hoped his Avis angel had gotten his message and waited for him.

Chapter 6

Schmitt pushed the bottom bell on the worn faceplate and stepped back. A voice over the intercom asked, "Who is it?"

"Werner Schmitt, Herr Buchmann. I am here."

"One second, Werner," came the reply. "First floor, back."

A buzzing sound followed.

The lock released. Schmitt pushed open the door and entered the dark foyer. Despite having been born upstairs in the front apartment of this three-story frame house, he found nothing that was familiar to him. When he was an infant, his parents took him back to Germany before the war. He was too young to have any memories of life in Bushwick, Brooklyn.

He passed the staircase. The musty odor of the old building caused him to hold his breath. He picked his way down the narrow hallway, over the floor's patched-vinyl squares, toward the rear. An elderly, gray-haired man in a tattered wool cardigan peered out through an opened door.

"Herr Buchmann, I am so happy to see you again," Schmitt said, as he extended his hand.

The man, bent at the waist with the weight of years, squinted above the glasses perched on his long nose.

"Werner, that is you? *Ja?* I haf not laid eyes on you since you were *das kind.*"

He opened his arms to receive him. Schmitt leaned over to accept the man's embrace. His father's oldest friend, overjoyed by the reunion with his godchild, grinned.

"It has been a long time, Herr Buchmann. Almost sixty-three years."

"Come in...come in," Otto Buchmann implored.

The old man stepped back to make room for Schmitt and gestured toward a sofa covered in a heavy, patterned fabric and nestled between the two windows of the tiny living room. "Sit...sit down. Please, call me Otto. Herr Buchmann is so formal. We are family, *korrekt?*"

Schmitt moved across the room, set his small suitcase down and took a seat at one end of the sofa. Otto Buchmann closed the door and faced his visitor. His pleased expression had not changed.

"Your letter surprised me. I could not believe you were coming. So many years and here you are." His grin widened. "You haf your *vater's* eyes. I can see that right away."

"Your memory is exceptional, Otto. When you last saw him, he was a young man." Schmitt said. "He had not turned thirty when he took us back to Germany."

"You are right," he said. "He was young. We will speak of him, but first, a taste of *schnapps. Ja?*"

Herr Buchmann disappeared into the kitchen at the rear of the apartment and returned with a bottle and two small glasses. He set them on the coffee table and eased himself into the overstuffed lounge chair to Schmitt's left.

"Let me think," he said, filling both glasses to the top. "We arrived here 1932. Maybe 1933. So long ago, I get confused. During the depression. Both of us twenty-five and ambitious. Your *mutter* was younger, like my Hilda, may they rest in peace." Buchmann picked up his glass. "*Prosit*, Werner. So good to see you."

Schmitt brought his glass to his mouth. "*Prosit*, Otto."

He sipped the *schnapps* while visualizing the beautiful face of his mother, Gherta. In her youth, she had been a vibrant woman. The years of struggle following the execution of his father destroyed her beauty and led to her death before Schmitt was sixteen.

"Both wives worked with us in the brewery for a while," Buchmann said, "until your *mutter* became pregnant with you. A few years later, your *vater* took you back to Germany full of *der enthusiasmus*. He could not wait to return to the homeland."

"Why was that?"

"Because of what was happening there with the movement. He felt he needed to be part of it."

"You stayed on with the brewery, did you?"

"*Ja*, another thirty years. Closed down two years after I retired, same as all the other breweries in Bushwick. They gave me a small retirement benefit."

Buchmann's eyes closed. He leaned back in the chair, his gray head pressing into the soft, frayed headrest. "After that, everything began changing," he said. "A nice German neighborhood when we came here. So, now...now a different color. Sometimes dangerous, you know." The old man nodded toward the bedroom door. "Haf to keep a pistol in my night table for protection."

"But you remain here," Schmitt said.

"I became a citizen in 1958. So where do I go? After Hilda died fifteen years ago, I was certain I would follow her soon. But God was not ready, and so..." Otto Buchmann raised his glass to salute his ninety-two years on this earth.

Schmitt nodded. He questioned if returning to Germany when his parents did might not have served Otto and Hilda Buchmann better. He hoisted his glass. "A blessing on your long life, Otto."

"So, Werner, now tell me why you have come. Business?"

A pang of guilt shot though him. As a feared member of East Germany's Stasi before the reunification, he had often spied on people he knew well. Now he was using his father's oldest friend for his purpose. He had not considered what the fallout might be for Otto Buchmann if his plan went wrong. A hotel somewhere in Manhattan would have been better, but he could not risk it, especially after Pennsylvania.

"I am here for a few days," Schmitt said. "I wanted to pay you a visit before I went to a hotel."

"Bah!" the old man responded. "Why spend money on a hotel? You stay here with me, *ja*?"

Schmitt expected the reaction. "If you wish, Otto. Until my business is done. Thank you for your generosity."

* * *

Flo slid the key in the lock. She nudged the door open with an elbow and entered her small townhouse unit. "Well then, darlin', we can always stay in. And I can cook you one of my bluegrass specialties."

Rizzo followed her in and dropped his overnight bag on the sofa. "That's not fair," he said. "Let me make the phone call first. We can find a cozy restaurant somewhere for a nice romantic dinner."

"Sugar, you think I can't make a romantic dinner right here in my own kitchen?"

She frowned like a hurt child, kicked off her shoes and disappeared into the bedroom.

"That's not what I mean," Rizzo said, tracing her steps toward the bedroom. "I meant, why should you have to cook dinner for us when we can—"

His words trailed off as he halted at the open bedroom door. Flo had shrugged out of her uniform jacket and slid the red skirt down from her hips as in the smooth, sensuous motion of a stripper. The garments collapsed together at her feet on the shaggy rug. She stepped out from the pile and reached up, undid the scarf from her neck and unbuttoned her blouse.

He stepped quickly through the doorway. "Here, let me help."

Down to panties and bra, she turned toward him. They were not leaving the apartment. The look on her face made that clear.

He pulled her toward him. "Okay, you win."

His arms circled her small waist, while the flat of her belly and pelvis pressed against him. She leaned back, her mouth forming a sly grin, and he smothered her lips before she finished. Passion heated his body during their deep, wet kiss. When he broke for air, he remembered the phone call.

"Can you hold this thought until I make that phone call?" he whispered. "Believe me, angel, if the call wasn't important, I'd be devouring you as my dinner appetizer right now."

"Darlin', I'm not goin' nowhere. You go ahead. Do what you have to do. Let me wash up. Then I can get things ready in the kitchen for your main course. When you're finished with the call, we can start with the appetizer."

His watch showed five-forty-five when he closed the bedroom door and sat on the corner of the bed. He hoped the conversation would not take long as he dialed the operator to place the call.

After several minutes, Amy Chatsworth's voice answered.

"Mr. Rizzo?"

"Yes, ma'am."

"Can you meet me in New York this coming Monday? Let us say noontime at the Waldorf Astoria Hotel. Call my room when you arrive."

"You coming to the States?"

"Yes. In addition, I need to retain your services for a while longer. Are you available?"

Rizzo pictured his empty calendar and waning bank balance. "I'm your man."

"Good. I'll pay your daily rate plus all expenses."

"Sounds fine. What's up with Scotland Yard, by the way?"

After a short pause, she said, "A fanatic bent on revenge killed my father. The Yard thinks they know his identity."

Rizzo shook his head. This was turning into an international problem, out of his league. "Mrs. Chatsworth, maybe you should contact the FBI."

"Mr. Rizzo, meet me in the Waldorf lobby at noon, day after tomorrow. I will explain everything then. Goodnight."

"I'll be there."

The phone went dead before he finished getting the words out.

When he entered the kitchen, Flo stood at the side of the sink paring a large carrot. She was barefoot, still in her panties and bra, with a half-apron tied around her waist.

"That was quick."

He put his hands on her bare shoulders and kissed the nape of her neck. She lowered her head to one side, moaned softly, savoring the moment, and dropped the carrot and paring knife onto the board.

"Dinner ready?" he asked while nibbling at her ear lobe.

She turned her small body around and took his face into both of her hands. "No, darlin'," she said. "But your appetizer is."

* * *

The next morning, Flo drove him to the airport. The ride was a mixture of awkward silence and self-conscious conversation. Rizzo had been able to book a nine-twenty departure to LaGuardia. The timing was perfect. Flo reported to work at eight-thirty, so he could go right to his departure gate without hanging around at the Avis counter, avoiding an uncomfortable, long goodbye.

They sped along Route 60. His growing indecisiveness seeped through his defenses. He felt conflicted. Was Flo the best bed partner he'd ever had? On the other hand, had she reached in and ignited a feeling he forgot was there? Whichever way, it worried him.

She parked the car in the Avis lot, and they walked toward the terminal building. When they reached the sidewalk in front of the building's sliding doors, Flo stopped. "Let's say goodbye here, darlin'. I don't want to give Velma reason to gossip."

He reached out and pulled her close. "Listen, Flo. I don't know when I can get back but—"

She put her hand over his mouth. "Shhh, no need to say anything, sugar. We had a wonderful time. No strings... no regrets."

He felt strange; anxiety had stoked old fears and uncertainties. He squeezed her hand and brought his forehead down to meet hers. He wanted to close his eyes. Instead, he forced them to stay open.

"I want you to know...uh...how special you are. I mean—" He could not finish. The word, *love*, had popped into his head, and the concept scared him.

"Darlin', I feel the same about you."

She tilted her head and their mouths found each other one last time.

Chapter 7

Rizzo moved to a cluster of overstuffed club chairs and sat facing the bank of elevators. Amy Chatsworth was on her way down, telling him when he phoned her room, "Elevators at the Park Avenue end of the lobby, Mr. Rizzo...be there in a minute."

He glanced around the vast Waldorf-Astoria lobby, at the abundance of elegance and plush appointments, happy he'd selected for this meeting his favorite Harris Tweed sports jacket to wear over a cotton crew-neck sweater. Thinking back to his rookie days on the NYPD, he realized many years had passed since his last visit to this New York City landmark art-deco hotel. Those assignments of providing security at various high-powered political functions always fell to the younger cops in his precinct. Easy, though not exciting, duty. He recalled the occasional close-up exposures to visiting foreign dignitaries. The last time he was here, Margaret Thatcher stopped to shake his hand on the way out to her waiting limousine.

Several people emerged from an elevator, crowding along the short corridor into the open lobby area. They separated, and Rizzo spotted the lone woman bringing up the rear. She hesitated, looked to her left and right before she looked straight at him. He rose from the chair. Amy Chatsworth approached with quick, deliberate steps while he stood riveted next to a tall, potted palm. She reached out, her face full of anticipation.

"Mr. Rizzo, how nice," she said with a gracious smile.

Rizzo took her extended hand. Her firm grip was one of authority and control. He searched for a resemblance to Frank Bard and found traces of his long neck and soft, golden brown eyes. She was of medium height, with chestnut brown hair, worn loosely at shoulder-length. Her delicate features, clear skin and laugh wrinkles around her eyes were appealing features, while her high cheekbones added a look of classy elegance.

"Mrs. Chatsworth. How are you?"

"Very well, thank you."

"I hope you had a good flight."

"Yes. Uneventful except for the long lines at Customs."

Hearing her speak, she called to mind the actor Emma Thompson — noticeably polished, liltingly British.

"Thank you for coming," she said. "I do hope you'll forgive the short notice."

Rizzo grinned. "Mrs. Chatsworth, even if I were that busy, I'd put aside everything to help you."

"That's sweet of you, Mr. Rizzo."

"You know, Mrs. Chatsworth, Frank Bard...your father, I mean...he was a wonderful, warm man, a good person. I got that sense of him in the short time we spent together. His murder really affected me."

Amy Chatsworth closed her eyes for a moment, revisiting the shock of the tragedy. When she opened them, she glanced around the lobby. They had been standing in the same spot since they shook hands.

"Are you hungry, Mr. Rizzo? Is there somewhere quiet we can go to have a light lunch and talk? Nothing elaborate. The FBI is not expecting us until three."

The Bull and Bear came to mind, a restaurant on the Lexington Avenue side of the hotel, always crowded and noisy. He dismissed it. However, the restaurant's name jogged his memory of a different animal-themed restaurant, one that he often used to meet with his drug-dealing snitches. The Dancing Crane Café, despite being out in the open, afforded him the privacy he wanted. *Hiding in plain sight*, Rizzo used to quote to anyone questioning his choice of meeting place. Despite it being the late fall, remnants of Indian summer blessed the city with a lingering warmth. The restaurant in the Central Park Zoo would work nicely.

His client wore a double-breasted, buttery-soft, leather, safari-type jacket, belted around her waist, and reached an inch above the knees of her black gabardine pants. The tan shade of the leather almost matched her eye color. She was hatless. He could see a white cotton turtleneck peeking out from under her jacket collar.

"Are you going to be warm enough in that?" he asked.

"I should think so," she answered, looking at his jacket. "Certainly as warm as you'll be in that."

"Good, because we're going to dine *al fresco* at the zoo."

"Oh, my. That sounds like an adventure. I'm glad I wore my safari jacket."

Rizzo pointed to the Park Avenue entrance. "Let's grab a cab."

They approached the revolving doors with Amy Chatsworth walking ahead of him. From behind, he had an opportunity to study the English woman. His eyes roamed over her figure. Her slender body had long, clean and symmetrical lines and a youthful appearance. She carried herself erect and moved with an air of self-confidence.

They reached the curb, where the uniformed hotel doorman held open the door of a waiting Yellow Cab. "Central Park Zoo," Rizzo told the driver.

They emerged at Sixtieth Street and Fifth Avenue. From there, they entered the park and walked the length of the bench-lined path to the zoo's entrance. Rizzo paid the admission fees and led her the short distance to the restaurant overlooking the seal pool.

"We can sit inside, if you'd prefer," Rizzo said, "or at one of these tables on the terrace."

"Oh, outside would be nice. If it gets too cold, we can always go in. Agreed?"

He chose a small table at one end of the terrace, away from those already occupied. The restaurant's menus were stuck between the napkin holder and the table's umbrella pole. Rizzo pulled one out and handed it to Amy Chatsworth.

"I apologize. Not exactly *haute cuisine*, but they do have interesting sandwiches.When you decide, I'll go inside to get it. No table service, I'm afraid."

"Lovely," she said, scanning the brief list of items.

Rizzo sat back and waited. He didn't need to look. He knew what he wanted.

"You know, I think I'd like the grilled veggie sandwich and a cup of coffee, no cream or sugar."

"Not tea?"

She narrowed her eyes and grinned. "The English drink coffee as well, Mr. Rizzo."

Five minutes later, Rizzo returned to their table, carrying a tray with their food. As he approached, he made a quick assessment of the surrounding area, taking in the faces of the dozen or so diners on the terrace, checking the perimeter to see if he spotted anything out of the ordinary. His vigilance might be overkill, but after what happened in New Brighton, Rizzo was not taking anything for granted. He reached their table, set down the tray and dropped into a chair across from Amy.

Tossing a look around, he said, "They renovated this place about twelve years ago. You know, I liked the zoo better when I used to come here as a kid."

"A traditionalist, are you?"

"No, not really. More like old-fashioned."

"I can see that by the way you insist on calling me Mrs. Chatsworth. That makes me sound so old. So let's try Amy and Luke, shall we?"

"A deal." He picked up his Coke, raised it, and said, "Here's to Amy and Luke."

* * *

Monday morning Schmitt had posted himself outside the Flatiron Building on Twenty-third Street where Luke Rizzo maintained a small office. He felt his patience rewarded when he spotted the detective leaving the building before noon.

Following him uptown by taxi to the Waldorf-Astoria had been easy, but the surprise that awaited him in the hotel lobby produced a rush of euphoria. He would now have an opportunity to redeem himself—another chance to kill Amy Chatsworth.

Standing less than twenty feet from them in the hotel lobby, he had listened through his ear buds to their conversation and to Rizzo's mention of the zoo. He departed the hotel in a taxi minutes behind theirs.

Schmitt pushed through the revolving turnstile, entered the children's zoo and made his way toward the pool of marine mammals, taking care to behave like another gawking out-of-town tourist. He arrived at the glass barrier protecting the circular perimeter of the harbor seals' playground. Adults and children scattered about, surrounding it, enjoying the aquatic show. He squeezed between two older children at the barrier and placed his elbow on top of the rail. The fishy odor of the tank filled his nostrils.

Leaning on the railing, striking a casual pose, he pretended to watch the show on the other side of the glass. Those children too small to see over the barrier squatted at his legs, pressing their faces against the cold, wet glass so they could see the action in the pool. They watched, transfixed, as the cavorting mammals disappeared under the dark water, only to break the surface several yards away with a flourishing leap into the air, repeating these antics again as they chased each other above and below the water. Two more earless seals perched on top of the rocky cave-like fortress in the center, produced a series of barking noises, each time bringing squeals of appreciative laughter from the children. Every so often, Schmitt's mouth turned up at the corners, unconsciously responding to the children's gleeful reactions.

His real interest was the two diners at the table on the restaurant terrace a hundred yards away, but well out of range of his ear-bud amplifiers. He stared at the woman and the detective locked in whispered conversation and smiled, thinking again how easily he had learned of the woman's quest to find her father. He knew if he were patient and clever, Rizzo would yield the photo he needed to identify Max Vogel, his second target.

Schmitt thought again of his errant shot in London. He would admit to losing a step with firearms, but certainly, he'd lost nothing with surveillance and stealth investigations. No one in his entire section was better at it. Working undercover all those years in East Germany primed his skills for this vendetta. His father, Lieutenant Walter Schmitt, would have been proud of him.

* * *

Rizzo got out of the taxi first and paid the fare. He looked at the fountain in front of 26 Federal Plaza, trying to remember the last time he had been in the building. As Amy slid across the seat to exit, Rizzo extended his hand, quietly admiring his client's decision to change her attire when they returned to the Waldorf. Amy had chosen a businesslike, two-button suit jacket and pencil skirt for their meeting with the federal agents, leaving behind in her hotel room, the expensive safari-casual look. They stepped off the elevator into the twenty-third floor waiting room. The receptionist politely directed them to the sofa while she dialed up Special Agent Jack Fields.

Fields emerged from within to escort them back to his office. "Please have a seat," Fields said, examining Amy Chatsworth with a glint of admiration. He pointed to the two chairs positioned in front of his large, efficient-looking desk.

Fields dropped into his high-back leather desk chair and reached out to the telephone console in front of him. "Mrs. Chatsworth...Luke...can I get you anything...coffee, a soft drink?"

She shook her head. "No, thank you. I'm fine."

"Same here," Rizzo said.

Fields pushed the intercom button and asked his secretary to hold all calls, but tell him when Tony gets in.

Rizzo pictured the face of the other half of the FBI's famous Batman and Robin team, Tony Condon. Condon, he remembered, was a serious, no-nonsense agent whose chiseled jaw-line and brush-cut never let you forget he was once a Marine drill instructor. Jack Fields, the senior agent, was the type of meticulous government man who operated quietly and always had everything under control. Tall, dressed in the Bureau's standard white shirt and blue conservative suit, he made certain his demeanor reflected an "all business" attitude when dealing with the FBI's affairs. Yet he could laugh at himself.

"So, Luke, it's been a few years since we shared a beer. You're retired now, I see," the agent said. "How's it going?"

"Fine, Jack. Routine P.I. work...you know...stuff like that. Nothing exciting like the drug-running case we had with you guys five years ago when I was on the Job."

"It was interesting, "I'll say that."

"But this assignment...I mean—" Rizzo glanced at Amy, who had her eyes fixed on Fields. "...that is, Mrs. Chatsworth's situation, it looks to be international. Way out of my league."

The agent leaned back. "You're right. The information Mrs. Chatsworth gave me yesterday over the phone would certainly indicate that. Why don't you start from the beginning? How did you become involved and what happened?"

As he did with Captain Albee Jarvis at the New Brighton Police Station, Rizzo took Fields through the details of his initial investigation: his trip to New Brighton to verify the death of Frank Bard; the interim stops made before his success at the VA office in Beaver. He recounted the meeting with the man who turned out to be Amy Chatsworth's father, Frank Bard, Jr., the unexpected call from Sergeant Maddox to return to New Brighton, and how he learned of Bard's murder from Captain Albee Jarvis. When he completed his briefing, he looked again at her.

"I called Mrs. Chatsworth to tell her what happened. She asked me to meet her in New York. She wanted to sit down with you guys, see if there was something we could do to find out who murdered her father."

Amy nodded with approval when Fields turned to her.

"After we spoke yesterday," the agent said, "I contacted Scotland Yard. They told me they now believe Mr. Bard's murder was a revenge killing for a wrong committed in 1942."

"Really?" Rizzo said. "That's a mind-blower. Whoever killed him has a long memory."

Amy shook her head as though she was having difficulty processing the information. "I don't understand. Scotland Yard told me the initials on the note posted to my home were those of a former East German Stasi agent. They believe he is the same person who shot at my husband that day in London. Am I to assume I'm also a target in this maniac's desire for revenge?"

"I think that's a safe assumption. This maniac, WS, is Werner Schmitt," Fields said.

"That's right," she replied. "That's the name they gave me. They said he might be someone with a grievance against my husband concerning a recent political issue." She rippled her brow. "But a wrong committed fifty-eight years ago by my father? My Lord, he was only four years old. And the Stasi didn't exist in 1942."

"You're correct," Fields said. "The Yard felt you should learn the details of this mystery from us, the FBI. That's why they suggested contacting me."

Rizzo now knew how Amy came by the name of Jack Fields at the Bureau.

"You possess the files on Werner Schmitt, I assume?" she asked.

"Well, no. Ahh...I mean, not on Werner Schmitt. On his father, Walter Schmitt. Scotland Yard maintains the files on Werner."

Rizzo noticed Amy's puzzled expression. "Okay, Jack, now you got us totally baffled. Was the WS in the note Walter Schmitt or Werner Schmitt?"

"Werner," Fields said. "The son."

Rizzo leaned in. "And he was...?"

"Seeking revenge."

"For something that happened fifty-eight years ago?" Amy asked. "Something Frank Bard did as a child?"

"Yes to the first question, no to the second. Something Frank Bard, Senior did in his thirties."

Fields stood and walked around the desk, sat on its edge and looked down into the bewildered face of Amy Chatsworth. "Mrs. Chatsworth, I don't mean to sound like I'm playing games. Are you certain you're ready for the full story?"

"Yes, damn it!" she snapped. "Now...please. You have my complete attention."

Fields slid off the desk and returned to his chair. He leaned back, pausing for several beats. He took a breath before he bounced forward and reached into his desk drawer, withdrawing a folder. He opened it and laid it out in front of him.

"Okay, then," he began, without looking at the folder. "You may remember reading in your history books that in 1942, at the early start of World War II, two German submarines put men ashore in the U.S."

Rizzo grinned like an eager schoolboy who knew the answer to the question the teacher had posed. He jumped in before Fields could continue. "One boat off Amagansett, Long Island, the other in Ponte Vedra Beach, Florida. I was a WW II junkie as a kid. Read everything I could lay my hands on. They were all captured, right?"

Fields laughed. "Move to the head of the class."

Amy Chatsworth remained motionless; her attention stayed with Jack Fields. "I guess my history education never covered that event."

"To continue," Fields said, "these invaders didn't arrive with the intent of seizing and occupying territory. Their mission was sabotage. Their targets were among the crown jewels of America's industrial might—major hydroelectric plants, important aluminum factories, critical railroad tracks, bridges and canals, and the water supply system of New York City."

"How does Frank Bard figure into all this?" Rizzo asked. "One of the saboteurs?"

Fields ignored him and merely pointed to the opened folder as though he wanted Amy and Rizzo to know he commanded the information contained therein. Rizzo remembered and admired how effective Fields could be, producing important details at will.

"Walter Schmitt, thirty-four, a scrappy, bull-necked man, was given command of the mission. He dubbed it Operation Pastorius, after an early German settler in America."

Rizzo listened to Fields with amusement. The man was a human fact machine. His memory was like a spread of liquid cement: it held anything that fell on it.

The agent went on. "Lieutenant Walter Schmitt, a longtime member of the Nazi party, also knew the United States well, having lived here for five years."

"And Frank Bard, Senior…part of the operation?" Rizzo asked again.

"Don't get ahead of me," the agent cautioned. "Frank Bard was not his real name. It was Kurt Luedecke. He was thirty-two at the time and a member of the first team."

"You mean my birth name is Luedecke?" Amy asked, taken aback by this sudden revelation.

"I guess," Fields replied. "As a teenager, Luedecke served as a Hitler Youth. At the age of twenty-four, he immigrated to America, where he worked as a waiter while active in the Bund. In '37, he impulsively went back to Germany, married a woman from Düsseldorf and had a son." He looked at Amy. "Your father."

"This is getting complicated," Rizzo said.

Fields continued. "The second man in the first team was Max Vogel, a Nazi who fled Germany in '33 for the U.S. to escape criminal charges for brawling. He lived, working as a cabinetmaker, in Detroit and Milwaukee, studying English and joining the National Guard. He was even preparing to become an American citizen. But in '37 Vogel suddenly headed home to rejoin the Nazi Party."

Amy rose from her chair, walked to the window and stared out. Without warning, she turned and looked at Fields. The edges of her eyes flared with annoyance. "Agent Fields, why are you burdening us with this long-winded history lesson? All these facts and details?"

"I'm sorry, Mrs. Chatsworth. I think it is important you understand why your grandfather acted as he did. Do you want me to go on or would you prefer I cut to the chase?"

Amy pulled at strands of loose hair as tears formed. Rizzo considered approaching her, but she moved back and sat down.

"Cut to the chase," she said.

"Okay, then." Fields put on a serious face and began. "Luedecke and Vogel, after a close call with a Coast Guardsman during their landing on the beach in Amagansett, were having reservations about the operation. They made their way into Manhattan, checked into a hotel and, over dinner, expressed their fears that the mission was doomed, and that the Americans would capture them. Both men decided to betray the operation. A week later they turned themselves in to the FBI in Washington D.C., gambling on the Feds' leniency for cooperating."

"You have all this documented?" Amy asked, her voice and face full of skepticism.

"Completely, Mrs. Chatsworth," he said. "That's why Scotland Yard wanted us to inform you."

The room was silent for several seconds. Rizzo glanced at Amy. She sighed, clasped her slender hands together and gazed at them. Her expression had changed to disappointment. She had based the original motive for finding her father on achieving closure to a bothersome loose end of her life. In the process, she learned her grandfather had been a German saboteur.

"What about the operation, the saboteurs?" Rizzo asked.

"Within two weeks the remaining six were picked up before they could do any damage."

"And...and what happened to them?" Amy pressed.

Fields reached across his desk. He slid the opened manila folder toward him and then pulled back in his chair. He looked up at her. "All eight were tried as war criminals by a military tribunal. By order of President Roosevelt, six were electrocuted two months after their capture."

Amy's eyes opened wide. "Oh, my God. But my grandfather—"

"No," Fields said. "Because of their cooperation, Luedecke and Vogel were sentenced to thirty years and were released after serving a shade over ten years. They were going to be sent back to Germany, but their lawyers intervened, convincing the Justice Department they would become targets for assassination if they returned."

"You mean, by the remaining old guard Nazis?" Rizzo asked.

"Right. For being turncoats. Don't forget, the war had ended little more than seven years earlier. The country still had a lot of angry Nazi zealots hanging around."

"What happened to them after they were released?" Amy asked.

Fields paused to look at her. "The two were offered the option of witness protection. They accepted and took on new identities. Both disappeared into the safety of American society, reporting to an assigned agent in the U.S. Federal Marshal Service for the next ten years."

Amy's wide-eyed expression was gone. She turned toward Rizzo and shook her head. "When I first set out to find my father, I never expected to experience the unraveling of my family's history in this fashion."

"And you didn't expect to become the object of some nut job's vendetta, either," Rizzo added. "Some turn of events."

Fields closed the document folder and stood. "There's not much more I can tell you, Mrs. Chatsworth. We have alerted the NYPD, and when we receive Schmitt's photo from Scotland Yard, the police will have it. How long do you plan to remain in New York?"

"I'm not sure," Amy replied. She took a deep breath through her nose, held it a moment then let it out very slowly through her mouth. "Agent Fields, I'd really like to see this man apprehended before I leave."

"So would we," Fields said, "but there's no certainty he's still in the U.S. He could have high-tailed it back to Germany by now."

Rizzo got to his feet. "How about the other man...Vogel? Wouldn't Schmitt hang around, try to find him, take him out too?"

"Yes, if he knew where to find him. At this point, his location is still a protected piece of information."

"He found Frank Bard, didn't he?"

Fields let the question hang in the air for several seconds. "No, Luke. You found Frank Bard...for him. He followed you to Pennsylvania, remember?"

Rizzo didn't miss the disdain in his tone. "Well, I wouldn't know where to begin looking for Vogel. You guys could locate him, though. Wouldn't the State Department have a record where he settled?"

"Assuming he remained there, yes," Fields replied.

Amy moved to Rizzo's side. "I should think Max Vogel needs to be warned, don't you, Agent Fields?"

"We've already started that process, Mrs. Chatsworth. We're just waiting to hear back from the State Department."

Chapter 8

Schmitt stepped off the elevator and eyed the small sign on the wall. The arrow pointed to the south end of the old building for office numbers 401 to 415. He turned in that direction and made his way through the neon-lit corridor, looking back over his shoulder as he walked. He reached the south end and made note of the metal emergency-exit door. His escape option.

He moved to an office door a couple of steps away and paused. Ever cautious, Schmitt surveyed the length of the hallway before he produced the lock-pick from his jacket pocket. The directory in the lobby had listed number 402 as the office of Lucas Rizzo, Private Investigator.

Schmitt had followed Rizzo and the woman from the children's zoo after their lunch to the Waldorf and then to a building in lower Manhattan, 26 Federal Plaza. In the lobby, he scanned the building directory and found a listing of the New York City headquarters of the FBI. He realized if they were meeting with the Bureau, he would have to be extra vigilant. Outside, he paused by the fountain in the plaza, wondering how long they would be. Should he wait? No, he would take the opportunity to visit the detective's office and look for the photo.

He defeated the lock and slipped though, leaving the door ajar so he could hear the chime signal of an arriving elevator. The office was small, and except for the detective's desk and a three-drawer file cabinet, it offered few places to hide the photograph.

Schmitt opened each desk drawer, going through the contents with meticulous care, leaving everything he handled looking undisturbed. He always prided himself for having a professional touch when involved with a breaking-and-entering assignment. He would often subject his Stasi subordinates to lectures on the importance of stealth-like break-ins. Schmitt was confident Luke Rizzo would have no idea he'd been there.

He opened the small closet and flicked on the overhead light. The few shelves lining one wall contained normal office supplies; a small safe sat on the floor. Schmitt studied the safe for a moment and dismissed any challenge of trying to defeat it.

* * *

The taxi pulled up to the triangle-shaped office building, its limestone and glazed terra-cotta façade reflecting the late afternoon sun. Holding the door while Amy slid across the seat, Rizzo reached in for her hand. Her tailored skirt hiked up as she swung her legs to the sidewalk, revealing her knees and a hint of thigh. His eyes flitted to her face. She hadn't seen him staring. They entered the brass-framed doors of the Flatiron Building's Broadway entrance and turned toward the bank of elevators at the Twenty-second Street end.

"I have to apologize," Rizzo said before the elevator reached the fourth floor. "My office is kind of on the smallish side. Not like Jack's."

"No apology necessary. I'm certain your office serves your purposes quite well."

"Been here since I opened the business. Good location, this building...built in 1902," he added, thinking she would be impressed with this piece of historical knowledge. "Probably one of the oldest commercial buildings in Manhattan...in use, that is."

"Seems like an active area," she said.

The elevator door opened, and Rizzo stepped aside to allow Amy to exit first.

"Down to the left."

He followed her into the narrow corridor lined with lighted neon tubes along the ceiling. They passed several doorways—the offices of the small publishing firms that had recently taken occupancy in the historic building—and reached number 402. Rizzo inserted his key, but he found the door unlocked. A noise from the end of the corridor stopped him: the sound of the closing emergency-exit metal door. He would often use this exit whenever he lost patience waiting for the elevator. His first impulse was to race after the intruder, but he couldn't leave Amy alone at his office door. Someone might be inside.

"What's wrong?" she asked as they both stared in the direction of the noise.

Rizzo put his hand on her shoulder. "Stay put. Don't move."

He eased open the door. The ten-by-twelve office was no larger than what many third-rate hotels had to offer their guests. His eyes scanned his desk, file cabinet, small sofa and the two armchairs flanking both ends of the desk. The door to the small storage closet stood open, the overhead bare bulb on. Rizzo could see the pint-sized safe tucked away on the floor in the corner. He secured his Colt Cobra .38 there when not carrying. The safe looked undisturbed.

He turned and took her elbow. "It's okay. Looks like someone has paid me a visit. Gone now, so come in."

"Werner Schmitt?" she asked, inching through the doorway and warily scanning her surroundings.

Rizzo closed the door and locked it. He strode to his desk and ran his eyes over the surface. "No calling card, but that'd be my guess."

He opened the desk drawers one by one. They had been gone through deliberately and neatly. Not much was out of place. Schmitt obviously knew what he was looking for. Rizzo glanced again toward the closet, reminding himself that the envelope Frank Bard had given him was secure inside the small safe.

"So he knows who you are...that you're helping me?" Amy spoke quietly but with an edge to her voice. She had taken a seat on the brown sofa, leaning forward with her knees locked together supporting her forearms, her fingers entwined.

"Damn, I'm really sorry," Rizzo said. "Give me a few minutes and we'll be out of here."

The experience shook her. He wanted to offer comfort. He had brought her to his office to give her the envelope, the envelope containing the mysterious photo. He had decided not to break the seal until he could discuss the contents with her. Now with the break-in, he was not sure his office was the place to do that.

Confident that Werner Schmitt knew how to bug a phone or a room, he would have a look around before they left. He approached the closet, knelt down and spun the dial on the safe. He could feel Amy's eyes on him as he reached in for the envelope and his .38. He placed the snub-nosed revolver into his holster and strapped the carrier under his arm. He hoped seeing the weapon had not alarmed her. The game had changed, and she would have to understand he needed to be armed.

He crossed the office to the sofa, bent down and put his face up close to hers. "Why don't we go back to the Waldorf?" he whispered. "Maybe have a drink at the Bull & Bear? Give us a chance to calm down a little."

"Luke, I'm not upset. No, not at all. I am wondering why the man broke in here. He was looking for something, yes? Something he thought you had?"

"Shush," he said, laying his index finger over his lips. He nodded and tapped the left side-pocket of his tweed jacket.

She narrowed her eyes. "Are you going to tell me?" she mouthed.

"Later. Let me give the place a once-over, see if he planted any listening devices. This guy may be nuts enough to come back here if we hang around."

* * *

Werner Schmitt had bounded down four flights with an agility that surprised him. Out of breath, he exited the building and picked his way across Twenty-third Street, dodging heavy cross-town traffic. At Madison Square Park on the opposite side, he took refuge among the afternoon strollers. From his bench on the Madison Avenue side of the park, he watched and waited.

A feeling of satisfaction washed over him as he repainted the broad canvas of events he had completed in his vendetta. It had been a long journey to this point. His plan began long before the German reunification when he ran an American spy who was a diplomat working in the U.S. embassy in East Berlin. Stasi agents had followed and photographed the man engaged in pedophiliac activities. Thereafter, under the threat of being exposed, the man remained in Schmitt's pocket, feeding sensitive information out of the embassy.

On a whim, Schmitt directed the compromised pedophile to research the cover names of the two traitors he wanted to locate. The spy could find only one: Kurt Luedecke, cover name Frank Bard. From that, Schmitt turned up information on Amy Chatsworth's birth by Frank Bard's son. Her marriage to Lord Chatsworth was public information.

After the reunification, he retired from the Stasi before the organization dismantled his operation. The diplomat-spy returned to the U.S. to a post in the Justice Department. Schmitt, still holding the strings, pushed him to find where Bard had settled in the States. Before he could uncover the information, the FBI arrested the pedophile. Prior to his arrest, however, he had confessed to Schmitt of seeing a photo of the two men taken by their caseworker. The photo had writing on the back. He told Schmitt he thought it was their cover names, and that the caseworker had given copies to their assigned marshals to mail to Vogel and Luedecke. Soon after, the pedophile was exposed and gone.

Schmitt checked his watch. He had been waiting on the bench for a quarter of an hour. Finally, he spotted Rizzo and Chatsworth leaving the building and getting into a taxi headed north. He guessed they were going back to the woman's hotel.

* * *

The taxi ride uptown proceeded at a crawl along Park Avenue's heavy rush-hour traffic. Rizzo directed the driver to drop them off at the Lexington Avenue end of the Waldorf Astoria, at the door to the Bull and Bear Restaurant.

The host showed them to a small two-seater against the window. Rizzo pointed to a large, curved booth toward the rear. "Can we sit there, instead?"

He glanced around the room, then at the booth. "Oh, of course. Take it. We're not that busy."

Rizzo gave their drink order to a waiter and waited until he departed before he turned to Amy.

"Your father wanted you to have this," he said, producing the envelope. "I was going to give it to you at my office."

"Then you know what's in it?"

"He told me it was a photograph of your grandfather and his best friend. That I should mail it to you."

Amy looked at him with curiosity. "On the surface, that appears innocuous enough. A photo of two friends? Not something someone would be desperate to get their hands on."

"Unless they're naked."

She snickered. "Wouldn't that be something?"

"Here, do the honors," he said, holding out the envelope.

The noise level of the restaurant was minimal, unlike the volume of chatter present during peak dining hours. Rizzo could hear her quiet breathing as she slipped a thumbnail beneath the envelope's seal. She reached in and removed the four by five, black and white snapshot, a remnant of decades-old photography. Holding the aged, cracked photo with the tips of her fingers like a fragile treasure, she examined the image of the two men. Rizzo watched her, taking in her soft eyes. She appeared relaxed. She had recovered from the earlier scare at his office.

Amy scrutinized the photo for several seconds before returning her attention to Rizzo. "I guess I'm missing something."

"Meaning?"

"Here," she said, offering him the photo, "Two chums posing with arms over each other's shoulders. What could be of interest to that Stasi maniac?"

Rizzo studied the snapshot. He puzzled over the secrecy Frank Bard attached to it, and the urgency to possess the photo by Werner Schmitt. Why all the fuss? Two men in their early forties, standing at the base of a meadow, wide grins signaling a brotherly fondness.

Behind them, the grassy meadow sloped up to a large, multi-level wood structure, a lodge perhaps, whose peaked, shingled roofline framed the lettering below: *MEAD'S*. Visible in the photo, four dormers dotted one side of the lodge. The front entrance, a staired portico, blended into a wide-open porch that encircled the building—older architecture from the '20s.

Rizzo examined the figures. The man on the left had a broad, friendly face that matched his strong, broad body. His head was half-bald, crowned with a circle of thinning hair. He was dressed in a plaid, long-sleeved wool shirt and jeans. His large-size knuckles resting on the shoulder of his companion were quite visible. Rizzo recalled the term, *for brawling*, employed by Agent Fields in describing why Vogel fled Germany in 1933.

The second man had a long, tapered face, narrow eyes, and was taller by a head. He had a slight frame, a full shock of neatly barbered dark-gray hair, and a strong familial resemblance to Frank Bard, Junior. Rizzo tried to picture him wearing a Steelers ball cap. His formal attire contrasted with Vogel's casual dress. He wore a three-button cardigan sweater over a shirt and tie; his pressed slacks touched the top of his wingtips. Rizzo concluded the two men had been leading different lives in America within their own socio-economic circumstances. Luedecke had settled in a quasi-cosmopolitan suburb of Pittsburgh, and Vogel…well…that was yet to be determined.

"So?"

Rizzo placed the photo on the table in front of him and continued his study. "There's gotta be something we're not seeing. Maybe that building behind them." He brought up the photo again, close to his face, but flashed the picture down when the server returned with their drinks. Once he departed, Rizzo resumed his examination.

Amy watched, sipping her Manhattan. "What's that on the back of the photo? It looks like writing. It's somewhat faint."

Rizzo turned over the snapshot and understood what had caught Amy's attention: two names written in pen, the ink now faded with the years. Smudges from fingers handling the photo further distorted the names, making them almost unreadable.

She slid around in the booth until she was hip-to-hip with Rizzo, their thighs grazing each other beneath the table. The sudden physical intimacy caught him by surprise. He felt a slight quiver, but feigned indifference to avoid embarrassing her. He moved the photo closer.

"A few letters in the last name of the first one…A-R-D, so I assume it's *Bard*."

"The second name is clearer," she said. "The last name appears to be A-V-O-N . . . *Avon*."

"His cover name," Rizzo said. "First name…looks like *Jack* or *Jake*."

"Jake," she said, squinting to bring the blurred image into focus. "Yes, spot on, it's Jake. She raised her head and chuckled. "This is funny, extremely funny."

"What is?"

"Who selects a fugitive's cover name?" She turned her head, looking into his eyes.

"Someone in the Justice Department, I guess. Probably have a special team for that purpose. Why?"

"Well, seems to me whoever invented theirs was a reader of William Shakespeare. The Bard of Avon?" She shook her head. "Come now. Surely, he must have had his tongue in his cheek."

"Ya think?"

Rizzo turned over the photo and looked again at the two saboteurs. Who snapped the picture and when? More important, where? This piece of information might be the clue that could lead the FBI to Vogel. He was curious about how Werner Schmitt knew of the photo.

"I hope our Stasi murderer never studied the classics," she said, smiling over her literary discovery.

"So Kurt Luedecke became Frank Bard," he said.

"And Max Vogel…Jake Avon."

Now Rizzo understood the urgency of possessing the photo. Schmitt knew about the cover names of both his targets inscribed on the back, no doubt from the same source that had revealed the photo's existence, but not what they looked like. The Bards were no longer a factor. Vogel, on the other hand, remained on Schmitt's hit list. Rizzo knew the Feds would drag their feet in launching any attempt to find him. Maybe he could find Vogel first.

"Do you think we can locate Jake Avon?" she asked, reading his thoughts.

"Maybe, now that we know his cover name." He picked up his ginger ale and took a long gulp, replacing the glass on the napkin with exaggerated care. "He could be anywhere in the U.S."

Amy remained with her hip pressed against his, maintaining their closeness on the curved seat. When she turned to speak, their noses almost touched.

"Are you drinking that fizzy drink for my benefit?"

"Excuse me?"

"Your drink. Are you behaving properly...avoiding alcohol because you think it's what I expect of you?" Her eyes captured his and held them, waiting, as if she had caught him in a white lie.

Rizzo released a loud snort and put his hand over his nose and mouth to stifle a guffaw. "I'm sorry...really," he said, and turned away.

"Why do you find that funny?"

"Well, for one thing, no one ever accused me of behaving properly."

"No?"

"Not that I can remember. The truth is, misbehavior is what led to my divorce. That and my out-of-control drinking."

Shamefaced, she looked down at her lap. "Forgive me, I didn't mean to—"

Rizzo slipped his arm behind her, across the back of the booth. "Not to worry. That's all behind me. I'm in AA now. Although I continue to be a bit of a reprobate...but I'm reforming—slowly."

Amy faced him, grinning. "I don't mind. Being a reprobate keeps things interesting. Besides, you don't strike me as someone who loses control."

Her reaction surprised him. He was hesitant about reading too much into it; nevertheless, he felt his neck warming. He removed his arm and straightened his shoulders.

"But let me ask you something," she went on. "The revolver you put in your holster looked terribly small to be dangerous. That isn't indicative of your…umm…personality? Is it?"

Rizzo chuckled. He brushed his hand over the slight bulge under his jacket's left breast. "Don't let the size of this snubbie fool you. It's small…a 3-inch barrel…but powerful."

Amy nodded.

"No, really," he went on. "It's a Colt Cobra .38. Holds six rounds, lightweight and has a smooth trigger action. It's no longer produced and has become something of a collector's piece." Trying to justify this spillage of catalogue facts, he added, "Jack Ruby used this same gun to kill Lee Harvey Oswald."

"Really?" She stared at the bulge in his jacket.

"Okay, let's get back to the photo," he said, as though he had caught her peeking in his window. He picked up the snapshot and pointed. "See this name on the building? Has to be a hotel or a lodge. Ya think?"

"Do you recognize it?"

"Mead's? No, I don't."

"Is it somewhere in the east?"

"Not a clue. We can do a little research at the library. See what comes up."

She raised her eyebrows.

"Yeah, believe it or not, I often go to the New York Public Library whenever I need to look up something."

"Well, then, why don't we begin there?"

"Okay, but we gotta hurry. They're open only until six on Mondays.

Chapter 9

The stone lions flanking the Fifth Avenue entrance of the New York Public Library greeted them like a pair of friendly giants. Rizzo and Amy climbed the tiered steps and passed through the arched portico into Astor Hall, the large, marbled reception area. They stopped long enough to take in the dual staircases in front of them before deciding on the climb to their right.

They reached the second level, and Rizzo grew aware of a familiar feeling— the almost church-like aura produced whenever he walked the rooms of this sanctuary of knowledge. He remembered coming here as a high-school student to do research for his assigned projects. The library made him feel connected to academia. Although never a great student—too busy with sports—he had enjoyed the learning process and opportunities to research new worlds of information. The library reminded him of that, but it also rang up his regrettable decision to opt out of going to college. He had a chance for a baseball scholarship to Fordham. Instead, he joined the police force. Like many who had made a similar choice, the question of *what if* always nagged him.

They continued the climb to the third level and found their way into the main reading room of the Research Library.

At one of the computers lining the wall, he searched the catalogued sources for hotels and lodges.

Amy leaned over his shoulder to watch his progress. After five minutes, she showed signs of impatience with his random searches.

"Put in *Historic Country Inns and Lodges.* See what that brings up," she whispered.

Rizzo's head snapped toward her. "Already looked there."

"No, Luke. We looked at *Hotels and Lodges.* That was too broad a description. The picture is over forty years old. The building looked like an antique even then."

He cleared the screen, typed in her suggested keywords, and clicked on *Search.* Seconds later an abundance of options filled the page. He scrolled down, examining each heading.

"Mead's Mountain Lodge," she repeated in his ear. "That would indicate the location was somewhere in the mountains. Wouldn't you agree?"

"Ya think?" Rizzo cleared the screen. "Has to be in the east, considering your grandfather lived in Pennsylvania. That would put the location somewhere between the Allegheny and Catskill ranges, including the Poconos, Adirondacks and Appalachians."

"So let's start there."

He entered *Historic Country Inns and Lodges* for each of the five mountain ranges. When he had a satisfactory listing of books documenting the kinds of history they were looking for, he wrote down their titles.

Amy waited at a table while he filled out a call sheet at the retrieval desk and returned to the table to wait with her. Ten minutes later, the lighted digital sign above the call desk posted his call number.

"Okay, let's get to work. You take these." He pushed across three of the six books.

They leafed through each volume, looking for anything that would provide a clue to the existence and location of

Mead's Mountain Lodge. Finally, in the volume titled *Country Inns, Hotels and Lodges of the Adirondacks and Catskills*, Rizzo paused. Within the section marked *The Golden Age of Catskill Lodges*, the descriptive narrative of Mead's Mountain House in smaller type leaped off the page.

"Home run!" he whispered.

Amy moved closer, trying to read the page opened in front of him. Their heads were inches apart. "That appears to be what we are looking for. Wouldn't you say?"

He turned and found himself looking into her golden brown eyes. Studying them for a moment, he realized how beautiful they were. Rizzo pulled away. She hadn't seen him smiling.

"Yeah, if it's the same place."

"It has to be," she replied.

"Look at this," he said, indicating the page that bannered the heading, *Archives and Records*. Below, in black and white type, it listed *Mead's Mountain House Registers, Ledgers and Account Books*. A long paragraph followed, describing the historic retreat: "*...that provided city dwellers an escape from the unhealthy air associated with hot urban summers. The Historical Society of Woodstock, named as the preserver of the resort's guest registers, had faithfully maintained them from 1919 to early 1953. The lodge was demolished in 1953 after thirty-four years of operation.*"

Amy looked up at Rizzo. "Bard and Avon's meeting at the lodge and the snapshot taken of the two occurred after their release from prison in 1952, clearly before the lodge's demolition. Wouldn't you agree?"

Rizzo nodded. He pointed to the small sepia photo of the building inserted at the bottom of the page. Alongside were several photo-stat-reproductions of sample lodge registers. The angle of the structure in the photograph differed from the one in the snapshot of Vogel and Luedecke. Nevertheless, Rizzo was certain they matched.

"The two buildings are the same."

"I believe you're right," Amy said.

His eyes came up to study her face. "We did it," he said, pushing his open hand at her. Amy stared back, puzzled. He pumped his palm at her saying, "C'mon, give me five."

When she grasped how he expected her to react, their hands came together with a loud slap. She broke into a giggle. "By God, we did do it."

"Yeah. How 'bout that? Now, it's a good bet Vogel settled somewhere in the east. My guess, not far from Mead's Mountain House in the Catskills. Two things we need to find out."

"What is that?"

"Is Vogel alive? He would have to be in his eighties by now. And if so, is he still living in this part of the country?"

She made a face. "My goodness, how do we approach such a monumental task?"

"Woodstock is in Ulster County. We're gonna start there with the Historical Society, and then the County Records Clerk...see where they lead."

"How far is Woodstock?" she wanted to know.

"A hundred miles up the New York Thruway. We'll need to rent a car. You game?"

"Sounds like another adventure. When? Tomorrow?"

"The sooner the better."

"Before we do anything else," Amy suggested, "we should put the photo in the hotel's guest-safe. No sense in tempting fate."

* * *

Schmitt's snail-paced taxi ride uptown had caused him to lose track of the detective and the Chatsworth woman for the moment, but he guessed they would eventually return to the hotel. He took a chair in the lobby, steps away from the bank of elevators from where he had seen the woman emerge earlier today. After activating his ear-bud amplifiers, he hid his face behind the opened pages of a *New York Post*. And waited.

Some time later, he saw the detective and the woman enter the hotel from the Park Avenue side and watched them approach the front desk clerk. After several seconds of conversation, the clerk handed a form to the woman, whereupon she made several notations and returned it. Rizzo scanned the area around them before taking an envelope from his inside pocket. It quickly disappeared into the security box the clerk held out. Schmitt did not need to eavesdrop to understand what had transpired. The hotel's safe would secure the photo for the duration of the woman's stay.

They turned from the desk and walked in his direction. He stiffened and raised the newspaper. The pair stopped a few yards short of where he sat.

"Okay," he heard Rizzo say, "Now let's see if we get lucky tomorrow. I'll pick up a rental and meet you at nine on the Park Avenue side."

"Is Woodstock where they had that famous concert?"

"Same area. It'll take us two hours, so we should get there before lunchtime."

Amy reached out and took his hand. "Thank you, Luke. We make a good team."

Over the top of the newspaper, Schmitt could see the woman pull the detective toward her, place her free hand around his neck, and brush her check against his. He lowered the page as Amy Chatsworth made her way into one of the waiting elevators. The detective had already reached the stairs leading down to the Lexington Avenue exit.

Excellent, Schmitt thought. The detective will be my guide to finding Herr Vogel. He reached into his pocket for his newly acquired cell phone. Time to check in with Felix Decker. He would know how to get to Woodstock.

* * *

Jack Fields sat behind his desk, going over a report. He looked up when Tony Condon came through the door. Condon was jacketless, and he had on the same necktie he'd worn three times in the past week—a regatta of sailboats against a background of canary yellow. Fields once asked him about the tie and received a strange look. "What's wrong? I like this tie," was all Condon would say.

Condon took a seat. "I was on the phone with Inspector Wiley of Scotland Yard."

"Any progress?"

The agent balanced a folder on his knees and examined his open hands. He rubbed them together as though he were trying to warm them.

"They found the bullet that missed Amy Chatsworth in a tree behind where she had parked the Jag. It came from a Walther PPK. Same model as those issued to agents of the Stasi back in the '80s."

"Fired from what range?"

"Not that far away," Condon answered. "They believe from across the street."

"And he missed?" Fields shook his head. "He must have been part of *The Gang that Couldn't Shoot Straight*."

"Or lost his touch with age."

Fields continued to waggle his head. "The Yard is amazing. They don't give up easily."

"Not when a member of Parliament is involved. I'll bet Lord Chatsworth raised hell, got them hopping."

"What about the shooter? Anything more?"

"Definitely the ex-Stasi thug, Schmitt...Werner Schmitt. The Yard is emailing the photo we asked for."

"Good." Fields remained quiet, thinking, before he pushed back in his chair. "Damned shame," he volunteered. "First the father and now an innocent security guard in Pennsylvania."

"A what?"

"One of those guards from a private security company. Pennsylvania contracts them to monitor their parks and highway rest areas."

Condon reached up to scratch the back of his neck. He rolled his head from side to side, attempting to work out a kink. "What happened?"

"This morning I put in a call to the New Brighton Police Chief...you know...the guy who questioned Luke Rizzo after Frank Bard was murdered."

"Right."

"I wanted to let him know about Schmitt's attempt on Mrs. Chatsworth's life back in London."

"Rizzo never told him?"

"Nope. Rizzo didn't know. He only found out after Chatsworth arrived in New York the other day. I also told the Chief about the note in German mailed to her home. He confirmed it was the same as the one found in Bard's vehicle."

"Which links the two shootings," Condon added, as though Fields hadn't made the connection.

"Anyway, that private guard must have had a run-in with Schmitt. It was at a rest stop off Route 60 on the way to the Pittsburgh airport. The guard was found shot to death in the parking area. Ballistics confirmed the caliber of the slug was the same as the one that killed Bard."

"Did you mention Schmitt might be here in New York?"

"Yeah. He asked if we thought Schmitt planned to return to New Brighton to take out the rest of the Bards."

"Unlikely, don't you think?"

Condon shrugged. "The guy he really wanted to get was the grandfather, Kurt Luedecke. Bad timing. He was already dead."

Fields pushed the report to one side of his desk. "How about the other guy, Vogel?" Fields asked. "Did the Yard know anything?"

"No, but here's where it gets interesting," Condon said, lowering his voice.

Fields adjusted himself in his seat and leaned forward, resting his forearms on the desktop. He knew Condon enjoyed this type of give-and-take.

"Both men got out of prison at the same time after serving little more than ten years."

"Jesus, we know that," Fields snapped.

"Right. What we didn't know is Luedecke had been in touch with Vogel after their release from prison, just before they were placed in the WPP."

Fields regarded him with a somber curiosity. "Where does that come from? Not Scotland Yard."

"Tyler Quimby at Justice. He continues to be involved in witness protection. I called him this morning, thinking he might know how Schmitt found out about Bard's cover. Seems Schmitt had someone on the inside of Justice."

"Makes sense."

"But here's the curious part," Condon continued. "When Luedecke and Vogel were turned loose in 1952, a Justice Department staffer named Felix Decker handled their placement paperwork. A short time later, Decker arranged a get-together between the two men. That was before a federal marshal could be assigned to each of them."

Fields rose and walked to the water cooler in the corner of his office. "Decker's the mole," he said matter-of-factly.

Condon waited until the water cooler ceased gurgling. "No, not him. Another staffer. C'mon Jack, no second-guessing."

Fields grinned. He knew Condon liked to control information.

"At Vogel's request," Condon continued, "Decker got permission to bring the two men together for a reunion weekend at an undisclosed lodge in the Catskills."

"Was there a connection between Decker and the two of them?"

"None that was known at the time. Decker was second-generation German. His bosses assumed he felt sorry for them. That's why they agreed to allow the meet."

"Did their contact continue?" Fields asked, sipping from the plastic cup.

"No. Justice assigned each of them a marshal right after that weekend. The marshals prohibited any further contact. Part of the relocation deal. That day in the Catskills, Decker snapped a photograph of the two men. He stupidly wrote Luedecke and Vogel's cover names on the back of the photo and gave copies to the marshals to mail to them."

Fields raised an eyebrow. "How's that stupid?"

"Before he gave the copies, Decker showed the snapshot to another staffer. The guy catches a glimpse of the names on the back and asks to see it. Decker refuses. Two weeks later, the Bureau revealed the co-worker was a spy, a pedophile they had been investigating. While he was posted at the U.S. Embassy in East Germany back in the '80s, this degenerate confessed he was being handled by a Stasi agent."

"Let me guess." Fields dropped the plastic cup in the trash by the cooler and walked back to his desk.

Condon laughed before Fields could answer. "Yep, you're right," he said. Holding up a binder a half-inch thick, he added, "But here's something else that'll blow your mind. Quimby researched the transcripts of the military tribunal that convicted the eight spies. He sent them FedEx to me last night. Got 'em about an hour ago." He dropped the binder on the desk.

Fields leaned over to pick it up.

"One transcript cites Walter Schmitt had confessed that the party intended to finance the operation with a large sum of money...$2.5 million, American. The money was transferred through an Argentine bank to an account in the States and kept in a safe-deposit box."

"Where?"

"A bank upstate."

Fields dropped back into his chair and paged through the binder. "And how were the saboteurs supposed to get to this cash?"

"All Walter Schmitt knew was the Nazi sympathizer in charge of dispensing the money was supposed to contact him. He never had a chance."

"So they never found out who he was...?"

"Yeah, they did. Would you believe, Felix Decker's father? Except his real name before emigrating from Germany in 1932 was Gerhardt Dietrich."

Condon placed another document on the desk. "Here's what Quimby came up with on Dietrich's background."

Fields picked it up and looked back at Condon with amusement. "You having a good time?"

Condon ignored the comment and listened while Fields began reading aloud:

"Gerhardt Dietrich had emigrated from Germany in 1932, settling in the upstate New York community of Saugerties with his wife and seven-year-old son, Felix, before opening his pork store off Route 28. A native of Munich, he became a naturalized U.S. citizen in 1938.

"Throughout the early years of unrest in Germany, Dietrich had become a devoted follower of Hitler and the Nazi movement. Dietrich had proudly taken his place at Hitler's side as a participating revolutionist during the 1923 Beer Hall Putsch, barely escaping prosecution after the government put down the revolt. His ties were strong and his reputation as a fierce defender of the National Socialist German Workers' Party was well known. He never questioned it when the party suggested changing his name before he relocated his family to the U.S. to become an agent. Gerhardt Dietrich became Gerald Decker, and only the party leadership knew his real identity. That was the reason they selected him to become the fiscal steward of the $2.5 million working fund they had funneled through a bank in Argentina and deposited in a U.S. bank at the end of 1941.

"Earmarked to finance the heavy cost of their elaborate sabotage mission, the party expected the elder Decker to dispense this enormous sum judiciously through the operation's leader, Walter Schmitt. The party, however, had neglected to offer a provision to return the money in the event the operation went bust."

Fields stacked the single page on top of the binder and looked up at Condon. "So Felix Decker's father was the Nazi sympathizer?"

"According to Quimby."

"And the Justice Department's background check on the son never made this connection?"

"Are you surprised?" Condon was grinning.

"So the father had control of the money?"

"Yep."

"You think Felix Decker knew about it?"

"Quimby doesn't think so. The son was away at college. He's sure the father kept him in the dark about everything."

"I take it, they never located the bank," Field said.

"No, they did. In Kingston, New York. By the time they got there, Decker had emptied out the box."

"The box was registered under a phony name, of course."

"Of course."

"Do you suppose it's what Werner Schmitt is looking for? Besides revenge, that is."

Condon shook his head. "I doubt he knew about the arrangement. He was around seven in 1942. Of course, as a Stasi agent, he could have found out later on."

"And Walter Schmitt never fingered the sympathizer because he didn't know?"

"Nor was the money ever accounted for."

"That Decker guy from Justice...the son...where is he?"

"Retired, twenty years ago, to Florida."

"Amazing," Fields said, shaking his head. "I guess Werner Schmitt needs that photo."

Condon nodded. "If he expects to locate Vogel."

Fields cupped his chin in one hand, supporting his elbow with the other. "I wonder why he never searched the house after he killed Luedecke."

"You want my guess?" Condon said. "He knew he wouldn't find the photo there."

Fields gazed across the room. His eyes landed on the empty chair, where yesterday Amy Chatsworth sat as he related the circumstances of her grandfather's capture and internment. He mulled over details of Luke Rizzo's search for Frank Bard and their meeting the afternoon of the murder. He looked back at Condon.

"Who do you suppose has it?"

Condon got up from his chair and faced his boss.

"Are you thinking what I'm thinking?"

Fields' eyes widened.

Chapter 10

S chmitt dropped the sheet he had folded on top of the pillow and comforter at the end of the sofa. He looked at the time and realized he had to be on his way into Manhattan to pick up his rental within the next hour. Decker had given him directions to Woodstock yesterday when he called him from the Waldorf, and suggested he buy a road map to be safe. Schmitt also needed a weapon. His opportunity sat in the next room—Otto's Beretta in the drawer of the bedside table.

His second night at Otto's had been a restless one. The sofa was too short, forcing him to dangle his ankles over the armrest for most of the night. In addition, the pulsing ache of his arthritic knuckles kept waking him whenever he managed to drift off.

Otto emerged from his bedroom, wrapped in a tattered bathrobe, his feet sliding across the bare floor in a pair of worn slippers. "*Guten morgen*, Werner. You slept well?"

"Yes, thank you," Schmitt lied.

"*Das ist gut.* I will shower quickly and then make you breakfast. *Ja?*"

"No, thank you, Otto. Not this morning. I have to meet someone in an hour. I will have breakfast with him. You go take your shower. I will let myself out."

Otto returned a look of admiration. "Okay, Mr. Businessman," he said, smiling. "I will be here when you get back." Otto turned, went into the bathroom and closed the door.

Schmitt moved to the door and cupped his ear. When he heard the old man turn on the water, he paused for another minute until he was certain Otto had closed the curtain and stepped under the shower. Schmitt dashed into the bedroom, to the night table on the far side of the bed, and pulled out the drawer. He reached in for Otto's .9mm Beretta and the 15-round magazine next to it. He shoved both Beretta and magazine into his pockets and closed the drawer.

He rushed out of the apartment after calling the cab company for his ride into Manhattan. He was sure he could pick up a map at the Enterprise garage on Forty-fourth Street. During his phone call, Decker had told him to get off the Thruway at Exit 20. "Be certain to arrive there ahead of the detective," he cautioned. "Follow from there, because following anyone on the interstate for a hundred miles will be quite difficult."

* * *

Luke Rizzo pulled the rental out from the curb in front of the Waldorf, dodging morning traffic up Park Avenue. He switched the Chevy Impala's heater setting to low, knowing the chilly but sunny autumn morning was bound to get a few degrees cooler as they headed north. He glanced over at Amy, who was dressed in a wool crewneck over a cotton button-down shirt and black worsted slacks. She had folded her leather safari jacket across her knees.

"You going to be warm enough?"

"I should think so," she said. "How about you?"

Rizzo patted the front of his zippered jacket. "It's lined, and besides, my .38 snubbie is all the warmth I need."

"I doubt that," she said, smiling.

At Ninety-sixth Street, they turned onto the FDR Drive heading north until they reached the New York Thruway twenty minutes later. The two-hour trip up through Westchester, Orange and Ulster Counties was a picture-postcard experience. The late fall colors were ablaze throughout the panorama of little towns and hamlets they passed.

Once they left the interstate at the Kingston exit, the drive for Amy became a series of "oohs" and "Look at that!"

"This is truly breathtaking," Amy said. "We never see this extent of nature's talent in England. What a colorful canvas she has created. Our changes of seasons are drab compared to this."

"It's why New York City people caravan into the Catskills every fall. Watching the leaves change is an annual ritual for the folks who live year-round in a concrete jungle. Too bad we're at the end of October. The peak show has already passed. See how most of the colors are beginning to fade?"

Rizzo held steady at forty-five miles-per-hour as they traveled Route 28 west toward Woodstock. Amy's head turned left and right, panning the scenery as though her eyes were a video recorder. He glanced at her face. Her expression was alive with pleasure.

Nearing the town, she said, "This reminds me of the hamlet where I grew up. These homes are more opulent and larger, you see, but the landscape is similar."

Rizzo remembered the photo of Frank Bard, Jr. she had sent, the shot of her young father standing on the side of a road lined with stucco and ivy-covered, thatched-roof cottages. Humble surroundings compared to this upscale community.

Enjoying his role as tour guide, he thought back to the article he read in the magazine section of *The New York Times*, published when the historic Woodstock Music Festival became a happening back in 1969, in the neighboring town of Bethel.

Recalling some of the details, he told Amy, "Woodstock became an artist colony many years ago...I think, at the turn of the century. In the 1930s, the artsy-crafty set from New York City's Greenwich Village discovered the place. Writers, artists, musicians, craftsmen and every free spirit you can name settled here. Practicing free love, would you believe?"

"My, that sounds intriguing." She looked at him and flashed a teasing grin.

Rizzo turned away and laughed. "Yeah, until the '60s and '70s when every hophead and hippie on the east coast followed the folk singer Bob Dylan here. They trashed the place but eventually moved on."

They arrived at the town center, circled the roundabout, and edged along Tinker Street, the main thoroughfare. Quaint specialty stores and restaurants looking for the tourist's dollar lined both sides. Despite the cooler weather, diners sat at outside tables, lunching, sipping cappuccino, and watching the many strollers dressed in their chic sweaters and jackets.

Rizzo drove by an official-looking, white-pillared building with a sign above the portico: Woodstock Town Hall. "That can't be it," he said when he spotted the hanging banner reading *Performing Arts of Woodstock*. He pulled into a parking spot in front of one of the touristy shops.

"Stay put," he said. "Let me go into this art gallery...see if they know where the Historical Society is." He stepped out onto the roadway. Before closing the door, he ducked his head back inside. "Hey, listen, if anyone comes along who wants to paint you, say no."

"Even if it's a handsome body-painter?"

"Not to worry; they're hard to find here. They're all down in Key West. I'll be right back."

Minutes later, Rizzo emerged from the gallery. "I got it," he announced and slipped in behind the steering wheel. "It's down this street about a quarter mile. There's parking in the rear if we can't find a spot out front."

A car full of tourists vacated a space ten yards before the building and Rizzo pulled in. Two steps up to the small front porch, they entered a boxlike building that was a combination insurance agency, real estate office and ice cream parlor. The small office of the Historical Society on the second floor had a musty odor. History is supposed to smell old, Rizzo told Amy when she remarked about it.

At the desk of the records-keeper, Amy queried the elderly, white haired historian about the building's origin. "Georgian Revival design," the lady said, "once the home of the town's mayor back in the '30s...before he fell on hard times and needed to commercialize it."

"That's so sad. Such charming architecture."

The worn-with-age, final year guest register of Mead's Mountain House yielded three names of interest: Bard, Decker and Avon. In the space for the guest address, Bard had written Pittsburgh; Decker wrote Washington D.C., while Avon scribbled the word Malden. The helpful records-keeper informed them that Malden, "pronounced, Mal-den, with a short A," was a small town on the banks of the Hudson River, ten miles due east of Woodstock and north of the town of Saugerties.

"You hungry yet?" Rizzo asked as they came down the stairs. "It's almost noon. I asked the records lady, and she recommended the Bear Café. It's back the other way...a mile or so."

"Hmmm...sounds like a nice fit, in keeping with those other animal-themed restaurants we've been to. The Zoo for lunch yesterday, the Bull and Bear at the hotel for drinks, and now the Bear Café. Let's do it."

They reached the cafe at the north end of town within five minutes. The parking lot was half filled—a little early even for tourists. The host seated them at a table against a window overlooking the dining terrace. A brook rushing down from the mountain behind them, roared below the wooden deck.

"This is picturesque," Amy said, gazing through the window. A scattering of more adventuresome diners occupied tables on the terrace.

"You rather sit outside?" he asked. "Lots of tables."

"A bit too chilly for me. Here's fine."

While Amy's attention was elsewhere, Rizzo studied her, noticing how the mid-day sun searched out varying shades of her hair. He'd become aware of how much he enjoyed her company. Her physical attractiveness turned him on. She was easy to talk with, intelligent without pretentions, and possessed a sense of humor that rivaled his own.

They hadn't shared much in the way of personal information, except for his own admission back at the hotel restaurant of being a drinker and a reprobate. He wanted to ask about her marriage and family. What was Lord Chatsworth like? Did they have children? Was she happy in their marriage? Thinking about it, he decided not to. She was his client; they weren't on a date.

Rizzo turned to the approaching server. She had the longest ponytail he'd ever seen, reaching below her belt line. As she walked, it bounced like a happy camper against the cheeks of her skin-tight jeans. She scribbled their order on her pad: an avocado omelet and house salad for Amy and a mile-high pastrami sandwich on seeded rye for him. When the server left the table, Amy looked across at Rizzo and wrinkled her nose.

"What?"

"You thought about pulling it, didn't you?"

"Ya think?"

* * *

Werner Schmitt sat behind the wheel of his rental, his eyes fixed on the doorway to the Bear Café. He had preceded the woman and detective up the one hundred miles of the New York Thruway to the Woodstock exit by thirty minutes. Waiting off to the side of the road at the tollbooth, he had spotted them as they stopped to pay the toll, and followed them into Woodstock.

He watched them enter the white building on Tinker Street. Did someone in there know Max Vogel, or where he lived? He considered returning there to investigate while the two were having lunch but dismissed the idea, fearing he would miss them leaving should their meal be a short one. The ex-Stasi agent understood the simple principle of surveillance all too well: never let the subject out of your sight.

The detective and the woman left the restaurant a few minutes past one o'clock and walked to the car. Schmitt had parked far enough away so that he would not appear suspicious if they happened to look his way. He slumped down on the seat anyway. He heard their engine turn over and the sound of crunching gravel as they backed out. He sat up in time to see them turn onto the main road and head back toward town.

Schmitt moved his rental toward the exit. A large SUV turned into the lot on the wrong side and caused both vehicles to slam on brakes. Swept-up gravel peppered Schmitt's undercarriage. The oncoming SUV clipped his front bumper and came to rest blocking the exit.

The young male driver that emerged from the SUV had a bandana wrapped around his forehead, holding down a cascade of stringy, blond hair. Schmitt looked him over and judged from his jeans, torn leather jacket and dusty black boots, he would be more at home on a Harley. He strode to Schmitt's window, hands gesturing wildly.

"Jesus, old man, what's your fuckin' hurry? You always race outta parking lots without stoppin'?"

Schmitt thought of reaching for the Beretta in the glove compartment. This turn of events was unfortunate. It cost him time and prevented him from keeping up with the detective. He had to settle matters quickly.

He stepped out, faced the angry driver and raised his palms. "I am sorry. I was not thinking. Did I hurt your car?"

The two bumpers had lightly grazed each other. Neither vehicle had suffered any damage.

The man walked around to the front of the cars. He looked down at his bumper where the two had made contact.

"You were damn lucky, old man," he said, without making eye contact. "Now, back up that piece of shit and let me pass."

Schmitt got into his rental, saying nothing. He glanced at the man as he climbed into his SUV. He imagined how much he would enjoy blowing away the brash, young pig. He remained silent, restarted the car and backed up far enough to allow the SUV to go by. The driver passed, failing to look at Schmitt, and headed directly to the back of the restaurant's parking lot.

Schmitt turned out onto the main road and drove in the same direction he had seen the woman and the detective take. They were long gone. He knew he had violated the most important tenet of Stasi surveillance. He had lost sight of his target. In East Germany of the 1980s, an unforgiving and punishing consequence would be waiting for him back at Stasi Headquarters.

He slipped his hand into his pocket and reached for his nitroglycerin spray. His muscles tensed. It wasn't there. In his haste to get out of Otto's apartment this morning, he had left the spray container in his suitcase. A flash of panic tore through hm. He would need to return to the apartment today. Without a prescription, he could not buy another one at a pharmacy, and without the spray, he would be at risk.

He cursed his bad timing, losing the detective and the woman. Perhaps he could learn where they went by vising the white building they had entered, discover what they found there. He parked at the rear of the building in front of Scoops, a purveyor of exotic ice cream cones and sundaes that occupied the back end of the two-story edifice.

Schmitt walked around to the front of the building. A directory posted to one side of the doorway indicated three occupants: the State Farm Insurance office on the ground floor to the left, and the Burns Real Estate office to the right. Inquiring at both, they informed him they had no visitors that morning. The third name on the panel, The Historical Society of Woodstock, was located on the second level.

He reached the top of the stairs and walked back to the door of the office. The posted hours of operation informed him he was too late: 9:00-1:00, Monday through Saturday. He looked at his watch - 1:15.

* * *

Rizzo backtracked through Woodstock, passed the Historical Society's building, and continued east on Route 212 instead of taking the route they had traveled earlier. He entered the thruway at the Saugerties entrance going south.

"Aren't we going to Malden?" Amy asked.

"Not right away, unless you want to knock on every door in town asking if they know where Jake Avon lives."

"You have an easier way, I presume?"

"We're heading down one exit to Kingston, the seat of Ulster County, where they keep the tax records. We'll save time by starting there."

Traffic in both directions on the thruway was light. Five minutes into the drive, he looked over at Amy and smiled.

"Why are you smiling?"

"I just remembered how different this traffic will be in three weeks, loaded with sportsmen and their pickups. That's when hunting season in the Southern Zone of New York State begins. One million white-tailed deer will be running for their lives."

"Such a shame, shooting those beautiful animals for sport."

"It's necessary," Rizzo said. "By this time every year, they've become overpopulated; they become a big nuisance to homeowners. Hunting them thins out the herd."

"I guess I understand, but it saddens me to imagine them destroyed."

"Listen, for too many of them, this thruway becomes their killing field...those desperate ones trying to cross while scavenging for food. They're a danger to themselves and the motorists."

They remained quiet for the reminder of the ride, until they reached the exit.

Kingston's Town Hall building was an easy find. A search of the tax rolls provided the information they needed. Jake Avon had been paying real estate taxes every year since 1962. The property address listed was 101 Malden Turnpike.

Rizzo retraced the ten-mile trip north on the thruway, got off at the Saugerties exit and followed Route 9W. At a railroad crossing, he noted a sign reading *Entering Saugerties, Antique Capital of New York,* and steered the car toward the center of town.

Amy turned to him. "Do they mean the town is an antique, or are they referring to the purchase of antique items?"

"From the looks of this place, maybe both."

Antique furniture stores lined Main Street on both sides. The short passage from one end to the other lasted three minutes. They continued north on 9W for another ten minutes, passing the Saugerties Grade School at the far end of town, the largest building on their route.

"That's it," she shouted when they passed up the turnoff to Malden.

"What? Did I miss it?" He braked and pulled to the side.

"The sign back there," she said. "It read Malden-on-the-Hudson. Could that be the same as Malden?"

"Yeah, maybe. More 'n likely a fancied-up name. Sounds like a summer resort, doesn't it?"

He backed the car down to the opening of the missed road. When he turned in, he spotted the street sign, Malden Turnpike, and laughed.

"What's funny?"

Rizzo moved down the road, taking the first bend at a slow pace. "Well, the street sign back there said we're on Malden Turnpike. Come on, now. Does this look like a turnpike?"

"Maybe, when the town was first settled."

"You mean when they traveled in covered wagons?"

Amy scanned both sides of the turnpike. "By the looks of the area, it doesn't appear to have enjoyed much modernization."

The landscape on the left offered a dense thicket of trees and overgrown foliage. Tucked in among the trees, a handful of modest homes sat on the occasional manicured lawn. Off to the right where the terrain sloped down dramatically, unhampered growth ran wild. A hundred yards farther, the slope fell away and opened below to a majestic vista of the Hudson River. They could see houses of more substantial construction scattered along the hillside. Sections of a winding road threaded down to the shoreline.

"Oh my," Amy exclaimed. "Look at that."

Rizzo threw a quick glance over her shoulder. "Wow! If nothing else, Malden-on-the-Hudson is scenic. Great view of the mighty river from here."

"What's the address we're looking for?" she asked.

"Hundred and one."

He slowed the car, trying to read the numbers on the mailbox to his left.

"That looks like number ninety-two. We're getting close."

Two hundred yards farther down on the right side, they arrived at 101 Malden Turnpike. Rizzo stopped in front of a two-story building with a Ford F-150 pickup parked on the gravel driveway of a detached garage.

Rizzo shook his head. "Could this be it?"

"If we have the correct address. That's 101 on the mail box."

Rizzo stared through the windshield at the spotless-white, two-story brick building with a green slate roof. The roofline sloped precipitously on both sides from its peaked center.

A miniature version of the building's profile perched on the forward end of the roof, looking like a belfry. Directly below the roofline, a circular window peered down at them like the eye of Cyclops, while a pair of tall, framed windows dotted the building's façade on each of the two levels.

A five-foot-wide broken cement pathway cut through the front lawn from the road to the entrance on the left side. A flagpole stood on the lawn to the right side of the path, with an American flag hanging from the top.

The entryway was a narrow, covered porch with two steps leading up to the green painted front door. On the brick facing of the porch under its peaked roof, they could make out the embedded words *Malden Graded School.*

"This can't be it," Rizzo said. "It's a damn schoolhouse."

Chapter 11

J ack Fields hit three numbers on his console and listened to the succession of fast beeps until Tony Condon answered.

"Yeah, Jack."

Fields looked down toward the phone console. "Tony, did you hear back from Tyler Quimby yet?" He pushed back in his chair and stared at the tray ceiling above his desk. The pencil in his hand worked through his fingers like a cheerleader's baton.

"Not yet. He said they would need a while to run the research. Maybe this afternoon."

Fields bounced forward and stood. "Jesus, you'd think that Justice would have this type of info available on their computers. I could get a listing of my last ten checks from my bank faster."

"The file is over forty years old. Maybe that's what's slowing up the research."

"Or maybe Quimby doesn't appreciate the urgency—"

"Oh, I'm sure he does. They'll get back soon, Jack."

Fields drew a breath through his nose and pushed air out his pursed lips. "Before Schmitt gets it, I hope. Or we'll have another assassination on our hands."

The pencil snapped in two.

"Give him another call...see where he is on this."

"I will."

"Keep me informed."

Fields hung up and moved to the window behind his desk, gazing out at the towers of glass and steel between Federal Plaza and the East River. The briefing he gave to Amy Chatsworth yesterday flashed in his mind. Why did she and Luke Rizzo elect not to say anything about the photo? He was sure they had it in their possession. If Tyler Quimby of Justice was correct and the photo did have the cover names of the two saboteurs written on the back, Max Vogel was in deep shit—unless he and Condon got to him first.

A half hour later, Condon entered the office. "Okay, Vogel's last known address…upstate, a town called Malden, ten miles north of Kingston."

"Kingston? That's where the bank was, where the Nazi sent the saboteurs' funds."

"Correct."

Fields shot his arm in the air and pumped a fist as if he had scored a touchdown.

"That's out of our jurisdiction," Condon reminded. "It's the FBI field office in Albany."

"Oh, that's right. So we're gonna need Karl to make a call for us." He gestured to Condon to take a seat while he punched in Karl Stevenson's numbers on the phone console. "Sylvie, Fields here. See if Karl will see us, will you? We have an emergency."

Ten minutes later, Sylvie ushered the two agents into the office of Karl Stevenson, the head agent of the FBI's New York City field office. Stevenson was at his large, dark mahogany desk, leaning back in a soft leather chair like someone ready to take an afternoon nap. The sixty-four-year-old head agent, dressed in a conservative three-button, dark suit with narrow lapels that shouted the '60s, had been with the Bureau since the Cold War. He claimed to have known J. Edgar Hoover briefly, when he joined the Bureau in 1970, a year before Hoover died.

To hear him speak of the former FBI Chief, one would think they had been friends since childhood. Stevenson was a man with a gift of gab, guilty of hyperbole and misquoting. Many in the Bureau, including Jack Fields, felt he had bullshit his way up the ranks through seven administrations.

"What's the problem?" Stevenson asked.

* * *

The sun knitted through the thickening cloud cover while a light shower of snow floated around them. Rizzo opened his door and stepped out. He looked up at the belfry on the roof's peak.

Amy asked, "Are you certain you copied the correct address?"

"I thought so…shit! Oh, sorry. I should have asked them to photocopy that page before we left the tax office."

"Well, what do you suggest we do?"

Rizzo scanned the area. He could see that the road ahead sloped down and disappeared around the end of the property line. Rizzo thought of continuing, but turning his head he caught a glimpse of a face staring down at them from one of the windows on the second level. Could the building be inhabited? Hard to imagine the place still functioned as a school.

"Looks like there's someone inside," Rizzo said. "Maybe they can shed some light."

Amy stepped out of the car, and together they approached the covered entry. Before Rizzo could knock, the door opened halfway. A short, stoutly built, bald man in a dark, nubby-wool crewneck sweater, peered out. He hunched over, and the collar of his flannel shirt, pulled up and covering his thick neck, made him look like a turtle peeking out of its shell. His shoulder leaned against the inside of the door, bracing the edge firmly in the meaty fingers of one hand, poised to slam it closed at the first sign of concern.

"Yes?" The old man squinted at the two strangers over the top of the specs resting on the bridge of his nose.

"Mr. Avon? Jake Avon?" Rizzo asked.

"I am."

Rizzo turned to Amy and grinned. "Mr. Avon, my name is Lucas Rizzo. I'm a private investigator from Manhattan. This is Mrs. Amy Chatsworth of London, England."

"What is this about?" Jake Avon asked. "Are you selling something?" His voice was soft with no residual trace of a German accent. His skin was ruddy and weathered, and his smooth shaven face gave off a healthy glow.

Rizzo grinned. How many bible salesmen knock at Jake Avon's door? "No sir, we're not selling anything. Amy...Mrs. Chatsworth, here...is the granddaughter of a person you know...someone from long ago."

"She is?"

Amy stepped forward and extended her hand. "Mr. Avon, my father was Frank Bard. You knew my grandfather, the senior Frank Bard."

Rizzo heard the old man take a quick breath. His steely eyes darted from her face to Rizzo. He continued to lean against the door, making no offer to take her hand. He remained in the same position for several seconds.

"Are you sure you have the right person?" Avon finally asked. He sounded like a hopeful questioner eager to prove his accusers wrong.

"We think so," Amy replied.

Rizzo did a fast computation. The man looked to be in his late eighties, around the age that Jake Avon, nee Max Vogel, would be today. He was confident they had the right man.

"Mr. Avon," he said, "we came here to alert you to a problem...something that could possibly put your life in danger."

Avon ignored Rizzo and turned back to Amy Chatsworth. "Tell me, please, where does your Frank Bard...your grandfather...live?"

"Until he died in 1973, he lived in New Brighton, Pennsylvania."

"And your father, how old is he?"

This was turning into an interview. Rizzo didn't blame the old man for being cautious. He had been living free for so many years, unchallenged and unthreatened, and now two strangers show up at his door with knowledge of his real identity.

"My father...my father is dead too." Amy swallowed hard. "He was recently murdered in New Brighton by the same person we feel will threaten your life."

The pained expression that painted Avon's face was either from fear or total bewilderment. Rizzo worried the man would close the door, shutting them out. He pushed a foot into the doorway.

"You come from New Brighton, Pennsylvania? Didn't you say you were from England?" Avon asked Amy Chatsworth, his voice filled with suspicion.

"I did, but—" she raised both palms and extended them outward toward the man in a supplicating gesture. "Mr. Avon, may we please come in? We can explain everything. It's something you need to hear."

The old man remained leaning against the door and shaking his head. He looked as though he was processing the meaning of this sudden intrusion, deciding if he should trust the two strangers in front of him. Abruptly, he stepped back and held open the door.

"Come in," he said. "Upstairs, if you please," pointing to the staircase hugging the wall.

* * *

Schmitt stood at the curb in front of the Historical Society building and looked around. His stomach felt empty. Except for the complimentary coffee and stale vanilla wafers at the car rental office in Manhattan, he had not eaten in the last eight hours. He spotted a small cafe on the other side of Tinker Street and crossed over.

He carried a bowl of lentil soup and a Rueben sandwich outside to one of the wrought- iron café tables. The trees around the sidewalk alcove had already surrendered their leaves to the changing weather. He watched the parade of locals and tourists pass while he grew angrier, thinking about losing the detective and the Chatsworth woman.

The early afternoon traffic was at its peak. Bumper-to-bumper vehicles moved at a funeral-procession pace. He finished the lentil soup and eagerly started the Rueben when a gray, two-door compact slowed to a stop in front of the café. The driver waited while three teenagers crossed in front. A glance at the man behind the steering wheel and female in the passenger seat caused him to drop his sandwich. The detective and the woman…he was sure of it.

Schmitt leaped to his feet as the compact moved off. He needed to get to his own car behind the building across the street. With traffic at a crawl, he hoped he had a chance to catch up and follow them. He could not lose the couple again.

He took off running, but his foot caught under a leg of his chair, causing it to topple over, while he tumbled to his knees onto the pavement.

A man at the next table jumped up and rushed to him. "Are you okay?" he asked, helping Schmitt to his feet.

"Yes, yes," he replied. He brushed off his trouser legs. Feeling a burning sensation on his knees, he shoved the pain to the back of his mind.

"Are you sure?" the man asked, holding Schmitt by the elbow.

Schmitt ignored him and stared out into the dense traffic, where the gray compact crept forward. "*Verdammt!*" he suddenly shouted, remembering the detective's car was a white Impala four-door sedan.

The man released Schmitt's arm and stepped away with a look of surprise.

Schmitt turned. "I am sorry. Yes, I am fine. Thank you for your help. I'm afraid I was clumsy." Embarrassed, he reached for the upturned chair and righted it. "Thank you, again," he said and sat down.

Schmitt tried to catch his breath. A sharp pain in his chest startled him. Was he having an angina attack? He picked up his uneaten sandwich, but his appetite was gone. Tossing the sandwich on the table, he rose and crossed Tinker Street to his car.

His shaky step and dry throat worried him. He turned the corner of the building and entered the ice cream store at the rear. He ordered a scoop of vanilla in a cup and walked to his car, where he sat, quietly enjoying his brief respite. The cold dessert soothed the rawness of his throat. After he finished, he pulled out his cell phone and dialed Felix Decker. Perhaps he could explain the detective's mysterious visit to the Historical Society.

"Schmitt here," he said when Decker answered. "I'm in Woodstock."

"You found him?"

Schmitt's jaw clenched. "No, not yet. I followed the woman and detective. They went to an office...the Woodstock Historical Society."

"I didn't know there was such a place."

"They left and went to a café for lunch. I lost them after that." His temples pulsed when he visualized the brash thug he encountered in the restaurant's parking lot. Decker failed to inquire what happened. "I went back to that building, the office of the Historical Society, to find out why they were there, but I was too late. They were closed."

"What will you do now?" Decker asked.

"I need to go to my hotel," he lied, "but I will come back tomorrow morning. Can you think of what they might be looking for in that kind of office? Maybe something to do with Max Vogel?"

Decker took several moments to answer. "It might have something to do with an event that happened in the past... something involving Max Vogel."

"Do you know what that could be?"

"No, I don't."

Frustrated with Decker's uselessness, he shut off the phone without saying goodbye. He sat monk-like with the car door opened, breathing in the cool mountain air, letting his anger settle. He knew now that in addition to killing Max Vogel, he would not return to Germany until he'd destroyed both the woman and the detective.

Chapter 12

Rizzo moved past the man into a dimly lit hallway. He looked up a steep flight of stairs that climbed to the second level with no interim break. A mounted chair rail lined the left wall and followed the steps to the top. The small, motorized folding seat with an operating lever waited at the bottom to transport the old man. To the right of the stairs, a wide hallway led past two closed doorways to a third door, opened and facing them. Broken trails of sunlight cast the rear room in light and shadows, while sawdust on the floor glinted like flecks of gold. The room looked like a wood workshop.

Amy nodded to Rizzo and started up, holding the banister on the right, taking each step slowly and deliberately. Rizzo followed. He could understand why Jake Avon had the chair lift installed since he could no longer safely negotiate the demanding climb. When they arrived at the top, they waited for the ascending chair to deliver their host.

"Please," Avon said after disembarking from his seat. He gestured to the open living area to their right. They entered, and gazing around, Rizzo imagined he had returned to an earlier century. The room had polished, wide-planked floors and was furnished with period furniture pieces that looked like they originated in the antique stores on Main Street,

Saugerties. Amy took a seat on a small, velvet-covered Victorian settee opposite the brick fireplace. Rizzo chose a ladder-back chair that creaked when he settled on the rush seat. An iron stove-insert placed in the mouth of the fireplace served as a supplementary source of heat for Jake Avon's living quarters.

"Please, Mr. Rizzo. Sit over there." Avon pointed to one of a pair of upholstered armchairs flanking the fireplace. "That Shaker ladder-back is nice to look at but not comfortable. Those Louis XV chairs offer a bit more hospitality, like the king they were named for."

"Mr. Avon, may I say you have exquisite taste in antiques," Amy said. "This schoolhouse...I mean, your home, is quite unusual."

"Thank you, but that credit belongs to my late wife, Ingrid. She owned one of those antique stores you passed in town."

"The chair lift," Rizzo said. "Great to have when facing that steep climb every day."

"Not my idea," he answered. "Ingrid's. She insisted on it." He tapped his chest several times. "After they put in my pacemaker in '85, she gave me the choice of that chair lift or move to a single-level house."

"Smart woman," Luke said.

Avon gestured toward the kitchen. "Would you like a cup of coffee? It's fresh." Without waiting for a reply, he walked toward the large, exposed functional kitchen, where appliances, cabinets, counter space and sink lined one wall. "Come," he beckoned, pointing to a long oak trestle table that took up most of the kitchen floor space. They followed and sat side-by-side on two high-back kitchen chairs.

Rizzo watched as the old man shuttled to the counter, removed three coffee mugs from the cabinet, filled them at the Mister Coffee, and meticulously placed the mugs on the table. He retrieved a creamer from the refrigerator, set it down and pushed across a sugar bowl. His callused fingers pulled out a chair on the opposite side. He sat down, looked across the table to his visitors, and his mouth curved into a self-conscious smile.

The old man was clearly uncomfortable playing the role of host. Rizzo doubted he entertained friends here in the schoolhouse, if indeed he had any friends. The furnishings were those of someone more interested in their collection value than their comfort value.

"But tell me. Why are you here? What is the danger I am supposed to fear?"

Rizzo launched into a retelling of his assignment to find Amy's father. He let her briefly explain her out-of-wedlock birth and the research she began years later to locate the father she never knew. Avon's attention remained focused on their faces during their narration. He listened but said nothing.

Rizzo described how he found Frank Bard and verified he was Amy Chatsworth's father. He recounted his meeting with him in the New Brighton tavern, of Bard giving him the photo before they left and went their separate ways.

"When Frank Bard arrived home, Mr. Avon," Rizzo said, "he was shot in the head before he could even get out of the car."

Avon gasped. "Oh, my God!"

"That's why we're here. The man responsible for murdering Amy's father is the son of someone you know."

"Who is it?"

"Before I tell you, you should know both Scotland Yard and the FBI have confirmed the man's identity. They also filled us in on what went down with you and Frank Bard at the start of World War II."

The old man's eyes flashed to Amy's face. "You may be sure I've spent many years regretting that. Happened so long ago, I almost never think about it...like it happened to someone else...not to me."

"I understand," she said. "I'm certain my grandfather felt the same way while he was alive."

Avon turned to Rizzo. "So who is this person that can't put the past behind?"

"He's the son of the man who was your group leader in that misadventure."

"Schmitt? Lieutenant Walter Schmitt?"

"Yes. One of the six executed. His son, Werner Schmitt, a retired Stasi Agent for East Germany before the reunification, has come to the States."

"Good Lord, I remember meeting Werner before we began training for the operation. He was a little boy then."

"All grown up now, and looking to avenge his father's execution."

Avon winced.

"Apparently," Amy said, "my grandfather spoiled part of his plan by passing away from lung cancer twenty-seven years ago."

Rizzo jumped in. "But Schmitt didn't know that. Somehow, his Stasi sources found the cover name given to Kurt Luedecke but not yours. When he tracked down Amy in London, he assumed her grandfather was alive."

Avon took a large gulp from his coffee mug, his face drained and pale. He looked at Amy. "So...so how did he find your father?"

Rizzo answered. "Schmitt discovered I'd been hired to find him."

"Scotland Yard believes he had our phone tapped," Amy said.

"The FBI told us he was a well-trained agent. He followed me to New Brighton, probably thinking he would also find the senior Frank Bard."

Avon's face pinched. "And when he didn't, he settled for killing the son?"

"That's right," Rizzo said. "After his attempt to kill Amy in London failed, he became frustrated. Made him more determined to get satisfaction."

Avon looked wide-eyed at her. "He tried to kill you?"

"Yes, in broad daylight."

"And you think he knows my name…where I live?"

Rizzo thought about the incident in the parking lot of the Veterans Administration. He remembered that later Frank Bard misspoke, trying to explain why he bolted. *"I thought you were someone else."* Rizzo suspected that something Schmitt did earlier must have alerted Frank Bard. He knew he was in danger but never spoke of it. Bard's admonition to Rizzo when he first turned over the photo to him now made sense. *"Tell her to keep it somewhere safe, away from prying eyes. Don't let no one know she has it."* He was more concerned about his friend's safety than his own.

Rizzo said, "We believe he doesn't know your cover name."

Avon raised his bushy eyebrows and peered over his spectacles at Rizzo.

Rizzo continued. "We think someone told him of the photo, that your cover names were scribbled on the back. He broke into my office looking for it. We had to find you first, to warn you."

"You discovered where I lived from the photo?"

"We did some digging," Amy replied, "but once we identified Mead's Mountain House, that gave us a clue for the section of the country where you might be living. The Historical Society of Woodstock and the county tax rolls solved the rest of the mystery."

Jake Avon's dazed expression was almost amusing. Rizzo could guess what was going through the old man's mind. "Don't worry, Schmitt won't find you that easily. To begin, he needs the photo to learn your cover name. That photo is secured in a safe at the Waldorf Astoria, where Mrs. Chatsworth is staying."

"And my copy is in a frame on a shelf in the library," Avon said.

"Nevertheless, we feel you need to be protected."

"And how would you do that?"

Amy pushed away from the table and stood. "We've already been in touch with the FBI. When we return to the city, we will fill them in…that we found you. They'll arrange for the protection right away."

Taking the hint, Rizzo checked his watch and got to his feet. "Yeah, we should get going."

"Please," Avon said, "you've come all this way. At least let me offer you dinner before you leave."

"Thanks," Rizzo said, "but we'll get something to eat back in the city."

"Nonsense. I have a pot roast prepared," he said, gesturing toward the baking dish on the stove. "German style, with onions. I was about to fire up the oven. Be ready before you know it."

Rizzo looked at his watch again, then at Amy for her reaction. He knew even if they left now, they would not reach the city before dark.

"Besides," Avon said, pointing to the window. "The weather's turned nasty. I don't think you want to drive in that."

Rizzo walked over to look out. The darkening sky offered up large, white flakes tumbling with remarkable velocity, clearly an early winter snowfall with troubling possibilities. The storm had already blanketed the ground in white and was rapidly building drifts.

"Well, I don't mind, if Amy is game."

She shrugged. "I hate to impose this way. Do you suppose the snow will let up in a while?"

"It usually does when it starts out heavy like this. It's early in the year," Avon said. "Still too warm to stick."

"Well, may I help?"

"No, young lady. I am better working alone. I learned to do that when Ingrid passed away twelve years ago."

Rizzo returned to his chair at the table.

"You two take a seat over by the fireplace. It is beginning to get chilly. I'll get the insert stove going...warm things up a bit."

Avon scuttled like a crab toward the stove and the large cradle alongside stocked with firewood.

Rizzo jumped to his feet. "I can do that."

Avon stopped. "City boy like you knows how to build a fire?"

"Hey, I used to be a Boy Scout. Earned a merit badge in fire-building."

Avon lowered his head and peered at him over his specs. "Okay, Boy Scout, you do it. Young lady, what kind of wine would you prefer? White or red?"

"Red would be nice."

"Go take a seat. I'll uncork a nice Shiraz."

"Nothing for me," Rizzo said. "Maybe ginger ale, if you have it." He cut his eyes to Amy. She flashed him a look filled with empathy.

Rizzo picked up several dried logs. He loaded them through the stove door and crisscrossed them on top of the remaining embers of an earlier fire. Splinters of one of the logs ignited quickly, surprising him. He placed another log into the flaming cavity. "Wow, this wood is like tinder."

"It should be," Avon responded. "It's been drying out all summer. The furnace in the basement is old. Puts out little heat, so I come to depend on that stove in the winter."

Amy returned to the Victorian settee with her wine. She looked to her left at the antique end table. "I shouldn't put my glass on this beautiful piece. Maybe I should use a coaster?"

Avon glanced over. "Don't worry, young lady. It is past the stage of any meaningful mistreatment. Ingrid and I used to play Gin Rummy on it every evening after dinner. It's an oak Victorian envelope-card table. The top opens up to a felt playing surface, although I'm sure the felt has been worn clean by now."

Amy leaned back into the velvet-tufted upholstery of the settee, watching Rizzo at the stove. When he had a good blaze lapping at the sides of the iron interior, he closed the stove door and reached for the glass of ginger ale Jake Avon held out to him.

"How long have you lived here?" Amy asked, taking a sip of her wine.

Avon turned and walked back into the kitchen. "Came to work here in 1953. Before that, took any odd jobs I could find. My cousin…the son of my mother's brother…he had a butcher shop out on Route 212 for many years. Decker's Pork Store. He arrived here with his family before the war and settled in this area. I lived with him for a little while, taking on odd jobs until the schoolhouse came along."

"Did you teach here at the school?"

"Oh, heavens no. This was a grade school. They needed a maintenance man, and my cousin recommended me to someone at the Saugerties School Board."

Rizzo remained standing by the stove, occasionally waving his hands across the iron belly to check on the heating progress. "How did this place become your home?"

Avon looked back over his shoulder. "The job came with a living arrangement. A small room on this level. I could live here free in return for looking after the building around the clock."

Rizzo went to the window again. Heavy flakes passed through the beam from the light pole at the rear of the building. The storm showed no signs of letting up. He worried they would be stuck longer than he first thought.

"The next nine years," Avon continued, "I became a fixture. The kids loved me. Mr. Fixit, they called me."

"When did it cease being a schoolhouse?" Amy asked.

"In 1962. The Saugerties school system chose to consolidate. This was the first school designated to be torn down."

Rizzo recalled passing the large school building on this side of town. He guessed that building now served as the central school for the many towns and hamlets in this area of Ulster Country.

"I had money saved. I offered to buy it," Avon said. "They agreed to sell if I paid the taxes and kept up the appearance, not let it become an eyesore. But the county kept ownership of the land."

Amy looked around. "It's clear you did a massive renovation over the years."

"I had to. After I met Ingrid at the Lutheran Church in Saugerties, I couldn't ask her to marry me without a home to offer."

"You do the work yourself?" Rizzo asked.

"All of it. I learned my trade back in Germany. I was considered what you in the U.S. would call a master cabinet maker." His voice was clear and filled with pride.

Amy gestured toward the kitchen area. "Those cabinets and counters are beautiful. The work of a real artisan. Certainly nothing shoddy about them."

The old man moved with purpose between the range and the refrigerator with an agility that belied his eighty-plus years. Over the chopping noise of his celery and carrot knife, he continued his recitation.

"After the school closed down, I worked for a year with a custom woodworking shop north of here, in Cairo. We built furniture and cabinets from designs that high-end decorators in Manhattan would send us. When the owner took ill and business slowed down, I set up shop right here…downstairs in what used to be the gymnasium. Soon those designs were coming to me." Avon stopped and walked to Amy Chatsworth carrying the wine bottle. "May I refill your glass?"

"Yes, thank you."

"How's your ginger ale?" he asked Rizzo.

"It's fine."

Avon remained for several seconds watching him.

Rizzo hoisted his glass in the air in a salute. He had seen the questioning look on the old man's face. "I'm in AA." He smiled. He hoped Avon would let it go at that. He did.

Avon turned back to the kitchen. "We'll be eating in about ten minutes. I hope you are hungry. When I cook, I always make an abundance of whatever, so I can enjoy it over the next several days."

Amy got to her feet. "May I set the table?"

Avon pointed to the cabinet at the far end of the counter. "Thank you. Dishes up there. Silverware in that drawer below."

Rizzo revisited the window. Early winter storm or not, they were not going to start back tonight. He remembered seeing a motel at the Saugerties exit off the thruway. Could they make the drive?

Chapter 13

Dark clouds filled with moisture had threatened Werner Schmitt's drive back to the city. After dropping off the rental at the Enterprise garage on Forty-fourth Street, he hailed a cab on Third Avenue. A mixture of light snow and rain fell from the dusky sky.

The taxi turned into Otto Buchmann's street in Bushwick, Brooklyn, at the same time an EMS ambulance raced by with its siren screaming and lights flashing. Schmitt caught sight of a police cruiser, light bar ablaze, parked at the entrance to Buchmann's building. Something was going on.

He directed the cab driver to pull over a half block away. He paid the cabbie, got out and remained standing on the sidewalk in front of a three-story brownstone. He watched for several minutes until a uniformed patrol officer exited the front door of Buchmann's building and climbed into the police cruiser. The blue-and-white remained at the curb with the engine running and the officer seated behind the wheel.

A short while later, a large black man came out of the building and popped open an umbrella. Dreadlocks hung down from beneath his knitted Rasta cap. He started in Schmitt's direction, but before he could go by, Schmitt put out his hand.

"Excuse me, what has happened there?" Schmitt asked, pointing to the police vehicle.

The man slowed, turned around and looked back over his shoulder to the flashing cruiser lights. "A mugging, mon. Nothin' unusual for this neighborhood."

Schmitt touched the man's arm before he could continue on his way. "Someone who lived in that building?"

"Yeah, my neighbor. An old German guy. Found him outside his door. Got whacked over the head by a damned piece-of-shit-druggie right outside his door. Took his motherfuckin' grocery money."

"Was he injured?"

"Hurt bad. EMS took him over to Wyckoff Heights Hospital. Motherfucker really did a job on the old guy."

The snowfall was heavier now, accumulating on Schmitt's uncovered head and shoulders. Moisture ran down his face and neck.

The stranger looked at him. "Hey, mon, get an umbrella. You're gettin' soaked."

He waved and took off.

Schmitt watched the police cruiser finally pull away. He waited until the car reached the end of the block and turned north before he moved. Feeling in his pocket for the apartment key Buchmann had given him, he began walking.

He was angry. Following the detective and the woman upstate had yielded nothing. He needed time to regroup. He felt terrible about Otto Buchmann's mugging and unexpected hospitalization, but Otto's misfortune provided him a safe haven until he could determine what to do next.

Poor Otto, in the hospital. He wished he had time to visit him, but that would be too risky. He had to be careful about Buchmann's neighbor, that black man. He had to avoid running into him again.

* * *

"Pull your car into the driveway next to the truck," Jake Avon said. "Get off the road or the plow will bury you in the morning."

Rizzo gave Amy a questioning look. "You sure you're okay with this?"

She glanced over to the window. "It doesn't appear we have many choices, does it? We can risk driving to that motel or accept Jake's invitation. I agree driving to New York City in this weather is out of the question."

Rizzo turned to Avon, who had bent over to refill Amy's glass. "Well then, looks like you have two overnight guests."

"Good," Avon said with a quick nod of his bald head. "Young lady, you take the guest bedroom over there. Luke can use the pull-down futon in the library. The Boy Scout is in charge of feeding the stove if you get too cold."

The old man disappeared to the rear of the apartment and reappeared carrying bed linens and a large comforter. "This is for you, Luke." He looked at Amy. "Your bed has clean sheets. If you feel you need more than the one blanket, there are extras in the chest at the foot of the bed." He handed the bedding to Rizzo and approached the stove. Adding wood to the waning fire, he spoke to him, sounding like a scoutmaster. "It needs to be fed again around three, but you'll know it's time when your toes go numb."

"Think you can handle it?" Amy asked.

"I don't know. I may have to wake you…get your help."

"Don't you dare."

Avon closed the stove door and turned to her. "It's past my bedtime. You two can find your own way. There is plenty of wine in the rack on the counter. I put you in charge of that. Help yourself."

Rizzo watched her move toward Avon, holding out her arms. The gesture stopped the old man. Avon raised his large hands and took her by the shoulders, preventing her from coming closer. Bending forward, he put up his chin and brushed his cheek across hers. Clearly, he was not comfortable with her sudden display of affection.

She stepped away. "Dinner was marvelous. Thank you so much for your hospitality."

"No, young lady. I should thank you for finding me, to warn me about Werner Schmitt. I am grateful to you and Luke." He nodded to both and padded off toward his bedroom at the front of the schoolhouse.

Before disappearing behind his closed door, he called back, "The ginger ale is in the refrigerator, and don't forget to move the car."

Rizzo grinned and walked the bedding to the library. He returned wearing his jacket.

"Be right back." He returned minutes later and found Amy sitting in the armchair closest to the stove. Her shoes were off, her feet tucked under her.

He remained standing, taking in her soft, gentle face. He admired the way she seemed to find comfort under any circumstance or situation. She adapted with ease. He'd known from the beginning there was something special about her.

She looked up. "What? Why are you staring?"

He dropped into the chair opposite, eyeing her half-filled glass of wine. The emptied bottle sat on the trestle table. "Nothing," he lied. "But I was wondering if this might be a good time to check in back home. You haven't made a phone call since we left the Waldorf this morning."

"You mean to my husband?"

"That's what I mean."

She drained her glass and placed it on the small table at her side. She inhaled slowly. "He knows where I am."

"But he doesn't know you're okay. Shouldn't that worry him?"

She leaned against the back of the chair and folded her hands behind her head, squeezing her eyes together. She stayed in that position for several seconds before she spoke. "It should, but I don't believe it does."

Rizzo made no reply. A pained tightness took hold of her face. He suspected the wine had opened a vein into something she preferred would go away. In the time they had spent together, she had not once mentioned her husband or anything about her life with him in London.

"You want to talk or drop it?"

She flashed a weak grin. A combination of exhaustion and wine made the whites of her eyes appear bloodshot. "It's an old story. Nothing original."

"There are no original stories. Only variations on the same theme."

"I guess you're right." Another weak grin.

Rizzo leaned over and touched her arm. "I'm sorry."

She walked to the kitchen, toward the wine rack at the end of the counter. Before she could select one, Rizzo came up behind and put his hands on her waist. "Are you sure you want to open another?"

They remained motionless for a time, saying nothing. When she turned to face him, she said, "I think I'm ready to turn in."

"You okay?"

"Yes. I'm fine."

* * *

Rizzo heard it, but he assumed the tapping noise was the creaking of the aged timbers of the schoolhouse. The library door crept open and Amy's whispering voice floated into the room.

"Luke...Luke."

He threw off the heavy comforter and bolted upright. "What's wrong?"

"I'm freezing," she said. "Shouldn't you put more wood in the stove?"

He pressed the stem of his watch to light the dial. Half past twelve. "No. According to Jake, not for at least another two hours." He could see her outline in the dark shadows. She was shivering.

"Can I sleep in here with you?" she asked. "My room is so far away from the stove, I can't feel any heat from it."

He held up the corner of the comforter and reached out toward her. "Get in."

She moved to that side of the futon. She looked down at him as though she needed one more assurance that what she was doing was okay with him. She wore an enormous flannel pajama top tucked into the waist of the giant pajama bottom, pulled together, bunched up and held there with a drawstring.

"Nice sleepers," he whispered.

She rolled in and he tossed the comforter over her. "Jake set them out on the bed for me. After all, I couldn't sleep in my knickers."

"Why not? I am."

She slid her hand under the sheet to his thigh and lightly touched the fabric of his boxer shorts with her fingertips. "Oh, my, you are. Aren't you cold?"

"Just a little."

She moved her body against his, turned and placed her head on his chest. "If we cuddle like this we should be able to stay warm. Ya think?"

He laughed and reached down to loosen her drawstrings. "Body heat is good."

* * *

Werner Schmitt poured a third glass of vodka, enjoying his buzz. The alcohol did nothing to lessen his anger, but he figured enough vodka would help get him through the night.

It was one thing to come up empty on surveillance, but quite another matter to lose track of your subject. He had failed badly today. His thinking and planning skills were less sharp; his ability to anticipate had become muddled and slowed. He was getting old.

During his long Stasi career, he had castigated many of his subordinates for performing at this same level. A few he'd had jailed, others, shot. He tolerated nothing but superior results, from them and from himself. His performance today was worthy of the same punishment. Fortunately, in his current retirement status, he was not required to report to anyone that would make that judgment.

"*Gott sei dank*," he heard himself mutter. "God has spared me."

Tomorrow, he would drive back to Woodstock and return to the Historical Society office. He was certain the detective and the woman had found something, something that would lead him to Max Vogel. He would uncover that same information and repair the stupidity of yesterday's performance.

After folding himself into the overstuffed lounge chair in Otto's small living room, Schmitt had drifted off into a stretch of broken sleep, awakened every few hours by a pounding in his head. When he could no longer get back to sleep, he sat up and glanced around the darkened room. He had no idea of the time. Two curtained windows looked out on the wall of the adjacent building, a distance of less than six feet away. The close proximity of the two houses inhibited any daylight from entering.

Schmitt stumbled toward the Tiffany-shaded floor lamp behind the sofa. He pulled the dangling chain and looked at his watch: Six-thirty. He needed to slip out of the apartment while it was still dark. The Woodstock Historical Society office opened at nine. He planned to be there near that time.

Schmitt tossed the Stolichnaya bottle he had emptied into the trash and heard his stomach growl. The few biscuits he'd found in Otto's kitchen were all he had eaten since his interrupted lunch at the café in Woodstock.

He showered and changed into a pair of cargo pants and wool pullover, then called the taxi service to deliver him to the Enterprise garage in Manhattan. He hoped the snow had stopped early enough during the night so that road conditions would not impede his return journey. Finding what the woman and the detective discovered yesterday was critical. He was sure their visit had something to do with Max Vogel. His investigative sense told him he was getting close.

Yesterday, upon entering the apartment, he remembered his near panic in Woodstock. He immediately retrieved his nitroglycerin spray container and slipped it into the cargo pants he planned to wear the next day. Turning to the door, he patted his pocket to make certain it was still there. Satisfied, he exited the apartment and locked the door.

Chapter 14

Felix Decker steered his Lexus into the empty long-term parking lot at the Southwest Regional Airport. The deserted lot looked like the one at Raymond James Stadium three hours after a Bucs game. The winter snowbird season in southwest Florida had not yet arrived.

His Delta flight would get to Atlanta in an hour and a half, leaving him with a fifty-five minute window to make his US Airways connection to Albany. He would arrive in New York State's capitol city late that afternoon.

Decker hated lying to his wife. He could think of only one excuse to give her for taking this trip. The bank in Kingston had called. His deceased father's account required an in-person identification and signature before they could release the contents of a forgotten safe-deposit box. She bought his explanation without question. He was to call her at their daughter's house in Atlanta when he returned to Florida.

He had forty minutes before he needed to board, enough time to enjoy a Café Mocha at the Starbucks kiosk before clearing the security checkpoint. He rolled his suitcase to a small table, set his coffee down and tossed his topcoat over the back of the chair.

He sat facing the floor-to-ceiling window that overlooked the wide expanse of tarmac and runways, his mind a jumble of worries. The image reflected on the glass was that of an overweight, balding man, grown content over the years in a worry-free Florida retirement, now threatened by a maniac bent on vengeance. Werner Schmitt was determined to kill his father's cousin, Max Vogel.

Decker had learned of this family connection only in 1980 — at the bedside of his dying father, who had wisely guarded the fact from him. Had Decker's superiors at Justice learned of this relationship, his career would have been over.

He squeezed his eyes and dropped his chin to his chest, remembering the conversation in his father's bedroom. He could visualize clearly Gerald Decker's sickly, ashen face, his temples pulsing and his eyes flaring with panic like someone worried that the Angel of Death would cut short his confession. His father struggled to get the words out.

"Must...must tell you this...before my last breath," he whispered to Felix in those final moments. "Max Vogel...more than childhood friend. A cousin. Didn't tell you. Would risk your job."

Felix jumped to his feet. He stood at the window, staring out, his anger burning in his throat. He remembered his father's phone call to him in Washington. "Please, he is my dearest friend. See what you can do." He could not believe how his father had used him, but shock and disbelief over this revelation was only the beginning. In retrospect, he remembered thinking the rest of his father's confession was worthy of a spy novel.

He heard his father's cancer-wracked voice beckoning him. "Felix, come."

Felix moved to the bed and looked down at the man he thought he knew.

"Sit...sit," the old man pleaded, his voice barely audible, the pain showing through his terrified eyes.

Felix dropped into the chair and his father continued.

"Before the war...German high command appointed me steward...large fund of money...to finance sabotage."

Felix took a quick, sharp breath. He had some vague recollection that his father had played a minor role in the early politics of the Nazi party in Berlin. However, he believed Gerald Decker had left all that behind once he brought his family to the U.S. Yet, to be given stewardship for the saboteurs' fund? Apparently, his father's role in the party had been more than minor.

"How much?" Felix asked.

"Two and...two and half million. Not used...everyone captured."

"Where did it go? You send it back?"

"No...couldn't. We would get caught."

"So what happened to it?" Felix asked, surprised that his interest had been piqued beyond simple curiosity.

"Half million...spent on family...cabin...Princeton...store expenses"

"And the rest?"

Felix waited for a reply. His father merely shook his head, and closed his eyes for the last time.

Decker long suspected his father had turned the money over to Max Vogel, after having reached an agreement for its dispersal. Whatever that was, he was not to be included. This long-held resentment convinced him to sign on to Werner Schmitt's plan. To find the money, he reminded himself, not to kill Vogel.

He picked up his topcoat, raised the suitcase handle and started toward the security checkpoints. He hoped he wasn't too late to dissuade his Stasi partner from committing another unnecessary murder.

* * *

Luke Rizzo flicked open one eye and examined his soundly sleeping bedmate. Her eager and unhesitating participation in their lovemaking last night had surprised him. Tender, passionate and natural, they had created the illusion of a long-time married couple comfortably enjoying their connubial rights. Would she have any regrets when she woke?

As though she read his thoughts, Amy's eyes fluttered open. She turned toward him, and, smiling, reached over to caress his stubby cheek. "Did you sleep well?"

"Like a brick. You?"

"I must say, you wore me out, but in a delicious way."

Amy's teasing expression brought back the image of Flo, his rent-a-car angel from Pittsburgh, mirroring the one she had displayed when he asked if dinner was ready and she answered. "No, darlin', but your appetizer is." For reasons he could not explain, he felt a twinge of guilt.

Rizzo swung his feet to the cold, bare floor. The room was frigid. He turned his head and looked down at the English woman lying at this side. "This change anything?"

"No, silly. We're adults, aren't we?"

"But—"

"But nothing. It was most enjoyable. Besides, weren't you appointed to keep the fires going? Both in me and in that damned wood stove out there. So be on your way. It's freezing in here."

Rizzo heard her snicker. He reached for his trousers and shirt. "I'm on it."

Jake Avon stood at the kitchen counter in front of the coffee maker, measuring scoops of Breakfast Blend Colombian. He turned when Rizzo approached. Rizzo glanced at the wood stove. Warmth radiated from within the cast-iron belly. He had failed in his assignment as the keeper of the flame.

"Didn't earn my merit badge last night. Sorry."

"No, not as a Boy Scout, anyway." The old man smiled. "Coffee in five minutes."

Rizzo pulled out a chair at the trestle table and sat down. He could make out the snow-laden tree branches at the back of the house through the frosted-over windows. "How much snow we get?"

"Radio reported a foot, falling in a ten-mile-wide swath from Albany down to upper Westchester. Earliest snowstorm we've had in ten years. And it stuck. Saugerties plows were out at dawn, clearing the roads." Avon removed a large cast-iron skillet from the hanging rack of pots and pans at the end of the counter. "There's a wall of snow behind your car, but my neighbor's teens will be over soon to dig you out. Bacon and eggs okay?"

"Oh? Sure, certainly. Hate to put you out more than we already have. You know, if the roads are okay, we can stop for breakfast at that motel by the toll booths."

"Wouldn't have it," Avon said, dismissing the idea with a wave of his hand.

"You think the thruway will be okay?"

The old man placed the basket of eggs on the counter and turned around. "That's the nice part of living in New York. They look after their interstate. Plows worked all night."

"I smell coffee," Amy said, padding barefoot from her room. She had slipped back into her slacks and button-down shirt, leaving the oversized sleep flannels on the bed.

"Good morning. Help yourself," Avon said, motioning to the filled carafe. "We're having eggs and Canadian bacon. How would you like your eggs?"

"I'm not fussy. Whatever way Luke wants his."

Amy looked relaxed. Absent was the wine-fed tenseness she had exhibited last night, before retiring. Rizzo slid a chair out from the table and motioned to her to join him.

* * *

"Okay, we'll meet you at Saugerties Police Headquarters," Jack Fields said. "Give us about two hours. Maybe longer if the roads become a problem."

He hung up and pressed his intercom. "Rachel, buzz Tony. Tell him the garage in five minutes. The Albany office is meeting us in Saugerties."

"Will do, Jack," the voice replied.

Twenty minutes later, Tony Condon steered the Lincoln Town Car onto the East Side Drive and headed north. Puddles left from the overnight rainstorm formed at the collars of the road, causing blowback from the cars ahead. Condon had the wipers going at full speed, and traffic moved along unimpeded despite the wet road condition.

The foot of snow that blanketed the area north of the city had dissipated into rain before falling on the lower suburbs. After passing the Mamaroneck Exit in Westchester, Fields no longer worried about travel on the thruway. The plows had the major roadway cleared.

"Did the Albany office have any information on Vogel?" Condon asked.

Fields shook his head. "Not a thing. Considering the WP program was in the early stages of development, they did a great job guarding Vogel's identity."

"And he was a model citizen all these years?"

"So it seems."

"Luedecke was too. Look what happened to him."

Condon picked up a thruway ticket at the Woodbury tollbooths, forty-five miles north of the city, and looked at his watch. "Looks like another hour. What time are we supposed to meet?"

"When we get there."

The Lincoln motored north, passing slower-moving vehicles. The two agents remained silent until Condon spoke. "Seems strange this guy, Schmitt, is still looking for revenge after all these years."

"Been thinking about that, have you?" Fields said, reminded that over the period of their partnership, Condon was tenacious about most things, particularly when a puzzle challenged him.

"Well, yeah. I mean, you'd think the fire would've gone out by now."

Fields chortled. "Hey, maybe the guy has nothing better to do with his time. Retirement from the Stasi must be hell. Nobody to torture or kill."

"No, I get the feeling there's something more to this."

"What?"

"The money. I know I said I didn't think he knew about it, but now I'm not so sure."

"You mean the funds to finance the saboteurs? Christ, that's got to be long gone."

"Maybe not. And if not, I believe Schmitt knows where it's buried."

"That would make things interesting," Fields said.

He looked out his window for several seconds, at the passing scene. Condon could be right. The $2.5 million had never been accounted for, and to the best of the Bureau's knowledge, never expended.

According to Quimby's report and the tax records of Gerald Decker, the Justice Department's background check revealed no excess spending during his lifetime. His son, Felix Decker, had gone to Princeton, true, but the old man's butcher business could have financed that without a stretch. Back then, you didn't need to sacrifice your first born to pay the tuition.

* * *

Schmitt pushed through the doorway and hopped down the two steps with an agility that belied his age. He stopped short on the sidewalk and looked back at the Historical Society building. Despite the scarcity of available information, he had been right on target by returning to the records office. The woman at the desk remembered the pair from yesterday. Unfortunately, she could not tell him anything more than they had inquired about Malden-on-the-Hudson, a small hamlet east of Woodstock. This, after they had examined a collection of old hotel registers. He pressed her for some details about Malden, thinking it might provide a hint as to what to look for when he got there. She apologized, and other than describing it as "a most quaint and picturesque hamlet," she had to admit she hadn't been there in some time.

Schmitt found a street map of the local area at a Rite-Aid store. A quick examination gave him the location of Malden-on-the Hudson, narrowing the chase a bit. Did he have enough information without having to inquire at every door in the hamlet? He knew the make, model and color of their car. He would start with that, assuming they had not left the area. The overnight snowstorm may have worked in his favor. If that wasn't enough, he would start knocking on doors.

Heading east toward Malden, Schmitt followed Route 212, keeping to the posted speed limit. On the drive earlier from the thruway to Woodstock, he had been surprised to find the local roads cleared and passable. The Ulster County's plows had left walls of snow lining the shoulders, but now the morning sun and rising temperatures were rapidly drying the road surface.

An excitement surged through him as he drove. He was getting close; he could feel it. Getting Max Vogel to give up the location of the money might take time—painful time if he resisted. A smile formed. The prospects of reviving his former interrogation techniques delighted him.

Schmitt drove twenty-five minutes before reaching the intersection of Route 9W and the road marked as Malden Turnpike. From this point, he could see very few homes. Did he have the wrong location? He turned down the road following the curve, hoping to spot the detective's car.

Schmitt stopped in front of a building resembling a schoolhouse. He watched two teenagers digging through the mound of snow blocking the driveway entrance. The late

144 - The Second Target

morning sun helped the boys' effort. Slushy piles of snow were scattered across the road's surface out front. Behind the mound on the drive, Schmitt could make out two vehicles parked side by side. A white blanket covered both vehicles. One was a car and the second vehicle was clearly a pickup truck. Did they both belong to the owner of the schoolhouse?

He rolled down his window and called over to the shoveling teens. "Do you live here?"

"No, sir," the smaller of the two replied.

"Does Max Vogel live near here?"

The boy looked toward his brother. When he received a shoulder shrug, he turned back to Schmitt. "We don't know nobody by that name...what lives here," the young boy said.

Schmitt nodded and rolled up his window. He suddenly realized he had used Vogel's name and not Avon's. He considered rolling down the window, but decided against it. Asking again, he feared, might raise suspicions. He should not have stopped. He needed to remain in the shadows to keep his advantage.

* * *

Their country breakfast finished, Amy cleared the table, loading the dishwasher with plates and cups. Rizzo busied himself preparing another pot of coffee. Without a word, the old man disappeared into his bedroom at the rear of the house. Several minutes later, Rizzo heard him cross to the staircase, take the chair lift down to the first floor and go out the front door.

"He's got the neighbor's kid digging us out." Rizzo said. "Plows buried the front of the driveway. Jake says we got a foot overnight."

Amy walked to the window, looked out at the frozen tree limbs, and turned back to Rizzo. "Will we be able to motor back to Manhattan?"

Rizzo patted the chair next to him and signaled her to sit down. He moved in close and   whispered, "Jake's not safe here. If we found him, so will Schmitt. We need to think of something."

Amy's eyes widened. "Do you really believe he'll be able to locate him the way we did?"

"Hey, it's possible. Don't forget, the man was a Stasi gorilla. They were ruthless bastards that hunted and killed a ton of their enemies. This guy has to have pretty fair investigative skills."

"What do you suggest?"

"For starters, get the FBI involved. Call Agent Fields. I don't know why we didn't tell him about your grandfather's photo. You kept his number, didn't you?"

"Yes," Amy said, but Rizzo failed to hear her. The loud roar of a truck engine drew his attention to the stairs.

Chapter 15

"Sit over there," Lieutenant Tom Lange said. "Sorry for the mess. We're in the process of renovating the main office downstairs, and they've relegated us to this rat hole until work is completed. Typical Saugerties bureaucratic planning, I'm afraid."

Fields liked him immediately. Lange was a tall, lanky man whose slenderness gave him an air of youthful energy. He had a plain, non-threatening face, with a bushy mustache that failed to camouflage his long nose. His close-clipped haircut reminded Fields of the way Condon kept his—the Marine Corps regulation cut.

"Lovely digs," Jack Fields said, as he and Tony Condon sat down on a small sofa that looked as though the local Goodwill had recently delivered it.

Lange ignored the comment. "Agent Brancuso called to say they'd been delayed in getting on the road. Might be about ten minutes late. Coffee?"

"Black," Fields said.

"Cream and sugar," Condon replied.

Lange disappeared into the break room and returned with two plastic mugs. He handed them to the agents, paused, his eyes following the length of his nose, and asked. "Is this a possible hostage situation?"

Fields shot a look at Condon. Clearly, the Albany office hadn't briefed Lange. Neither agent had given the hostage idea much consideration. Fields turned back to Lange and seeing the man's wide-eyed expression, he resisted smiling. The idea that Schmitt would find Max Vogel first did not appear on their radar. Unless Schmitt had tapped into a Justice Department source they didn't know about.

"We don't believe so," Fields answered. "That doesn't remove the need to act fast, find our subject and put him into protective custody."

Relief formed on Lange's face. "That's good. We're a small precinct here. A hostage problem would mean we'd have to recruit from Albany's SWAT team resource. That's not something we like doing."

"I'm sure the Albany office has already covered the possibility," Fields assured him. "Should that become necessary."

During the next several minutes of waiting, Fields and Condon learned Lange's parents were first generation German, but he was born in Kingston, ten miles away, and raised in neighboring Cairo. After a four-year enlistment in the Marine Corps—Fields and Condon smiled in tandem at this revelation—he entered the State University of New York, Albany Campus, and graduated with a degree in sociology. He prided himself on his knowledge of the area's geography and residents. "Not too many places to hide that I don't know about," Lange told them.

The door opened and the sergeant-on-duty ushered in the two Albany FBI agents. Lange rose to greet them. "Agents Hart and Brancuso. Nice to see you again." He motioned to Fields and Condon. "I guess you guys know each other."

Brancuso, the lead agent, stepped forward. "Hey, Jack, it's been a while." He turned toward Condon, who had stood to greet them, extended his hand and said, "Hi. Ralph Brancuso. My partner here, Keith Hart."

Ignoring the standing Condon, Hart looked directly at Fields. "Ralph mentioned you two worked together in the past."

Fields nodded. "True, a couple of years back."

Lange rolled two desk chairs to the vicinity of the sofa and motioned to his two new visitors to sit. "My apologies." He carved the air with an opened, upright palm. "Kind of make-shift, I know."

Brancuso kept his topcoat on when he sat down. Mid-forties, he was a short man with a stocky build and a broad forehead. He tended toward baldness, was clean-shaven, and dressed in the obligatory blue suit and white shirt with a tomato-red tie under his belted Burberry topcoat. Fields knew him in the early '90s when they shared an office at Federal Plaza, before Brancuso had transferred upstate. Fields remembered him as a tenacious bulldog, a good law officer given to uttering expletives that would make a dockworker blush, particularly when the FBI's bureaucratic restrictions frustrated him.

Agent Hart was dressed similarly, but in a suit immaculately tailored to his athlete's build. Fields guessed him to be crowding early 30s. He had straw-colored hair, trimmed in a length somewhere between an earlier crewcut and a full head. He sat ramrod straight, feet flat on the floor to keep the chair from rolling, and smirked.

Fields looked him over. Ivy League. He came off as arrogant, and his polished appearance and confident demeanor fit that image. Four years of that elitist environment guaranteed their graduates this personality endowment. No such inheritance from Ohio State. Fields, aware of Hart's extraordinary contrast with Brancuso, wondered about their partnership's compatibility.

Lange stood by, silent until he offered coffee to the two new arrivals.

"No thanks," Brancuso said.

"No thanks," Hart parroted.

"Okay," Brancuso said, looking at Fields, "whadda we got?"

* * *

Schmitt eased along looking for signs of the detective's car. He followed to the bend of the road, creeping forward to where the two lanes traversed the top ridge of the sloping terrain. They had plowed the road earlier, and the shaded surface of this area was slick with a light coating of ice.

Houses dotted both sides with most driveways hidden from view. To the left, a maze of narrow lanes and driveways fed the houses strewn about on the steep hillside that ran down to the river's edge. On his right, a tributary of driveways led up to those houses situated on the upslope. He had difficulty seeing any parked vehicles. The likelihood of spotting the detective's car grew dimmer with each house he passed.

Driving for several minutes, Schmitt finally reached the point where the road dead-ended. He backed up, attempted to U-turn and hit a wall of snow. When he painstakingly completed the maneuver, he started back in the other direction. At the top of the bend, he slowed to a stop and studied the schoolhouse a short distance away.

The boys were gone, but a short, stocky man, hatless, wearing a heavy wool jacket, was brooming the windshield of the pickup. He guessed him to be around the age that Max Vogel would be today. When the man finished cleaning the driver-side door, he tossed a small suitcase across the seat, glanced back at the schoolhouse and got in.

The truck's motor turned over immediately. Schmitt watched as the old man sat for several seconds, waiting for the truck to settle into a smooth rumble. Without warning, the man pressed down on the accelerator, causing the engine to roar. He backed out onto the road and took off in a hurry, skidding briefly on the wet snow.

Schmitt followed. His gut feeling told him the old man was Max Vogel. If he was wrong, he could always return to the area later. The truck turned right onto Route 9W and travelled north at a speed that allowed him to keep the vehicle in sight with little trouble.

He thought of running him off the road and into a snow bank. Taking him captive would be no problem. Nevertheless, he could not risk attacking the wrong man. Instead, he stayed in pursuit, keeping his eyes riveted to the taillights of the truck.

He would wait until the driver arrived at wherever he was going. In time, he would have an opportunity to create a harmless close-up encounter, ask him a few questions, size up the man, and make a determination. Schmitt had the element of surprise on his side. He didn't think Vogel knew he was a hunted man.

* * *

Amy went to the counter to refill her coffee cup. Rizzo's attention stayed fixed to the top of the stairs. The loud noise he heard came from the outside, the unmistakable roar of a truck engine. He got to his feet and approached the stairs, squatting to look down. The chair was at the bottom position. He could see the closed front door. "He must have gone outside to start up his truck," Rizzo said, walking back to the table. "He's probably worried about the battery."

"Will our rental have a problem?"

"Shouldn't," he said. "It's a new model."

Amy sipped her coffee while Rizzo drummed his fingers on the tabletop. Would Avon accept the FBI's protection? The old man was strong-willed and might object to the Feds confining him under their wing. He had spent the last forty-eight years since his release from prison taking care of himself. However, this was different. Schmitt was threatening his life. Rizzo doubted Avon, at his advanced age, could defend himself against a professional killer like the Stasi.

Amy glanced at Rizzo, then down at her watch. "He's been gone a long while. Do you imagine he might be having a problem?"

"I don't know. Let me go down and see."

Rizzo approached the stairs. A sudden wave of worry overtook him. He flew down the steps two at a time. Pulling back the door, he peered out hoping to see the neighbor's kids shoveling the drive and the old man supervising their efforts. Instead, the empty scene that greeted him had the impact of a gut punch. Avon and the kids were nowhere in sight. Neither was his pickup.

"He's gone," Rizzo shouted when he hit the top of the landing.

"Who?" Amy asked, confused. "The boys?"

Rizzo shook his head. "Jake. He took the truck and left."

"Well, perhaps he gave the boys a ride home."

"I don't think so. They live close by...couple of houses down the street."

"Is he...is he coming back, you think?"

Rizzo swallowed his response. He walked toward the back of the house, to Avon's bedroom. Several bureau drawers left open displayed their contents in disarray, as though the old man had gone through them in a hurry. A small overnight suitcase remained on his double bed, unopened. The imprint of a second larger bag was visible on the comforter. The one he had packed and taken with him.

Rizzo checked the library where he and Amy had slept. He spotted the framed photo of Avon and Bard standing on the middle shelf of the bookcase. Under the frame, Avon had placed a sheet of lined paper and a house key. Rizzo picked up the paper and read the message written in Avon's shaky hand:

> *Sorry to leave you like this. Here is the key to the house. Please make yourselves at home. Stay as long as you like. Luke, if Werner Schmitt comes looking for me, you have to protect Amy. Suggest you alert Lieutenant Lange, Saugerties Police. He will know what to do. In addition, Luke, the Boy Scout, do not forget to tend the wood stove at night. Jake.*

Rizzo sat down at the table next to Amy, took the coffee cup out of her hands and swallowed a mouthful of tepid liquid. "This needs warming up," he said, as he placed his hand on her shoulder.

Amy's eyes fixed on him for several moments. He took in her bewildered look and handed over Avon's note. He walked to the microwave, put the cup into the compartment, and set the timer for thirty seconds. When he was done, he turned and waited for her reaction.

She lowered the note. "Doesn't appear he'll be returning soon, does it?"

"That would be my guess. Time we called Jack Fields." He reached in his pocket for his cell phone. "What's his number?"

Amy retrieved her purse from the bedroom and recited the ten digits.

"I'm sorry, Mr. Rizzo, Agent Fields is not in the office," his secretary, Rachel, announced when he was connected.

"Well, can you at least get a message to him that I called? It's urgent. He needs to know what I have to tell him."

"I can try. What's the message?"

Rizzo took a deep breath. He hated when officious secretaries stalled him that way. He looked over at Amy, grimaced, and held the Star Trac cell phone out from his ear.

"Jesus H. Christ!"

"Mr. Rizzo, did you hear me?"

He brought the instrument back and replied. "Miss, please tell him to call me as soon as possible. Here's the number." Several seconds of silence followed, during which he assumed the agent's secretary was writing his number. "Did you get it?"

"Yes, I did, Mr. Rizzo. I'll try to reach him."

"Thanks. And I'm sorry if I sounded short with you, but this is an emergency."

"I understand. I'll convey that to him," she said. "Bye, Mr. Rizzo."

He closed the phone without replying.

Chapter 16

Tony Condon finished relating to Brancuso and Hart the circumstances of Frank Bard's murder in New Brighton, Pennsylvania. He was about to go into the killing of the private security guard at the rest stop near the Pittsburgh airport, when the desk sergeant opened the door and took a half-step through.

"Agent Fields, phone call. Your office. Take it out here, if you like."

Fields rose to his feet and walked to the doorway. "Finish up, Tony. Don't wait for me," he said over his shoulder.

The sergeant stepped back, holding the door open, and pointed to the desk against the back wall. "The red button," he said, as if Fields had never seen a telephone console before.

Fields nodded and sat down on the edge of the desk. "Rachel?"

"Jack, that P.I. from the other day, Luke Rizzo, called a short while ago all in a lather. He wouldn't tell me what he wanted," she said, "only that you should call him ASAP. He left his phone number."

"Okay." Fields took out a small spiral note pad and grabbed a pencil from the coffee cup full of pens and pencils. "Shoot."

When he finished writing down the number, she said, "Jack, he said it was an emergency."

"Uh-huh. Thanks, Rachel." Turning to the sergeant behind him, he asked, "How do I get an outside line?"

"Press nine first, sir."

Fields dialed the number and waited. "Luke Rizzo," the tense voice answered after three rings.

Fields turned his back on the desk sergeant and lowered his voice. "Luke, Jack Fields here. What's up?"

"Jack, I found Jake Avon...I mean, Max Vogel."

Fields remained quiet for several seconds, thinking about what he'd heard. He was about to ask him who was Jake Avon, but stopped quickly before repeating the name aloud. "Who's the first guy you mentioned?" he said.

"Jake Avon. It's Max Vogel's cover name, the name on the back of a photo Amy's father gave me in Pittsburgh."

Fields eased off the desk. "And you never mentioned the photo when you were in my office?" He heard Rizzo take a deep breath.

"Bard had the photo in a sealed envelope. He gave it to me before Schmitt killed him. He wanted me to send it to Amy in London."

"Why didn't you?"

"Never had a chance," Rizzo replied. "Amy told me she was coming to New York, so I held up until she got here."

Fields remembered the Yard had called him to set up an appointment with her a few days after her father's murder.

"We didn't open the envelope until after we left your office. That's when we discovered the names on the back."

"Names?"

"Yeah, Jake Avon and Frank Bard."

Fields rolled the pencil through the fingers of his free hand. How in hell did Rizzo locate Vogel with nothing but his cover name? There had to be a logical answer, or this guy was one hell of a sleuth. On the other hand, maybe he had a connection with Felix Decker.

"How were you able to locate him?" Fields asked.

Rizzo described the photo, related how he and Amy had researched the lodge's name at the library and discovered the Woodstock Historical Society's role in maintaining the demolished hotel's records. "The guest register listed his location as Malden. His tax records at the county seat in Kingston gave us an address."

"Where are you now?"

"Upstate. Jake Avon's home…a converted schoolhouse… north of Saugerties and Kingston."

"Don't leave. Stay with him until we get there."

"That's the problem."

"What?"

"The old man took off about a half hour ago. Finished having breakfast with us and slipped out without saying a word. He packed a bag, so I'm sure he's not returning soon."

"No idea where he was going?"

"None."

Fields snapped the pencil in two and tossed the parts onto the desk. "Stay put. We'll be there in ten minutes."

"Ten minutes?"

"Yeah, damn it," Fields answered. "We're at the Saugerties Police Station." He slammed down the phone and strode into the other room.

Tony Condon, having completed his briefing of the two Albany agents, looked up at him from the sofa. Fields knew Condon could read him whenever he was pissed about something. That was the reason they worked so well together.

"What happened?" Condon asked.

Fields shook his head, not believing the turn of events. "Our friend, the P.I., got to Max Vogel ahead of us."

"No shit," Brancuso uttered, keeping in character with his reputation. "How the fuck did he find him?"

Fields looked at Condon. "A photo of the two saboteurs, their cover names written on the back. Frank Bard gave it to Rizzo before Schmitt shot him."

"And he found Vogel by knowing his cover name? Unbelievable," Agent Hart said.

"Yeah," Brancuso agreed. "We better get the hell over to Malden, pick him up before this bozo, Schmitt, finds him too." Looking over at Lange, he asked, "You know this guy, Avon? Where he lives?"

Condon jumped in. "We have an address."

"I know the place," Lange offered. "It's a converted schoolhouse. I also know Jake Avon...have for years. He's a good friend, our neighbor. Lives two doors away. One of the nicest people you will ever meet. It's hard to imagine him as a WW II German saboteur."

"Hold up a minute," Fields said. "The P.I. told me Avon flew the coop a while ago. Packed a bag and took off."

"To where?" Brancuso asked.

"Rizzo didn't know," Fields said, "but maybe we should have a look around the schoolhouse. See if he left anything that would give us a lead."

"Good idea," Hart said. "Is the P.I. there?"

"He better be," Fields answered.

* * *

The pickup truck turned onto Route 32, traveling north. After several miles, Avon turned into the small graveled parking lot of a general store on the northeast corner of a rural intersection. Werner Schmitt slowed down. He watched the old man get out of the truck and disappear into the store's front entrance. Schmitt drove past the lot and stopped twenty yards away on the shoulder of the two-lane road. The store's entrance was visible through his side-view mirror.

His mind ran through possible scenarios: How he would confront the old man; how he would go about testing his identity; how he would subdue him without a scuffle. The

Beretta in the glove box came to mind. He would have to be careful if he needed to threaten the old man. There would be serious consequences from accidentally killing the wrong man. The police would launch a massive manhunt, inhibiting any further effort to find the turncoat, Vogel, and the money. Moreover, if the old man turned out to be Max Vogel, killing him before he could learn where Vogel had hidden the money would dismantle his project. Felix Decker, he knew, would not be happy with that turn of events.

Schmitt looked at his watch. The man had been in the store for a long while. Several people had entered and exited during this time. Should he look in, make certain the old man had not slipped out? He immediately dismissed the notion. Someone might see him and later be able to identify him.

His patience stretched, Schmitt finally relaxed when the man came through the door cradling a large box filled with groceries. He crossed the driveway toward his truck. He deposited the box on the passenger seat and closed the door. The old man circled the front of the pickup and climbed in under the steering wheel.

The man's behavior had him wondering. Why would he drive so far to shop for food? Where was he heading? He was inclined to believe the old man was not Max Vogel, but his intuition fought back the notion. Before the pickup could pull out onto the road, a young bearded man hurried out of the store.

"Wait, Mr. Avon, wait," the young man shouted as he ran toward the truck. "You forgot this," he said, handing something to the old man through the truck window. The clerk returned inside the store, and the pickup rolled out of the parking lot.

Schmitt stiffened. "Aha! I knew it," he cried, slamming the heel of his hand against the steering wheel. He threw the Ford into gear and moved out to pursue.

After crossing the intersection, the car bounced along on a badly paved, snow-packed road lined with small, fenced-in homes surrounded by shrubs shrouded with blankets of snow. He stayed back at a safe distance, and within a mile, the grade of the road increased, twisting and turning. As he followed Avon's truck ascending the Catskill Mountains' foothills, the houses disappeared, and a thick forest flanking each side of the thoroughfare embraced both vehicles like a tunnel.

* * *

Looking like the tail end of a funeral procession, headlights on with Tom Lange in the lead, the three cars came to a stop in front of the schoolhouse. Lange exited his Range Rover, waved to the teenagers shoveling his driveway two houses away and walked toward them. "Donnie," he said to the older one, "how long have you been out here?"

The boy dropped his shovel into a mound of snow. "Maybe an hour, Dad. Why?"

"You did finish Mr. Avon's drive, didn't you?"

"Yeah we did. A while ago." Then looking toward the two Lincoln Town Cars lined up behind his father's Crown Victoria, Donnie asked, "What's goin' on?"

Lange ignored the question. "Did you see Mr. Avon leave?"

"No," Jesse, the younger son, answered. "After we finished, we went inside."

"Hot chocolate," Donnie volunteered. "Mr. Avon was outside when we left. He wasn't there when we came back out."

"Okay," Lange said, and started toward the schoolhouse.

"Hey, Dad," Jessie called.

Lange stopped and turned. "What?"

"While we were digging out Mr. Avon's drive, some man came looking for a guy, supposed to live 'round here."

Lange walked back to Jesse. The two boys liked to play an occasional joke on their serious-minded father, but Lange was certain this wasn't one. "What did he look like, Jess? You remember?"

"Nah, I don't. Old, I'd say. I'm not sure. I didn't get too close to his car."

The answer, on one level, was the response Lange wanted to hear. *Be wary of strangers, especially in cars.* The boys understood that lesson well. However, on another level, the information wasn't helpful.

"What kind of car?" Lange asked, hoping to have something more tangible to go on.

Jesse shrugged. "Sorry, Dad."

"Ford, I think," Donnie offered. "Black."

Lange turned to leave, but Jesse's next comment stopped him.

"He had an accent. Sounded like Mr. Kleinschmidt down at Ace Hardware."

"Did he say who he was looking for?"

"Vogel, I think. Yeah, that's what he said. Vogel."

Lange felt a rush of adrenalin. "How long ago?"

Chapter 17

After twenty minutes of driving far enough behind Avon not to become suspicious, Schmitt caught sight of the pickup turning off the road and darting through an opening in the trees onto a narrow trail through the woods. He followed into the opening, and within a few moments, Schmitt decided it was a route more appropriate for trail bikes. The old man's truck seemed to manage the passage without trouble. It disappeared into the dense foliage as though a giant vacuum had swallowed it. Avon's truck was nowhere in sight.

Schmitt continued on, and moving forward, the Ford labored to stay in the trail's rutted tracks under the layer of snow. His rental lacked snow tires and kept slipping and sliding like a skater with weak ankles.

Each time the trail route veered, Schmitt gunned the car into the turn, scraping past the brush on either side. At one point, the trail divided, breaking off to the right, too late for him to notice. He drove on straight ahead. Tree boughs laden with snow grazed his windshield. The V-6 engine struggled against the incline. He worried the vehicle would not handle the test much longer. With no room to maneuver a U-turn, his only choice was to press forward.

A hundred yards farther, the pitch of the trail suddenly leveled and sunlight broke through the trees. He stopped the car, and as though stepping from a darkened room into sunlight, he squinted through the windshield at a broad clearing beyond the tree line. Melting snow left the ground cover spotted with bare chunks of grass, but with no indication of Avon's tire tracks. That puzzled him. In the distance, at the base of a stand of trees, a log cabin nestled against the mountain. Behind the cabin, the mountainside climbed straight up, its face pockmarked with rocky outcroppings, hosting a forest of its own.

Schmitt backed up the car far enough to remain under the cover of the heavy brush. He stared at the cabin, wondering how to approach without the old man spotting him. Driving up to the cabin door would be announcing his arrival. His option was to circle the perimeter on foot, climbing through the thick growth, an exercise better suited for fatigues and boots than his street shoes and trousers.

He remained at the wheel, searching for a different tack. Moments later, he reached into the bag on the passenger seat, removed Herr Buchmann's 9mm Beretta and opened the car door.

He slogged his way through the brush, stopping every ten yards to wipe the dampness from his eyes and face. Perspiration trickled down his neck from his forehead and temples. The wet branches that slapped across his body each time he neglected to hold out an arm had soaked his jacket and trousers. Frustrated, he realized that a direct approach to the cabin would have made more sense. Even if the old man had spotted him driving up, Vogel would not have recognized him or guessed the reason he was there.

He came out of the brush about twenty yards opposite the north side and made his way toward the cabin. He could see no facing windows. A wide stone chimney dominated that side of the building, narrowing as the shape climbed the sidewall of logs to well above the gabled roof. He spotted the pickup truck parked at the rear of cabin, then edged to the front corner and peered around. A small-elevated deck wrapped the face of the structure, and two steps up provided access to the covered entrance.

Schmitt raised the Beretta to ear level and moved toward the steps. He couldn't decide if he would politely knock or simply put his shoulder to the door and push. Before he could reach a decision, a calm voice from behind spoke to him.

"Herr Schmitt, I suggest you toss the pistol on the ground and turn around."

Schmitt went rigid. He lowered the Beretta but held on firmly.

"Please do as I say, or I will have to remove your head from your shoulders."

Schmitt released his grip, and the gun fell to the ground.

"Now turn around."

He hesitated and slowly twisted his head, but not far enough to see the speaker.

"All the way around, please."

This time the Stasi complied. When he did, he faced a double-barreled shotgun and, behind it, Jake Avon, nee Max Vogel.

"Let's go inside…have a chat, why don't we? Move, please."

While Avon retrieved the Beretta, Schmitt edged toward the front of the cabin. He stumbled on the second step but regained his balance before he could fall into the door. The trek through the brush had exhausted him, an unwelcome reminder that his sixty-five-year-old body was in sad shape.

Avon poked his back with the shotgun. "Open the door…slowly."

Schmitt did as directed.

"Move inside and walk left to the fireplace."

He entered the spacious room and made an immediate left, stopping in front of a flagstone fireplace. He faced the deep, open fire pit where, within its cavernous mouth, logs crisscrossed on top of an iron cradle. A raised stone ledge two feet high ran the full width of the fireplace, and on one end, a set of andirons hung from their rack like soldiers awaiting orders. A large iron cradle sat at the opposite end, stacked with dried logs.

Avon pointed to one of two rustic cedar chairs that flanked the hearth. "Have a seat, if you don't mind."

Schmitt obeyed as Avon moved to the back of the chair and out of sight. In the next instant, Schmitt felt a hard blow to his head. Everything went black.

When he opened his eyes, he raised his chin to look around. His eyelids blinked rapidly as he tried to focus. Disoriented, he attempted to raise a hand to rub the back of his head, but he couldn't move. Both wrists lashed to the arms of the chair and his ankles secured to the chair's legs made him the old man's prisoner.

"I'm sorry to treat you so ungraciously," Avon said, "but you arrived armed. You gave me no choice. Would you like some water before we begin our chat?"

* * *

"Did you look in the front bedroom?" Fields asked, starting toward that end of the schoolhouse.

"I did," Rizzo said, "but you go ahead. Maybe I missed something."

Hart turned from the address book he had been scanning at the counter in the kitchen. "I guess you did miss something," he said aloud. "Like, Jake Avon, for starters."

Rizzo bristled but said nothing. Hart had confirmed his first impression. He was a horse's ass, full of himself. He had walked in and bombarded Amy with questions, forgetting about any introductions. Clearly, his purpose was to impress her.

Tom Lange appeared at the top of the staircase, out of breath from taking the stairs two at a time.

"Where's Brancuso?" he asked, looking at Hart. "He was here...I mean the guy looking for Jake. My kids saw him... spoke to him. I'm sure he's the one."

"Wait, wait. Slow down. Who the hell are you talking about?" Hart asked.

"My two sons were out front digging out the driveway when a car stopped. The driver wanted to know if anyone named Vogel lived in the neighborhood."

Fields returned from the old man's bedroom and stood at the trestle table. "Do your kids know who Vogel is?" he asked.

"Of course not. How could they? Hell, I didn't know until Brancuso called."

* * *

Condon and Brancuso had gone down to the first level to scour the large work area, the room that had served as the gymnasium when the building functioned as a schoolhouse. Condon unlocked the door at the rear and looked out. The door opened onto a wide, flat area, now covered with snow, which once served as the playground area for the school.

Their search uncovered an old, heavily scarred workbench, a small two-drawer cabinet next to it, one drawer filled with buckshot, and a shelved closet where the old man stored his paint and wood-finishing material. Across the broken cement floor, old sawhorses cluttered the surface along with several smaller worktables with splintered legs, none in any useful shape. Half-cut planks of oak leaned against the wall in one corner.

Another door on this level led to a smaller storeroom where Avon kept his woodworking tools, neatly organized in bins, others on hanger hooks from overhead beams, and the larger equipment—such as table saws—covered with painter's drop cloths.

Brancuso looked around, noting that Jake Avon attended to the tools of his former trade with a lover's fervor. "Christ, I feel like I walked into the fucking church sacristy," Brancuso said. "This guy must be some kind of anal compulsive personality."

Condon laughed. Using two fingers, he picked up one end of a drop cloth that shrouded a large piece of equipment, as though he expected something to jump out at him. The turning lathe mounted on a worktable was in pristine condition. He released the cloth. "Well, the guy certainly keeps his tools in great shape."

"Let's go back upstairs," Brancuso said. "Nothing here tells us anything we can use."

The agent looked up at the steep climb ahead of him, eyed the chair on the rail at the bottom of the steps and looked for a second that he would use it. Instead, he puffed his way up the steps without stopping, as if to prove his fitness to Condon. When he hit the top step, he moved into the kitchen area and, pausing, caught his breath.

* * *

Fields watched his counterpart taking in deep breaths. Brancuso's stomach looked like a fireplace bellows. Fields choked back a sarcastic remark.

"Find anything downstairs?"

Brancuso shook his head. "A lot of sawdust, that's all." Red in the face, he waved his hand toward the chairs around the trestle table. "Lange, Rizzo, come sit down. We're chasing our tails with this thing."

Amy and Rizzo sat together at one end, with Lange at the other. Fields and Condon remained standing at the corner alongside of Hart, while Brancuso announced his intentions.

"Jack, you and Condon must have bigger fish to fry than chasing after this old geezer." He nodded toward Hart. "I know we do. We're heading back up to the office unless you think this goose chase deserves more time."

Fields recalled the call from Scotland Yard several days ago. He had agreed to meet with Amy Chatsworth. The Yard hadn't asked him to take on this search for Schmitt, simply to do what he could to help within the bounds of his jurisdiction. The killing of her father in Pennsylvania was a local issue, now in the hands of the New Brighton police. He cut his eyes across to Tom Lange.

"I think we'll head out, too," Fields said. "The charge for this situation rightfully belongs to the Saugerties police. There isn't much more we can do that Lange and his staff couldn't accomplish. If the guy returns to the city, Tom can give us a call and we'll get right back on it." Fields reached into his inside jacket pocket. "By the way, this is what Werner Schmitt looks like." He removed two 4x6 photos and slid them across to Lange at the end of the table.

* * *

Rizzo watched the four Federal agents reach the bottom step and disappear out the door. He rolled his eyeballs. That's the Feds for you. If a case did not produce headlines in *The New York Times*, the Feds could be damned dismissive.

Time to come to a decision. He and Amy could hang around, wait to see if Jake Avon would surface again, or they could turn over the concern for the old man to Tom Lange and the Saugerties police, as Fields suggested. The cold-blooded murder of Frank Bard, Amy's father, remained a raw memory, and the likelihood of Avon coming to a similar end angered him. He didn't want to bail out now. It was important. He needed to finish it; see it to completion; prove to his ex-wife she was wrong about him. Still, it was Amy's choice. She was the client. He thought he knew her well enough to predict what she would say.

"Would you like me to make coffee?" Amy asked when he returned to the kitchen.

Rizzo sat down at the table and watched Lange, who stood at the window gazing out. The late afternoon light cast shadows across the pane, and tree branches rustled noisily at the rear of the house. What was going through his mind?

"Luke, coffee?"

Rizzo spun around. "Oh, sorry. I wouldn't mind a cup, thank you."

"Officer Lange?"

"No, thanks," he said. "Something's bothering me. I need to get back to the station house...put out an alert on Jake. If something turns up, I'll let you know."

Lange left. Rizzo sat across the table from Amy. He held the coffee cup to his mouth, blowing into it to help it cool. She hadn't said a word about the departure of the FBI agents. Should he open the subject?

Amy was already there. "Luke, will your business commitments permit you to stay here with me for a while longer?"

He raised his eyes and lowered the cup. "Amy, I want to see this to the end. I have nothing I'm working on that's more important."

"Good, because I'd feel terrible if something happened to Jake, something that we could have helped him avoid."

"Me too. I'm in as long as you say."

She stood and walked around to his side of the table. He could sense her presence behind him, and thinking she had gone to refill her cup, he was surprised when she embraced his shoulders. She pressed her lips against his cheek. "Thank you."

He reached up and patted her hand. "Okay, now that we got that out of the way, I feel better. If we're going to remain here much longer, I could use a change of clothes. How about you?"

"Well, since I don't think anything in Jake's closet would fit me, as evidenced by his sleep wear last night, we might consider shopping for a few things to carry us. Let's hurry downtown to that shopping center."

Chapter 18

The dried logs caught quickly and soon the chill left the cabin. Jake Avon took the chair opposite his captive-guest. The two men stared into each other's faces, silent for several minutes before the old man spoke.

"After these many years, Werner, you've come all this way to seek revenge? Is there no statute of limitations on your anger?"

Schmitt sat with his chin against his chest, his pale lips pressed together, the blood drained from them. He wanted to scream at the man, tell him how much he hated him, how he wanted to see him dead. His head ached from the blow, and the ropes securing his wrists to the chair were cutting off circulation in his arms.

Despite the warmth from the growing flames in the hearth, Schmitt's soggy shoes and soaked-through trousers were painful distractions. He kept his eyes squeezed shut, afraid that if he opened them, the man would be gone, depriving him of the opportunity to kill him.

"I am sorry for the years of anguish you and your mother suffered over the loss of your father," Avon said. "Surely you might find this difficult to believe, but I do regret being the instrument that caused that loss. We never guessed, any of us, that we would face execution. We were wrong. *Das, was gemacht wird, wird gemacht.* I cannot undo it."

Schmitt ground his molars. "*Verräter,*" he hissed.

"True, but to a flawed assignment, not to Germany. Planning and support was amateurish. Your father, Walter, was leading us into certain failure. He knew it but felt compelled to carry out his orders."

Schmitt raised his eyes and glared across at the old man. "Walter Schmitt was a soldier, a hero. You do not deserve to say his name."

Avon rose to his feet and crossed the room, disappearing into a back bedroom. Schmitt watched, waiting for his return. He struggled against the ropes around his wrists, testing their give. Once he had time to work at them, he sensed they would be assailable. He could not guess what the man had in mind, or how long he intended to keep him tied, but he was not going to wait to find out. Once he freed himself, he could easily overpower the old man. Then he would see how long the traitor's arrogance held up while he coaxed the money's location from him.

* * *

Jake Avon returned with a tape recorder and placed the machine on the table next to Schmitt. He took note of the frozen expression on his captive's face, eyes darting curiously from the recorder and back to Avon, a fixed, angry look as though set in concrete.

"It's time to have our chat," Avon said. He raised the glass and pitcher resting on the fireplace ledge and held them out to Schmitt. "Before we start, Werner, would you like a sip of water?"

Schmitt said nothing, his chin again finding his chest.

Avon set down the pitcher and glass and reached over to turn on the recorder. "Well then, let's start."

Avon sat in the chair opposite, leaned back and crossed his legs like someone about to have a cordial give-and-take with an old friend. He looked across at the Stasi. "Werner, why have you come here...to the States?"

Schmitt ignored him, raised his eyes and stared into the flames climbing the sides of the hearth. The crackling of the burning wood filled the silence. Avon did not press. For his plan to work, Schmitt's answers could not appear coerced. He would need to offer facts or admissions voluntarily. He let a stretch of heavy quietness work on Schmitt's nerves, aware that eventually the silence would put him on edge. As a former Stasi interrogator, the man was not accustomed to someone else having control. He should be the one asking the questions, not responding to them.

"Did you come to here to find me?" Avon asked.

Schmitt glared into Avon's eyes, holding them with blatant hatred, but not answering the question. Avon sensed that the man was about to explode with a furious tirade of expletives. The Stasi's chest heaved in an effort to keep himself under control before settling back to a normal breathing rhythm.

Again, Avon offered the water glass and the pitcher, holding them out to Schmitt. Once more, he refused. Avon brought the glass to his mouth and drained it.

"I'm amazed you found me, Werner. Considering your father's slowness in grasping a lost cause, I would not have thought you had the ability to solve the riddle of my whereabouts. Congratulations."

"*Fick dich!*"

The words, filled with venom, came from the back of Schmitt's throat. Eventually the man would lose control. Avon needed to hear his rage. He stayed quiet, allowing the silence to do its job.

Watching him, Avon drifted back to a time when he was a strong, hotheaded youngster and his fists did the talking. At his advanced age, he could no longer entertain such notions. He was glad for that. He had to be careful. Nothing elicited by force would stand up in a courtroom. He could not live with Schmitt escaping prosecution for killing Frank Bard.

The old man walked behind Schmitt's chair. He paused to examine the clot of blood left on the Stasi's head. He could fetch the First Aid Kit and attend to cleaning up the wound, but he would not. No reason to give the man the idea that he cared at all. His objective was to antagonize him.

He moved to face him again. "Tell me, Werner, why the necessity to kill Amy Chatsworth? She is completely innocent of any wrong done to you."

"She is the bastard offspring—"

His words trailed off, but Avon viewed his incomplete response as a first step.

"She didn't know her grandfather...or even her own father. Why would you hold her responsible?"

Schmitt sat with his eyes closed. A burned log in the fireplace broke in two and fell onto the embers. No longer able to contain his rage, Schmitt let go with a rant. His words sputtered like a defective carburetor.

"She is the blood of...uh...uh...a traitor to Germany...a cursed bastard. She does not deserve to live...she is...she is...a *nutte-tart*." He halted, catching his breath.

Schmitt appeared to have run out of invectives. On the other hand, was he merely attempting to build a case on air?

"If you had killed her, Werner, your search for her grandfather and me would have ended. Didn't you think of that?"

"I had other means."

Avon crossed in front of the fireplace and sat down. He faced his captive. Beads of perspiration formed on his forehead. He couldn't tell if the cause was the heat of the fire or the man's emotional condition. With deliberate enunciation, Avon said, "I don't think so."

Schmitt twisted his mouth and spat. "How would you know?" he shouted. "I had sources you could not have known about."

"Rizzo, the private detective?" Avon made no effort to stifle his snicker. "Killing Amy Chatsworth back in London would have ended his search for her father. You had no one else to lead you to New Brighton, or to here. Your attempt on her life was stupid. Wouldn't you agree?"

Schmitt's head swiveled left and right as though he were seeking something in the room. A weapon, perhaps? He appeared overwhelmed by his agitation.

"But he did lead me there, did he not?" he screamed, as if he had achieved a large victory.

"To what end? Herr Luedecke was already deceased. You didn't know that, did you?"

"I knew, but his son was alive," he blurted. "I had my revenge on him."

Avon leaned back in his chair and folded his arms across his chest, waiting. "How so? The detective says he called him when he returned to New York."

"That is not true. He lied. I put the bullet in Luedecke's head. He could not have lived."

There. He had the admission before Schmitt realized he had uttered the guilty words. Avon changed the subject.

"And now, I'm your second target. After you kill me, you can go back to Germany feeling vindicated. You will have settled the score. Is that your plan?"

"You will learn soon enough."

Avon felt a surge of anxiety overtake him. He rose and walked to the front door. Standing on the small deck, he gazed out through the waning daylight, taking the crisp, clean mountain air into his lungs. He pushed out the air and expelled it with a force between his lips. He repeated the exercise several times. In seconds, he felt the pace of his heartbeat slow down and his head begin to clear.

Before returning inside to his captive, Avon had to decide what to do with him. If the cabin were equipped with a landline, he would immediately call for help. His neighbor, Tom Lange of the Saugerties Police, would come to his rescue. He could kick himself for obstinately refusing to have a telephone line pulled into the cabin when he took it over from his cousin years ago. Even now, in this modern world of cell phones, he stupidly resisted buying one. If he drove down to the general store to phone Tom Lange from there, he would have to secure Werner Schmitt in a more permanent way before leaving the cabin. Avon had no idea how he was going to accomplish that. He frowned. And sighed.

Chapter 19

At the local Janesway Department Store, Rizzo and Amy found a selection of country-style clothing suitable to carry them for a few more days. Amy was in the guest bedroom putting away her fashionable finds, as she referred to them. Halfway into building a fire in the stove, Rizzo heard knocking on the front door. He hurried down the stairs and reached it during a second series of sharp raps. A jittery Tom Lange stood under the portico, shifting his weight from one foot to the other like a kid needing a bathroom break.

"Hey, what's up?" Rizzo asked.

"Let's go upstairs. I'll tell you what I've been thinking."

The two men climbed single file to the top. They entered the living room and Lange took a chair next to the stove.

"Give me a minute," Rizzo said.

He lifted the iron poker from the rack and knelt in front of the stove's opened doors, probing the logs that were beginning to ignite, adjusting those that hadn't. He glanced several times at Lange's concerned face. Satisfied he had a fire going, he closed the stove and pulled up another chair.

"Okay. What's going down?"

Lange leaned forward, elbows resting on his knees. "Jake has another place about thirty miles from here."

"Really? Another house?"

"No. A log cabin up on Black Head Mountain, just below Haines Falls. We go there every year for a long weekend during deer season."

Lange sat back, nervously pulling on the collar of his jacket. He turned when Amy stepped out from the bedroom.

"Oh, hello, Tom." She looked at Rizzo, her eyebrows lifted. "I heard voices and wondered whom you were talking with. Any news, Tom?"

"No news, but an idea," Lange said.

Amy approached and sat down on the settee.

"I was saying," Lange began, "Jake, me and the boys would go up to his cabin in the mountains for a long weekend of hunting, during deer season. It's a pretty secluded spot, and unless you've been there with Jake, it's hard to find."

"Does he own this cabin?" Rizzo asked.

"Yeah, he does now. The cabin once belonged to a cousin of his. When old man Decker passed away, he left the place to Jake."

"The butcher?"

"That's right. Jake tell you about him?"

"Only that he lived with him for a short while after his release from prison."

"You believe Jake may have gone there?" Amy asked. "To hide?"

Lange inched his chair closer to the stove. "While I was at the station house getting out an APB, I remembered Brancuso saying something about finding a box of shotgun shells in the room downstairs where Jake stored his tools."

"How is that relevant?" Amy asked.

"Well, it reminded me...I mean...that we had talked of going up there at the end of this month. Jake must have forgotten about that box of shells. Ordinarily, he stores all of his guns and ammo in the cabin."

"Can we call him...find out if he's there?" Rizzo asked.

"No phone. Jake vowed whenever he went up to the cabin, he wanted complete isolation. No contact with anyone. There's telephone service on the mountain, but he never had a line pulled in." Lange laughed. "He's afraid of a cell phone. His pacemaker."

Rizzo was not surprised. He remembered how private the old man was. "Did you say it was thirty miles from here?"

Amy rose from the sofa. "Why don't we drive—"

Lange cut her off. "It's not a trip to make at night. Too easy to get lost. We need to wait until morning. Luke and me can take my Range Rover and head up there. Jake has plenty of firepower in the cabin to protect himself."

Rizzo sneaked a look at Amy. He knew she would want to go along, but in the event things turned nasty, he couldn't risk putting her in harm's way. "That okay, Amy?"

She squeezed her eyebrows.

"Look, you can come with us if you like, but I—"

"No, it's fine. I'll stay here."

"I just feel you'll be safer…you know…if we run into any trouble when we get there."

"I understand," she said. Her tone was flat.

"While we're gone, Jake comes back, you can call me. Okay? We'll turn right around."

Amy tilted her head and smirked.

"Tell you what. I'll leave my snubbie with you…keep you company."

Lange jumped in. "My wife and the kids are a couple of doors away. The boys know where my .38 is and how to use it."

"Oh, my," Amy exclaimed, her voice rising. "Another adventure. How exciting."

Rizzo grinned. He loved the woman's sarcasm.

* * *

Rizzo finished clearing the table and started up the dishwasher. The fire in the stove insert had died down and a chill was settling in. He needed to add more logs. Amy had disappeared into the bedroom to retrieve the denim jacket she had recently purchased. He knew she would be on his case, for sure, if he neglected his Boy Scout duties again.

He fed several logs into the stove insert and watched the fire rebuild. Several loud raps on the door downstairs caught his attention. Rizzo made his way down, thinking that Tom Lange had returned.

A short, round, plainly dressed man, wearing a tight-fitting topcoat that pulled around his middle as if the garment once belonged to a slimmer person, appeared at the door. He was hatless. Thin curls of brown hair plastered to his skull covered his tanned, high-crowned head. Looking him over, Rizzo expected him to announce that he was the town's mortician. Instead, the man said his name was Felix Decker, and he was Max Vogel's cousin.

Rizzo's hand tightened on the edge of the door. "Who?" he asked, not certain he had heard the man correctly.

"Max Vogel. He goes by Jake Avon now."

The words hung in the air.

"He lives here, doesn't he?"

Rizzo stepped forward and looked into the man's anxious eyes. "Who the fuck are you?"

"Look, I know this is unexpected, but you have to understand."

"What?"

Decker's high forehead wrinkled, and his dark eyebrows merged. "Is Jake here?" he asked. "It's urgent I speak with him."

Rizzo hesitated. Lange had mentioned Avon's cousin who owned Decker's Pork Store years ago, but he told him nothing of his family. Was the man standing at the door Decker's son? If so, how did he come to know Avon's cover name? Get more answers, he thought, before admitting to anything.

He pushed the door back, remembering that his .38 snubbie was upstairs. "Why don't we go up...see what the problem is and what we can do about it?"

Decker remained standing, his hands in his topcoat pockets. After several moments, he moved through the door and breezed past Rizzo without speaking.

"Wait here," Rizzo said when they reached the top step. He entered the library, pulled his overnight bag off the closet shelf and reached in for the .38. He tucked the snubbie into his belt and pulled his shirt over the weapon before returning to the waiting Decker. "Let's go in here," he said, "and see what's worrying you."

Amy looked up from the antiques magazine she had in her lap.

"We have a visitor," Rizzo announced. "Mrs. Chatsworth, this is Mr. Decker. He has a problem, and we're going to see how we can help him."

"You're the private detective, aren't you?" Decker said after removing his coat and falling into one of the two armchairs opposite the fireplace.

Rizzo pulled up like a reined-in pony and stared down at him. Red flags went up all over the place. Decker appeared to know things things that put him on the inside of what was going down.

"We have an opened bottle of white wine in the refrigerator," Amy said, rising to her feet. "I'm going to have a glass. Would you like one, Mr. Decker?"

Rizzo fought back a smile. Amy had a difficult time being anything but gracious. He was ready to rip the man apart, and she elected to play the courteous host.

"Thank you. That would be nice," Decker replied, nervously stroking the fabric of the topcoat that lay across his knees.

"How do you know I'm a private detective?"

"That would relate to why I'm here."

"Really? What's your story?"

Amy returned with two glasses, handing one to Decker before sitting down. "You can rest it there," she told him, remembering Avon's comment about the abused card table.

"Why are you here?" Rizzo asked.

Decker started to answer but paused for several seconds. When Rizzo leaned in from his chair, Decker spoke with a ringing finality. "Werner Schmitt."

"Okay, let's not dance around. How do you know Max Vogel and Jake Avon are one and the same?"

"I worked at the Justice Department handling the placement of Max Vogel and Kurt Luedecke into the protection program. Justice gave me their assignment because I was fluent in German. That's how I knew their cover names."

"That was okay with the Justice Department...you being related to Avon?"

"They didn't know. In fact, neither did I. Max Vogel was my father's first cousin. I didn't learn that until he told me... at the time of his death in 1980."

Smiling, Amy said, "My, that was quite a coincidence, wouldn't you say?"

"So what's your connection with Werner Schmitt?" Rizzo asked.

Decker set his glass down. "He contacted me last month with a proposition involving a good deal of money. I had no idea he also intended to commit two revenge killings."

"Kurt Luedecke and Max Vogel?"

"That's right."

Amy drew a breath and shivered noticeably. Rizzo saw her reaction. Questions buzzed around in his head like hornets. He looked back at Decker. The man had to have known about the execution of Walter Schmitt, Werner's father, along with the five other captured saboteurs. His position with Justice certainly gave him access to that historic event. The real questions were how did he come to know Werner Schmitt, the son, and what was the proposition Schmitt offered him? Rizzo needed a lot more answers.

* * *

Schmitt watched as the old man leaned over to stop the tape recorder. The Beretta lay on his lap, and when he stood to pick up the machine, the Beretta slid to the floor. Avon kicked the gun under his chair and disappeared into the back bedroom.

While Avon had taped their conversation, Schmitt managed to loosen the ties around his wrists. Avon, absorbed in baiting his captive, failed to see him rhythmically straining at the ties, pulling up and relaxing, until the poorly knotted ropes gave up their tautness.

His left wrist released first. He undid the knot securing the right hand and slid from his seat to his knees. With his ankles bound to the chair legs, he brought the chair forward so that it folded over his back. He stretched out across the floor and seized the pistol, then righted himself and the chair and scrambled back onto the seat. He tucked the gun inside his jacket and waited.

Avon returned carrying a shotgun under his arm. When his gaze fell upon the chair he had vacated, he froze. The Beretta was gone. He flashed to Schmitt. He was in the same position as when he left the room. Before he could elevate the shotgun, Schmitt slid the Beretta from beneath his jacket and pointed it at the old man.

"Put the gun down."

Avon raised the shotgun to his shoulder and Schmitt fired. The round buried itself in the plank flooring. Splinters flew up against Avon's leg. The warning shot served its purpose. The old man let go, the shotgun bounced on the floor, and his body crumbled.

"Get up, you old fool and undo these ties around my ankles."

Avon strained to get to his feet. He was perspiring and dazed.

"Untie me, *dumme,* before I shoot you where you stand."

Avon moved toward him, looking down at the pointed gun barrel. He shook uncontrollably. Schmitt motioned toward his feet. The old man dropped to his knees and fumbled with the knots. When he had both ankles freed, he looked up. Schmitt raised one leg and slammed his heel into Avon's chest. The old man sailed across the floor, banging the back of his skull on the hard wood surface, coming to rest with his legs twisted under his torso. He lay motionless as Schmitt straddled him.

"Do not die on me now, old man," he shouted.

Avon's breathing slowed, his mind closed down.

* * *

Jake Avon opened his eyes, confused over why he was staring at cedar beams climbing the ceiling up to their vaulted peak. He thought of the Lutheran church he and, Ingrid, used to attend. The church had the same ceiling treatment. In fact, he was sure that his cousin, Gerald Decker, took the idea from there when he built this cabin back in the late '50s. He wasn't in church, so why was he staring?

"It's time you woke up."

Avon turned his head toward the voice. He found that was the extent of his mobility. Schmitt had him spread-eagled on the cabin floor, his wrists and ankles tied to metal pinions pegged to the floorboards. The surging pain through his head and shoulders jolted his memory of Schmitt's attack before he went unconscious. He felt his body go rigid.

"I have waited a long time for this, Herr Vogel. We need to talk. We have an issue to resolve. If you cooperate, I might spare your miserable life."

Avon knew those were merely words. Short of a miracle, Schmitt would kill him. He turned away from the Stasi monster standing over him and tried to imagine what issue Schmitt had in mind. Whatever it was, he was certain his fate in the hands of this lunatic meant death. He was ready to accept that.

Avon had no sense of how long he had been out. Dusk showed through the one window within his view. He remembered it as the time when he and Ingrid would stroll the property with their *Gespritzer* cocktail to see who could spot the first star of the evening. Now Ingrid was gone, and he would soon follow.

"I wish my father could see you," Schmitt said. "He would *lachen* at you, and how this turned out."

Avon doubted that Schmitt's father had ever laughed. During their training period before the mission launch in 1942, Walter Schmitt never showed a relaxed side. If he had been as proficient in his planning skills as he was at being a pontificating and arrogant group leader, perhaps the operation would have had a different ending.

Schmitt moved in between Avon's spread legs and looked down. "Tell me. Were you and that traitor, Luedecke, there when they executed my father? Did you see him die?"

Avon turned his head to the other side.

"Well, did you?"

The old man squeezed his eyes and sucked in a deep breath, preparing for Schmitt's expected onslaught of anger.

"Answer me, *dumme!*"

Schmitt's foot landed between Avon's legs with the force of a mule. The old man's testicles contracted with the blow, shoving them back into his abdomen. A white flash of pain electrified his entire body, while he exploded with a bone-chilling scream. His expulsion of breath left him choking uncontrollably for several minutes. He was on the edge of passing out again before Schmitt stepped away and walked to the fireplace.

"Perhaps you will now answer my questions when I ask them."

Avon sensed his heaving chest slowing as he regained control of his breathing. Tears had bathed his eye sockets, causing the once-symmetrical cedar beams above his head to appear as dim, shapeless lines. He felt his testicles receding to their normal position, but the pain in his groin continued beyond anything he had ever experienced. He lay still, grinding his molars until his jaws ached. The Stasi remained behind him, out of sight, but Avon could hear him laboring as he piled logs onto the fireplace grate in an attempt to rebuild the disappearing fire in the hearth. Avon took it as a sign that Schmitt intended to remain in the cabin for a while.

Avon thought about his impetuous departure from the schoolhouse. Not leaving a clue about his destination was a stupid move. He had not wanted to involve Amy and Luke any more than he already had. The cabin was his safe haven. He could not have known that Schmitt was there when he drove off from the schoolhouse, and would follow him.

Schmitt dragged a chair from in front of the fireplace and positioned himself at Avon's head. He sat looking at him upside down.

"So, old man, are you ready now for a little conversation?"

Avon rolled his eyes up toward the voice, but he was unable to bring Schmitt into focus. He turned his head toward the window and could see that night had arrived in the mountains. He doubted he would be alive to see daylight again.

Schmitt leaned in with his head directly over the old man's face and grinned. "One of my Stasi officers told me of a two-and-a-half-million dollar transfer of funds that was made to your cousin, Gerhardt Dietrich, in 1941. To finance the mission my father led. It was never used because of your traitorous decision."

Avon closed his eyes, attempting to shut out the image of Schmitt's smirking face. It failed. The image had already etched itself on his brain.

"Are you listening?" Schmitt asked, full of anger. "What do you know about that? I was told you and Dietrich had access to it."

Avon breathed in deeply and pushed the air out from his lungs. He felt lightheaded. "It is gone."

"Gone? What do you mean, gone?"

"Spent."

Schmitt leaped to his feet, tipping over the chair. "You are lying."

Avon tensed, readying his body for another attack. This time Schmitt directed the kick to the old man's rib cage. Avon yelped like a wounded animal, his body recoiling and straining at the restraints to his wrists and ankles. When the shock passed, Avon realized that Schmitt had used the side of his foot, similar to a soccer kick, and not his toe. It meant the man was not through with him.

"Where do you hide the money, here or in that damned schoolhouse? You would not live in an old, run-down school if you had spent it. Answer me or you will suffer a slow, cruel death. I promise you. Is that what you want?"

Avon tried to stifle a smile, enjoying the psychopath's vexation. He doubted he could convince Schmitt of the truth, that he could account for the fund's disposition, and that no balance remained. Schmitt would continue to think he was lying. Either way, he was dead. Nevertheless, he could try. Perhaps then, Schmitt would grant him a quick death.

"Answer, *dummkopf.*"

Avon recoiled from the second kick, wincing at the shooting pain in his side. He coughed and wheezed until he managed control of his breathing. This time he was certain the kick had cracked a rib. He could not absorb many more blows like that before the wires in his pacemaker would shake loose, certain to interrupt the electrical pulses to and from his heart. Dear God, he prayed, make it so.

Chapter 20

"Okay," Rizzo said, "begin explaining why Werner Schmitt would contact you with this money-making scheme? You bring to the table what?"

Felix Decker, trying to find a more comfortable position, set his wine glass down and shifted his weight in the chair. "For one thing, he needed someone to finance the trip to the States. He had little means of his own."

"Okay, but why you?"

Decker addressed Amy. "Didn't Scotland Yard tell you? Werner was a career Stasi agent."

Amy looked to Rizzo.

"We know that. But how the hell did he know about your connection to Vogel?" Rizzo had a hard time keeping his anger in check. Back when he was on the Job, he would have been in the man's face in a heartbeat.

Decker picked up the wine glass, sipped, then set it down. "Werner told me he learned of it from his sources in London." Decker took a breath, looking unnerved. "During his years in the Stasi, Werner had access to many sensitive State Department files made available to the East German secret service. Even some from within Scotland Yard."

Rizzo grew impatient with Decker's roundabout answers. "What kind of information?"

"About the money...about my father...about me."

Amy returned from the kitchen after refilling their wine glasses. She handed one to Decker and sat down. "Money? What money?"

For the next ten minutes, Decker spun the story of his father's pro-Nazi background, stopping at intervals to sip his wine. The tale covered Gerhardt Dietrich's name-change and relocation to the States, as well as his assignment as steward of the $2.5 million fund for the saboteurs' mission in 1942. Amy and Rizzo sat engrossed, listening to what sounded to Rizzo like a scenario from a World War II movie. However, he knew they weren't hearing Hollywood fiction. Too many pieces falling into place made the story credible. Before Decker finished, he had emptied his wine glass again.

"And Schmitt thinks the money is buried somewhere?" Rizzo asked with a snigger. "Since 1942?"

Decker's face reddened. "Well, it's never been accounted for, except for the half million my father kept for himself."

"Did Werner Schmitt assume you knew who possessed the balance?" Amy asked.

"I tried to convince him I knew nothing about the money. He didn't believe me."

Rizzo screwed up his face. "So?"

"He threatened to leak my connection with Max Vogel to the Justice Department, knowing that would jeopardize my government pension."

Amy stood and picked up Decker's empty glass. "Another wine, Mr. Decker?"

"Yes, please," he answered, sounding like a drowning victim who'd been thrown a life preserver.

"That's why you agreed to help him?"

"Yes. I told him my father had spent his half million, but I thought he had turned over the rest to Max Vogel...I mean Jake Avon. That's when he made his proposition. He'd find Vogel and the money if I financed his trip.

"What were you getting out of it?"

Amy returned with two glasses, handing one to Decker. Rizzo noticed her wine intake was keeping pace with Decker's.

Decker took the glass and looked at Rizzo. "Half."

"Did you tell him where he could find Jake?"

"No. I didn't have that information. I guessed he might be somewhere in Ulster County, based on that weekend I brought Vogel and Luedecke together after their release. That location was Vogel's choice. Where he lived was protected information. At the time, I was completely in the dark about his connection with my family. I never knew he was staying with my father."

Rizzo sat back. His fingers drummed a tattoo on his thigh as he stared into Felix Decker's face. "Did you know Schmitt wanted to find Luedecke and Vogel to kill them?"

The glass of wine poised at Decker's mouth tipped under a shaky grip. He set the glass on the card table and began looking around for something to soak up the spilled liquid. Amy rose and hurried to the kitchen to fetch paper towels.

When Decker finished blotting the wine from his shirt and tie, he looked toward Amy. "Sorry."

Amy nodded with understanding.

Rizzo waited, wondering if Decker would plead ignorance of Schmitt's murderous intentions, or admit that one million dollars was worth the life of a relative. In the next moment, Rizzo had his answer.

"I knew it, I'm ashamed to say. Somehow, I never believed he would carry out his boast. I tried to talk to him, but he was determined. After he phoned to tell me he had killed Kurt Luedecke's son...I mean...God, I'm so sorry." He looked at Amy, "I tried to tell him we could find the money without another murder. He ignored me. So I took the risk and called a contact I had in the Justice Department. She almost said no, but she found Max Vogel's location for me as a favor. I booked a flight to Albany and drove down here to try to stop that lunatic from killing again." Decker pressed forward, covering his face with both hands, and sobbed. "I'm so sorry...oh, God...I'm sorry."

Rizzo saw tears welling in Amy's eyes. Was she buying into the man's story? He was not there yet.

Decker looked up. Paper towel in hand, he dabbed at his wet cheeks. "Is Max Vogel here?"

"No, he's not," Rizzo said, volunteering nothing more.

"Well then, is he somewhere safe...where Werner can't find him?"

"Yes."

Decker stared off in silence for several seconds, his eyes moist from tearing. "I hope so. Oh, God, I feel so responsible."

"Look, if Schmitt shows up, Jake will have plenty of protection," Rizzo said. "Don't worry about that. Meanwhile, you plan to hang around for a while?"

"Ah...yes, yes, at least until Werner is apprehended. I am booked into the Holiday Inn near the thruway.

"Good idea. The local police may want to have a word with you before you leave."

Rizzo didn't say it, but he believed Felix Decker could be held as an accessory to Bard's murder. He financed Schmitt's vendetta.

"We'll contact you tomorrow...let you know where things stand."

Amy had helped herself to another glass of wine while Rizzo escorted Decker down the stairs and watched him drive off. He noted the time of his departure, returned upstairs, and called information to get the phone number of the Holiday Inn.

"Yes, sir," the hotel operator said, "Mr. Decker is staying with us. Shall I connect you?"

"No, that's okay. I'll call him tomorrow." He closed his cell phone and turned to Amy. "How many is that?"

"What?"

"Wines."

"Oh, are you keeping track for me?"

He sat next to her on the settee and put his arm across her shoulders. "It's not my business, I know."

Amy tilted her head against his arm. "Unless you want it to be."

"Hey, I shouldn't have said anything. I'm sorry."

"No, it's fine. I did tip the bottle a bit much. Would you believe me if I told you I was merely trying to keep Mr. Decker oiled so he would be more forthcoming with his information?"

Amy's deadpan expression sent Rizzo into a fit of laughter. "What's that," he asked, "an English form of torture?"

She pulled away and shook her head. "No, you smartass. I was merely joking. Why are you so suspicious?"

He remembered her reaction when he reminded her she hadn't been in contact with her husband. She hinted that Lord Chatsworth didn't care. Perhaps it was more the reverse.

"I'm sorry, but I get a feeling you're trying to drown something in wine. Are you? You want to talk about it?"

Amy's eyes fixed on the stove insert across the room for several seconds before she got to her feet. She looked back at him with downcast eyes. "No, I don't...at least not tonight. It's getting late."

Rizzo stood and took her by the waist, pulling her into him. "Ya still think I'm cute?"

She laughed, reached up and took his face in both hands, fusing their mouths for a long kiss. As they broke apart, she said, "You're still cute, but it's time for bed."

"Your place or mine?"

"Yours, silly. It's closer to the stove and the fire you're about to build."

"Oh yeah, that's right."

Amy started toward the bedroom and stopped. She turned back to him, smiling like someone with a secret.

"You know, of course, you'll be expected to build my fire as well. Are you up to it, Boy Scout?"

"Trust me. It's part of my oath."

"I do, but hurry, please. It's getting terribly chilly in here."

"I'm on it," he said, raising his hand to his brow in a three-fingered salute.

* * *

Avon caught his breath and looked up at the Stasi. "Werner, sit down, please. Let me try to give you the facts."

"I do not want to hear a story. Tell me where you hide the money," Schmitt said as he returned to the chair.

"No. I'll tell you the facts." Avon puckered his cheeks in frustration. "You are wasting your time. Please believe me."

"Why should I?"

"Werner, you can choose to or not. I do not care. I am old. I will die soon anyway."

Schmitt laughed.

"At least hear me out," Avon pleaded. Thinking of Amy and Luke, he added, "I don't want you hurting anyone else. That is all I ask."

"So tell me," Schmitt said, as though resigned to listening to Avon's lies. "But I believe you hide the money somewhere here. If not here, then at the school."

Avon closed his eyes, resting, trying to regain a semblance of calm. He cleared his mind and visualized the night Gerhardt Dietrich told him about the money.

"I lived with Gerhardt for a few months after my release from prison," Avon began. "Did you know that?"

Schmitt stayed silent.

"We were on a hunting trip...the two of us...camped in these woods. After a night drinking beer and talking about the past, Gerhardt told me about the money. Ten years of secrecy...the pressure of worrying that someone would discover his role with our mission became too much."

"Where did he keep the money?" Schmitt asked.

"At first in a bank safe deposit box. After the mission failed, and the men were captured, he moved the money to a location under the floorboards of his pork store."

"Then the money is there?"

"No. The store is long gone. He spent a half million slowly for his own personal use over the next thirty-five years. He was fearful that someone…the government…would notice if he spent it quickly."

Avon heard Schmitt swear. He ignored him and continued.

"When the Malden school closed in 1962, Gerhardt offered me a half million dollars from the balance."

"You expect me to believe that? Why would he give money to *ein ficking verräter*?"

Avon sighed. "Werner, I knew about the fund. Remember, he was my cousin. He wanted me to buy the schoolhouse and enjoy a decent retirement. That money is gone now." He lifted his head, straining to catch sight of Schmitt's face to see how he was reacting. He was too far away.

"And the rest?" Schmitt's voice rang with skepticism

"He transferred another half million to Kurt Luedecke's bank in New Brighton. The remaining million he put in a trust, and named me the beneficiary with certain conditions. When Gerhardt died, the balance came to me."

"Then there is a million dollars somewhere in this cabin. Yes?"

This was the part Schmitt would find difficult to swallow. He was certain the mere thought would inflame his anger. "That million is gone too."

"You spent it? You *arschloch*."

"I didn't spend the money, Werner. I donated it. That was the way Gerhardt had set up the trust, with the understanding the remaining million went to charities."

Avon stared at the beams overhead, comforted that had Ingrid known what he did, she would have sung his praises from her place in heaven. Avon waited for Schmitt's reaction.

He expected an explosion. Instead, the Stasi surprised him by laughing, then stomping his feet on the floor like a drunken fan at a hockey game.

"Do not insult me, old man," he shouted. "You cannot expect me to believe that."

"It's the truth, Werner."

Schmitt went silent for several seconds. "Who did you give the money to?" he asked, as though half-believing him.

"In 1988, my wife, Ingrid, died. Every year for ten years, on the anniversary of her death, the trust gave one hundred thousand dollars to a charity, donated anonymously. The bank officer in charge of the trust chose the charity."

"And it is all gone?"

"All gone," Avon echoed in a sarcastic tone.

Schmitt released a guttural sound, coming from deep within his throat and dissolving into a gush of high-pitched screams. When he regained control, he got to his feet and walked to Avon. Schmitt bent over Avon's face and spit, leaving gobs of saliva covering the old man's forehead and cheeks. Avon pressed his eyelids together and shook his head like a dog emerging from the water.

"Do I look like *ein dummkopf?* No more fairytales, *Got verdammt es!* Where do you hide the money?"

Schmitt had reached the end of his patience, but he would not kill him yet, at least not until the Stasi was certain he would not find the money.

"I told you. It's gone."

With a surprising burst of energy, Schmitt turned away and bolted into the bedroom. For the next hour, Avon listened to him tearing into drawers, dumping the contents on the floor, and overturning what little furniture there was. He reappeared and charged to the fireplace ledge to grab an andiron from the rack. Avon, for a fleeting moment, thought Schmitt intended to use the tool to kill him. Instead, gripping the andiron, he raced back into the bedroom. A loud banging noise filled the cabin as Schmitt rapped on the log walls like a maniac, looking for any hollowed-out sound.

After Schmitt had gone over every inch of the cabin in this manner, examining furniture, fixtures and walls, looking for any clue that might lead him to the money, he returned to the chair opposite Avon. He threw himself down, exhausted, and looked over at the old man.

"Unless you buried it outside," he said in a weakened voice, "I do not think this cabin is where you hide the money."

"I told—"

"Shut up, *dumme*. Tomorrow I search the school. You stay here. You will not leave this cabin...ever." Schmitt got to his feet and slogged back to the bedroom.

The fire Schmitt built earlier had died, yet the numbness that engulfed Jake Avon's entire body prevented him from feeling the cold. He lay staring at the ceiling, wondering if it were possible to intentionally swallow his tongue and thereby choke himself to death.

Schmitt had closed the bedroom door and for the next several hours entertained Avon with a variety of loud snoring. It reminded Avon of the many times Ingrid complained about his own snoring. He was certain those vibrating noises emanating from the bedroom far exceeded anything he could have produced.

Schmitt's threat that he would never leave the cabin was expected. The Stasi intended to kill him soon, before leaving for the schoolhouse. Avon was not afraid to die; in fact, he would welcome death if he could figure a way to become the instrument of his own demise. He would enjoy cheating the bastard out of the satisfaction of dying at his hands. He closed his eyes to sleep, praying that God might show him a way during his dreams.

* * *

Amy waited under the comforter on the futon. The light from the lamp on the bookcase shelf cast a dim glow in the room. Rizzo could still see her form curled up in the center of the bed. This time he left the door ajar to allow passage for the stove's heat.

He stood in his shorts at the side of the bed, gazing at the woman who had entered his life as a client, but had become personally important to him. He could not help wondering where the relationship would lead. Unlike the way he felt during his brief tryst with Flo, his rent-a-car angel in Pennsylvania, his feelings for Amy transcended anything he had experienced since his divorce. He worried that the complications of a relationship might drag him in over his head. His gaze caressed her form as she waited for him. He would put off worrying until later.

He pulled back the comforter as she rolled onto her back and reached up for him. His gaze traveled over her face and searched her eyes. "I don't know what it is about your eyes, but I get turned on each time I look into them. Maybe it's their golden color."

"You are such a sappy romantic. Do you know that?"

She wore Avon's oversized pajama bottoms, pulled tight around her waist. She had forgone the top half. He leaned over and took one of her hardened, gumdrop-size nipples between his lips then circled it gently with his tongue. When he lifted his head, he asked, "Are you cold or just happy to see me?"

She gave his shoulder a playful slap. "Get in here, you idiot."

He removed his shorts and eased into bed. After pulling up the comforter, he reached across to Amy's pajama bottom and undid the tie. "Let's get rid of this gunny sack."

She raised her hips. "Luke, be loving to me. You don't have to say anything. Simply make love to me like nothing else matters."

"I can do that. I have an Eagle Scout badge in passion."

She rolled to him, and he folded her into his arms, locking his mouth onto hers.

Chapter 21

Rizzo swung his feet to the small throw rug on his side of the futon. He pressed the stem of his watch and lit the face. Three A.M. He slipped off the futon, trying not to wake Amy. When he stepped onto the cold floor where the rug ended, he let out a faint whimper. A quick look back at the sleeping woman told him she hadn't stirred.

The bed of red embers covering the base of the stove insert looked to be on its last legs. His previous wood feeding had lasted more than three hours, and the little remaining heat failed to quell his shivering. He worked fast, jamming in and crisscrossing new logs. The dried out splinters on one of the logs touched the hot embers and ignited a small flame. In no time, he had the beginnings of a first-class fire, and the chill in the room had disappeared.

"Jake would be proud of you."

Rizzo turned from his kneeling position. The light coming from the opened stove doors revealed Amy shrouded in the comforter. She stood at the edge of the living room, studying him.

"Thought you were sleeping."

"I was, but I heard you out here and came to see if you needed help."

"I got the job handled, but I'm freezing my buns off."

Amy padded toward him, opened the comforter and held out one end. She was back into her oversized flannel sleepers.

"Here, get in. You'll catch your death kneeling there in your shorts."

"Okay. Let me feed in one or two more logs. That should do us until morning."

In minutes, he had the insert pumping heat at full capacity. He clanged the door closed and locked it after making certain the vents remained opened. The smell of burning wood hung in the air and in his hair.

"Let's stay out here for a while," Amy said. "Just until the icicles on your shorts melt." She moved toward the settee and lit the small hurricane lamp on the gaming table. She held up the end of the comforter again. "Come, we can chat for a bit before going back to bed."

Rizzo got to his feet. He remained standing, examining her face, as he liked to do. He had never been close to a woman of her extraordinary class and maturity. Amy could display a fierce and determined side, yet be sweet and thoughtful in the process. She carried water for no one, and he loved her for it.

"Do you want me to put on coffee?" he asked, while he snuggled at her side.

"I don't need any. Do you?"

He took her earlobe between his lips and mumbled, "Noop."

Giggling, she pulled away and looked at him. "All right now. Let's chat."

"About what?"

"About me...about my husband. That's what you suggested we do earlier. Did you forget?"

Rizzo bolted upright, like a student called for slouching at his desk. "You sure?"

Amy faced him with knitted eyebrows. "Yes, unless you'd prefer we didn't."

"No, no. I meant…well, you've been so dam
mouth. I didn't think…you know…if you wante osed
any personal stuff. I wasn't about to pry. Hell, I d are
know if you have kids."   en

"Well, we don't. Not that we haven't tried. That i
become a major sticking point in our marriage."

"I'm listening," he said, puffing his cheeks and hol
thumb over his mouth. No interruptions. Time enough
for a Q and A. Let her set her own pace, reveal wha
personal baggage she wanted him to know. When he wa
the Job, he always puffed his cheeks while he interrogate
perp. He discovered they volunteered more information th
way. Much more than if he simply fired questions at the perp.

"I couldn't get pregnant," she said, following a long pause.
"He took the position I was at fault. Refused to see a physician.
'Terribly embarrassing,' he claimed." She pulled up on the
comforter and tucked the edge under her chin, resting her
head on her knuckles.

Rizzo could feel her breathing deepen.

She turned to look at him. "Why are your cheeks inflated?"

He released the air with a *poof* sound. "My way of fighting
the impulse to interrupt, that's all. I didn't want to cut you off
with questions."

"Oh, silly. You're permitted to ask questions. Ask me
anything you wish."

"Okay."

She reached up, took hold of his chin and, turning his face,
brought their lips together for a long, tender kiss.

"Do you know how sweet you are?"

"That's because you infuse me with sugar. Go on. What
about adoption? Did you think about that?"

"A pompous point of honor for him. He would not consider
it. Before long, he began avoiding any opportunity for
intimacy. Weeks would pass without the smallest expression
of caring. I was puzzled."

sensed her discomfort. The admission was as though
umed most of the guilt. He was certain she had nothing
with the way her husband reacted. The woman was a
on, by anyone's standards: warm and giving, sensuous
passionate. Either Lord Chatsworth was making nice
th someone else, or he was a closet gay. He wouldn't say
at to her, but he might give odds on it.

"When did all this start happening?"

"Two years ago. Nevertheless, that wasn't where our
problems began. A year after we were married, when I first
launched my effort to find my father, he objected."

"He say why?"

"He wanted me to drop my search. He worried how his
constituents might perceive the family's image...his position
within the House of Lords, really. I continued on the sly. He
found me out and became greatly perturbed."

"Let me guess. He wasn't thrilled with you coming to
the States?"

"Not in the least. He said he would file papers for a divorce
if I left."

"But you left anyway."

"Luke, after being the target of a deranged gunman, who
happened to be the same man who murdered my father, I
became determined to get to the bottom of these attacks. Do
you blame me?"

"No. In fact, I applaud you. Hey, I count myself lucky. We
got to meet."

She squeezed his hand. "Thank you. No regrets?"

"None."

"See, you are a sweet man."

* * *

Werner Schmitt pulled on his pants and looked around at
the mess he had created in the bedroom where he spent the
night. First light seeped through the edges of the window

shades. He held up his arm to examine his watch. It was five-thirty.

After dressing, he entered the adjacent bathroom to throw cold water on his face in an effort to get his circulation going. He was surprised how deep his sleep had been. He remembered why. He had all but demolished the cabin, spending several hours searching for the money. When he flopped down on the mattress he had tossed to the floor earlier, he dropped off to sleep immediately.

He passed through the small kitchen and exited the door leading to the rear of the cabin. The base of the mountain stood twenty yards away. The sheer rise of trees and boulders made him wonder if his captive ever worried about rock avalanches.

Schmitt's body ached as he shuffled toward the black pickup truck parked at the far end of the cabin. He was delighted to find the key still in the ignition. A graveled roadway led away from the cabin, opposite to the side of the property from where he had left his rental. The graveled road disappeared into a wide opening through the brush. He realized Avon had taken this route when the rutted trail they followed had forked to the right. Schmitt had missed it.

The propane gas canister resting on a cement slab at that end of the cabin caught his eye. The connecting line ran from the canister into the base of the cabin wall. He opened the hinged door cut into the side of the cabin. Inside the tall storage closet, he found a forty-gallon water-heating tank wrapped in insulation. The tank rested on a concrete slab. A fan-assisted PVC pipe vented the tank through the wall to the outside.

He re-entered the cabin and approached the old man. "Did you have a good sleep, *mein freund*?"

Avon's body remained pinned in the rigid, spread-eagle position. He showed no signs of movement or breathing. Schmitt leaned over the man's face and looked down into his frozen eyes. He waited several seconds for a response. None came. After placing his hand under the old man's nostrils, he pressed his finger on the carotid artery. That moment he understood what had happened. Jake Avon, nee Max Vogel, had died sometime during the night.

* * *

By eight-thirty, Tom Lange's Range Rover turned off Route 32 onto the two-lane, blacktop road leading up to Black Head Mountain. Rizzo, studying a map of the local area, looked up for a moment and caught a glimpse of a pickup pulling away from the general store at the corner. The truck quickly disappeared, heading south on Route 32.

Lange steered the vehicle with a confident one-handed grip on the wheel, while his other hand held the small coffee thermos up to his mouth. The Range Rover continued for several miles before beginning its twisting climb along the tree-lined road on the dense mountainside. The temperature had dropped into the low 30s during the night, but the morning sun had melted most of the snow left by the storm. They had expected to get an earlier start, but Lange had to take care of precinct business in Saugerties before he could shake free.

"I'm glad the road is dry," Rizzo said, looking out the window at the precipitous drop off to his right. "It must be a bitch making this drive when it's covered in snow."

Lange chuckled, set the thermos in the cup holder and gripped the wheel with both hands.

"It's hairy even on a good day. Can you imagine making this climb at night?"

Rizzo was relieved that Amy agreed to stay back at the schoolhouse. He suspected she would be enjoying the ride if she were with them. She thrived on adventure.

Under Lange's deft driving, the Range Rover handled the steep, twisting climb without challenge. The turns got tighter at each bend in the road. Fifteen minutes into the drive, Lange's cell phone sounded.

Rizzo watched him let go of the steering wheel with one hand, reach to the holder on the dash and pick up the instrument. Rizzo raised his eyebrows.

"Lange," he answered

Lange said nothing for several seconds, listening, until he shouted, "Holy shit!"

Rizzo bolted upright, listening.

"Yeah…yeah…uh huh… how long ago?...Yeah…okay… we're five minutes away. Bye, Carl. Give you a heads up when we get there."

Rizzo stared. "What happened?"

Lange kept his eyes on the road. "The cabin is on fire. A neighbor on the mountain above Jake heard an explosion from down below. He went out to the edge of his property and could see Jake's cabin in flames. The volunteer fire department from Haines Falls got there ten minutes ago."

"How's that possible? We didn't see any fire vehicles."

"They came down from the Falls, from above, off the main road. Coming in from below is the long way around. We're taking the short-cut trail into the property. In fact, here's our turn."

Lange turned off the road through an opening in the brush that Rizzo was sure he would have missed even if he were looking for it. The Range Rover managed the rutted path, making the climb without a problem, turned right at a fork and onto a wider trail.

"Jake blazed this part."

"What with, a machete?"

Lange stopped where the thick brush opened onto a graveled roadway leading to the cabin. Scattered in front of the cabin in the open area were four Haines Falls fire trucks: a tanker/pumper spewing water over the rear of the cabin roof top, a ladder truck, a 4 X 4 brush truck standing ready should the fire reach the treed perimeter, and a fire rescue vehicle.

Lange and Rizzo jogged toward the fire rescue truck parked closest to them. The sight of the burning cabin produced a knot in Rizzo's stomach. Had Jake managed to get out in time? They neared one of the firefighters standing next to the fire rescue vehicle. He turned when he spotted them approaching.

"Hey, Tom, you got here fast."

"We were already on the way when I got the call. What's the situation?"

Lange took the firefighter's extended hand. He turned to Rizzo. "Gary Moore...Luke Rizzo. Luke is a P.I. on a case involving Jake."

Moore's face turned grim. He lowered his eyes and said, "Not good, Tom...about Jake, that is."

"He was in the cabin?"

Moore bent over to examine his boots, searching for an answer. He straightened, shook his head as he raised his eyes. "In addition to being in there, someone didn't want him to ever leave."

"What's that mean?"

Moore kicked at an invisible obstacle. "We found him inside, pinioned to the floor near the fireplace in a spread-eagled position. He was already dead. Not from the fire. The flames hadn't reached that side of the cabin yet."

Rizzo sucked in air between his teeth. It had to be Schmitt. "Shot, was he?"

"Not that we could tell, but after the coroner's exam, we'll know more."

Rizzo glanced back at the cabin. "How'd the fire start?"

"Best we can tell, propane leak. Looks like someone intentionally ignited it. Anyway, that's what caused the explosion. We've got the fire pretty much under control now."

Stunned, tears had fallen on Lange's cheeks. "Where do you have him?"

Moore nodded at the vehicle next to him. "Waiting for the EMS ambulance to transport him down to the M.E. in Kingston." He put his hand on Lange's shoulder and squeezed. "I'm really sorry, Tom. I know you two were close. When we got here, I didn't think Jake was anywhere around. No pickup parked behind the cabin in the usual spot."

Rizzo flashed on the black pickup he'd observed earlier leaving the country store. An alarm sounded in his head. He looked around for another vehicle and spotted the front of Schmitt's rental car nosing out of the brush across the open perimeter a hundred yards away. Pointing, he shouted, "There's Schmitt's fucking car."

"Who?" the confused Moore asked.

"The guy responsible for this," Lange said, flipping his thumb back at the cabin.

Rizzo took off like a frightened rabbit. He sprinted toward the Ford at an Olympian pace with Lange on his tail, leaving a bewildered firefighter beside his emergency truck.

Rizzo and Lange combed through the car, looking for any clue that would indicate where Schmitt might have gone. Rizzo reached under the front seat and pulled out a map of Ulster County. He searched the glove compartment, hoping to find the rental contract, but came up empty. He was not surprised. He figured Schmitt, always the cunning Stasi, had taken the document with him. They walked back to the rescue truck where Avon's body awaited the EMS bus.

"Find anything?" Gary Moore asked.

"Nothing, unfortunately" Rizzo told him. "But I have an idea, Tom. Can you call your deputy, have him trace the rental agency's ID from the license plate?"

"Sure, but what's that gonna tell us?"

"I'm sure he used a rent-a-car company in the city. If he did, he's required to put an address on the contract. I'll ask Jack Fields to contact the rental garage, see what address he listed."

"You think he'd be going to that address?"

"Who knows? Could end up being bogus. Fields can send a couple of agents to check out the location. It just might be where that maniac's heading."

Lange walked back from the Range Rover after making his call. Rizzo stared across the field to Schmitt's rental and felt a sudden shiver. The black pickup he had seen earlier leaving the general store...that was Schmitt. He was sure of it. He spun around to face the approaching Lange and screamed, "Oh, good God!"

"What?"

"The schoolhouse...Amy."

Rizzo sprinted toward the Range Rover with Lange twenty yards ahead of him. Reaching the vehicle, Lange called his Chief Deputy to dispatch a team to the schoolhouse. He whipped the Rover around and sped into the opening of the trail.

"Jake's number?" Rizzo asked. "You got it programmed?"

"Yeah."

Keeping a hand on the wheel, Lange fast-dialed. "Here." He handed Rizzo the phone.

Rizzo listened, his irritation increasing with each unanswered ring. "You sure you got the right number?" he snapped.

Lange shot a peek at the phone display. "That's the number."

"Fuck!" Rizzo shouted and banged his fist against the side window. "I hope she's not afraid to use my snubbie."

Lange looked at him. "Snubbie?"

"My .38."

"Oh, yeah, I forgot."

Rizzo banged his fist again.

* * *

Amy posted herself at the window in Jake Avon's bedroom, keeping an anxious watch for Rizzo and Lange. The Colt .38

that Rizzo left with her had made her nervous. She put the weapon in her handbag and placed it on the futon in the library. As soon as she spotted Jake's black pickup pull into the driveway, she dashed down the stairs to the front door. The words tumbled out even before she had the door opened. "Jake, we were so worried about—"

A fist landed on her cheek, cutting off the rest of her words. The impact sent her reeling backward to the floor. Schmitt was upon her in a flash. Kneeling on her chest, he grabbed her by the throat, squeezed and jabbed the Beretta against her temple.

"Unless you wish to die right here, you will not make a noise. Do you understand?"

Dazed, Amy felt the cold metal on her skin. She looked up into Schmitt's face but could not see him. Her eyes, watering from the shock of Schmitt's punch, were unable to focus. She choked as his vise-like grip at her throat cut off her windpipe. In the next instant, her jumbled mind went black.

Chapter 22

Schmitt dragged Amy Chatsworth into the large workroom at the rear of the schoolhouse. With an adrenalin-charged effort, he hoisted her onto Jake Avon's woodworking bench. Exhausted and out of breath, he scoured the area until he found a length of rope, cutting it into four sections. He turned the woman onto her stomach, stretched out her arms and tied each wrist, lashing the ends of the rope to the corners of the cross brace between the table's legs. With each ankle tied in the same fashion, he secured the ropes to the ends of the brace. Done, he stepped back to assess his effort.

The Chatsworth woman had on form-fitting jeans and an oversized "I LUV NY" sweatshirt that he had pushed up in his struggle to get her up on the bench. His eyes ran over the milky-white skin of her exposed back and traveled down to her well-shaped buttocks. Her curved mounds tweaked a reaction of rare sexual excitement. He could feel the needling in his groin. He remembered the last time he had intercourse. It was with the prostitute in Berlin who would grant him sexual favors in return for help in feeding her drug habit. His erection pushed against his fly. If he wanted to take advantage of the situation, he could yank down her jeans and enter her from behind. Even if she came to, she would be unable to stop him.

Before he could take temptation to another level, a noise at the front entrance stopped him. He retrieved the Beretta and moved behind the workshop door. The gun clasped tight in his hand, he waited.

The shuffle of feet, a pause, more shuffling, and then a heavy step of someone making the climb up the long staircase. Schmitt counted ten steps before a man's voice called out, "Jake Avon...are you there?"

Schmitt knew the answer. In fact, he had not expected to find anyone in the schoolhouse. The driveway was void of any vehicles. The woman had surprised him when she opened the front door.

The speaker's words went unanswered. Getting no response, he continued to climb. Schmitt counted five more steps before the man halted again.

"Jake Avon. Are you home? It's Felix Decker."

Schmitt gripped the edge of the door and slammed it back against the wall. He rushed to the base of the stairs and looked up at the overweight man wrapped in a topcoat, trying to catch his breath.

"Decker," Schmitt screamed.

The shocked man twisted where he stood, lost his balance and reached out to the staircase banister to steady himself.

"*Gott verdammt!*" Schmitt shouted. "What are you doing here, you fool?"

"Werner?"

"I thought we agreed you would not interfere."

A shaky Felix Decker climbed down, stopping before he reached the bottom step. He looked at Schmitt and stammered, "I know...I didn't...I mean, I wasn't going to, but—"

"*Dummkopf,* now you will spoil everything." Schmitt shot a look back toward the workroom, worried Decker would panic if he saw the woman. "Why have you come? Did you not think I would keep my end of our agreement?"

Decker's eyes landed on the Beretta in Schmitt's hand. "No, no, no, that's not it."

"What then? Have you changed your mind? You wish to back out?"

"Werner, I am merely interested in finding the money. That was our agreement. I cannot condone killing anyone. You have to—"

"Stop talking. Move back there." He waved the Beretta in the direction of the workroom.

No longer concerned about Decker's reaction, Schmitt made up his mind. He would dispose of both of them. He would finish his business here and get out. The two-gallon gas can he had purchased at the country store was in the truck. He intended to use it to set fire to the schoolhouse. Before he left, the schoolhouse would be blazing.

Schmitt could not accept Vogel's account that the money was gone, but he realized there was little time to complete a thorough search of the schoolhouse. He could taste the frustration; however, getting out of the country alive was now his most important worry.

Decker had not moved. Schmitt shoved him forward with force. The man stumbled through the doorway of the workroom and went to his knees a few feet from the bench. Looking up, he saw Amy.

"Werner, what have you done?" he screamed. "Are you out of your mind?"

Schmitt moved in quickly, and before the man could utter another word, the Stasi placed the gun to the back of Decker's head and pulled the trigger. The bullet tore open a hole in the base of the man's skull and exited below his jaw. The loud report of the Beretta echoed in the high-ceilinged, empty room. The sound faded as Schmitt became aware of a different sound: a police siren off in the distance.

Racing to the front door, he peered out. He could hear the whining siren closing in. He returned into the workroom and retreated to the door at the rear. Schmitt stared out at the wide expanse of the open play area behind the schoolhouse. The police siren stopped. He cut his eyes back to Amy, hesitated, and bolted out the door.

Schmitt crept to the corner of the building and, back flat against the wall, sneaked a look around to the street. No sign of the police cruiser, and the pickup was not blocked. He waited several seconds, wondering if he could make it to the truck unseen. He took a second peek and froze.

A uniformed police officer appeared at the front corner of the building, snuffed out a cigarette, and began making his way down along the side of the house. Schmitt stepped back and raised the Beretta. The officer reached the end of the building and turned into the Beretta's muzzle as it exploded. The officer went down holding his chest. Schmitt sailed past him, reaching the truck in seconds. A voice from upstairs in the schoolhouse floated down as the pickup's engine turned over.

"Frank, what the hell happened? You okay?"

* * *

Rizzo's feet hit the pavement the same instant the Range Rover skidded to a stop in front of the schoolhouse. Jake Avon's truck was not in the driveway. Rizzo felt a surge of panic. Had the Stasi taken Amy hostage? Maybe he hadn't returned to the schoolhouse. Rizzo prayed for the latter.

Lange leaped out of the Rover and followed Rizzo to the door. "Luke, hold on," he called, raising his Glock to ear level. "Unless you're armed, let me go in first."

Rizzo backed up a step and watched in silence as Lange inched open the door. Both men pressed against the building on opposite sides for several seconds. Lange nodded and started to enter.

"Lieutenant, back here," a voice shouted from the rear of the building.

Lange froze. He turned to Rizzo with a puzzled expression. "That sounds like one of my guys."

"I'd be careful. That crazy fucking Stasi could have a gun on him."

Lange nodded and moved to the corner of the building. "Baggs, that you?"

The officer poked his head around. "Lieutenant...Frank's down. He's been shot. I got EMS on the way."

Wary of a setup, Lange asked, "Leave him a second, Baggs. Come up here to the front of the house."

"God, Lieutenant, I hate to leave him here."

"Just be a minute."

"Ah, okay."

Augie Baggs had to be the youngest officer in the Saugerties precinct. He stumbled toward them; his whole body shook like someone about to freeze to death. His blood-smeared hands hung at his sides. Judging from the red rings around his eyes, Rizzo guessed he had been crying.

Lange pointed to the rear of the house. "Augie, what the fuck happened there?"

The young man gulped twice before he could get out any words. "We...we...that is, we got here...about a half hour ago. Frank sent me into the house to secure it. He wanted to have a look around the property...you know...to make sure. While I was upstairs checking the rooms...I got confused. I mean, no one was home. Who were we supposed to protect?"

"Wait. Slow up." Lange said. "You didn't find Amy Chatsworth anywhere in the house?"

"No. No one. Like I said, I checked all the rooms. Empty." Baggs looked across to Rizzo as though he were seeking confirmation.

Rizzo turned to Lange. "If Amy wasn't in the house, you think she might have gone over to yours?"

"That's a possibility. I'll call there in a minute."

"Christ, I hope so."

"So, what then?" Lange asked the shaking Baggs.

"Well, I heard a shot outside. I ran to that window," he said, pointing up. "I couldn't see anything, so I yelled down to Frank." Baggs stopped to gulp a breath.

"Okay," Lange said, and waited for Baggs to continue.

"I started to turn away, but I spotted a guy running to the pickup parked in the drive. I raced downstairs. The truck disappeared up the road before I got there. I found Frank in back of the house," he said, pointing with a bloody finger.

Rizzo took off sprinting ahead of Lange and Baggs. The fallen officer lay on his back. He knelt over him and recognized Baggs' feeble attempt to stem the bleeding. He ran his hand under the officer's nose. The man was very dead. No doubt, the first time the young Baggs had looked into the face of death.

The wail of the EMS siren broke through, bringing Rizzo to his feet. "Too late. He's gone."

Lange stood frozen, looking down at his deceased team member.

A gust of wind caught the rear door of the schoolhouse, left open by the fleeing Schmitt. The door slammed against the building, catching Rizzo's attention. "Officer Baggs, did you look in any of the rooms downstairs?"

"No sir. No chance."

Rizzo moved to the wind-blown door and caught it. He stepped into the opening and scanned the workshop interior. Amy's prone form stretched out on the bench in the middle of the room came into focus. His words exploded with a fierceness meant to frighten the devil: "God damned son-of-a-bitch bastard!"

* * *

Jack Fields stood looking out the window. The buzzing intercom brought him back to his desk.

"Yes, Rachel?"

"Jack, Lieutenant Lange, Saugerties police on line one."

Fields punched in the number and sat down. "Tom, what's up?"

"Jack, we have a major problem. We're gonna need you guys involved again."

Fields heard the stress in the officer's voice. He admired Lange's dedication, but he felt the lieutenant could be a tad uptight. "Tell me."

"Jake Avon's dead. When he took off from here yesterday morning without telling anyone, he headed up to his hunting cabin near Haines Falls. Schmitt somehow found the schoolhouse. He must have seen Jake leaving and followed him there."

"This all happened before we got there, right?" Fields said. "How did you discover where he went?"

"The Haines Falls Fire Department got a call-out. A neighbor reported the cabin was in flames. The firefighters found Jake nailed spread-eagled to the floor opposite the side of the explosion. The fire never got to him. A quick inspection of his body revealed he had been tortured before Schmitt set the fire. The fire chief thinks Jake's heart failed and that's how he died."

Field felt a twinge of guilt. Perhaps their departure was a little hasty. "Any idea what happened to Schmitt?"

"In a nutshell, the son-of-a bitch returned to the schoolhouse...killed one of my deputies when he surprised him. I had sent two of them there to protect Mrs. Chatsworth. Schmitt also killed a man who used to live in Saugerties...a Felix Decker."

"Good God!"

"Yeah...and the bastard had the Chatsworth woman tied up in the workroom downstairs. He would have killed her too if my deputies hadn't arrived in time. He still got away."

"She okay?"

"Shook up, not harmed…'cept for the black eye she got when Schmitt belted her. She's being checked out down at the Kingston hospital. Rizzo's with her."

"Any lead on where Schmitt's headed?"

"Yeah. He left in Avon's pickup, which cut us a break."

"How so?"

"I already had an APB out on it. Got a call minutes ago from the Rhinecliff precinct across the river. When he lit out, he drove across the Kingston-Rhinecliff Bridge. They found the truck parked on the southbound side of the Rhinecliff railroad station."

Fields made a quick damage assessment. Schmitt was responsible for two killings in Pennsylvania, and now two more in New York State. The Stasi might be over the hill, but he had proven to be quite lethal. Fields shook his head in disbelief.

"What's the window between the time he left Saugerties and the call on the truck?"

"From about noon to a half hour ago."

Fields looked at his watch. "Well, if he caught a train right away, he's halfway to Manhattan by now. We'll get a team over to Penn Station right away, but there's no telling he didn't get off somewhere between Rhinecliff and Manhattan."

"You think he'll try to get to JFK…jump a flight back to Europe?"

"Not right away. You never know. We'll cover all the airports. I'll get right on that."

"Keep me in the loop, will you?"

"Yes…of course. And Tom, I'm sorry about your deputy. Maybe if we'd have stayed around — "

"I don't know how that would have changed anything, Jack."

"No, I guess not. Bye, Tom." Fields pressed the intercom. "Rachel, see if Tony is in."

Fields doodled on a small pad next to the phone console. He had mentioned to Condon earlier he thought they bailed too soon. Losing Avon in that cabin fire bothered him.

Tony's voice came through the speaker, "Yeah, Jack?"

"Get Abrams and Freni and come to my office in five."

"Okay. Any news from upstate?"

"Yes. Werner Schmitt is loose somewhere in the metro area."

"That come from Lange?"

Fields fell silent, his doodling pencil in his hand. He let several beats go by. "Yeah, a few minutes ago. And Tony, I want to be there when we nail him."

And we will, Jack."

"Right," he said as the pencil scribed an X on the pad.

Fields returned to the window in the corner of the office. He looked down on City Hall several blocks away. Farther down he could see the tops of the Twin Towers looming over the smaller buildings south of him. Gazing out over lower Manhattan, he tried to assemble the events of the past few days. Several pigeons swooped down from above then disappeared out of sight. The magician's line, *Now you see it, now you don't,* occurred to him. The line fit the elusive Stasi murderer, who showed up in Pennsylvania one day and upstate New York the next, always one-step ahead of the Bureau. Looking out, he drew in a deep breath and slammed a fist into his palm. Another pigeon disappeared from view.

* * *

Silence engulfed Rizzo like a heavy blanket. Amy had not spoken since they exited the examining room of the hospital. Seeing again the raw discoloration on her left cheek and the blackened area around her eye caused his teeth to grind. The choke marks on her neck from Schmitt's bruising grip were visible, as were the rope burns on her wrists and ankles. All were painful reminders of Schmitt's brutality.

Rizzo had seen her stained jeans when he freed her from the workbench. She had wet herself during her frightening ordeal.

The spot had dried and disappeared, but the embarrassment in her eyes lingered.

During the drive between the Kingston and Saugerties exits, Rizzo kept glancing at her. Amy sat with her temple pressed against the window glass. Her squeezed eyes made her appear like a frightened child trying to block out an evil image.

"Jesus, Amy, I am so sorry...so God damned sorry."

A weak smile appeared.

He remembered how she had pushed to go with them to the cabin, that he had convinced her to stay in the schoolhouse. "I should have never left you alone," he said after a long pause. "What the hell was I thinking?"

"Luke, it's not your fault." Her shaky voice made an effort to assure him. "I should have used more caution before opening the door to him."

"But I was supposed to protect—"

"Stop it, Luke. I'm okay. That's what matters."

"Yeah, thank God." Rizzo fell silent again.

Two miles before the Saugerties exit, Amy reached over and touched him on the shoulder. "Luke?" Pools of tears covered her golden brown eyes. "I don't want to go in."

"Amy, you don't have to. Stay in the car. I'll get everything together. We'll head back to the city right away. You okay with the two-hour drive?"

She hugged herself and turned up her chin. "I'm fine." She shook, while tears streamed down her cheeks.

Leaving the thruway, Rizzo steered to the side of the road and stopped the car. He turned toward Amy. Stretching out his arms, he took her by the shoulders and pulled her toward him. "It's okay...it's okay," he whispered.

He held her that way for several moments, foreheads pressed together. When her shakes quieted, he wiped the moisture from under her eyes with his palm. Then he kissed her nose.

Rizzo stopped the car at the curb in front of the schoolhouse and got out. Before closing the door, he leaned in. "You gonna be okay alone for about ten minutes?"

"Yes, I'll be fine. Please hurry."

"I will. Lock up."

He remained standing until he heard the door locks click and then turned toward the schoolhouse. Tom Lange waited on the path.

"Got a minute?" Lange asked as Rizzo approached.

"Yeah, sure, Tom. Just going upstairs to collect our things. We're heading back to the city ASAP."

Lange looked back at the car. "How'd she check out?"

"Only bruises...nothing broken. But scared shitless." Rizzo unlocked the schoolhouse door. "Come in with me. We can talk after I gather up our stuff."

Rizzo found the few items in the library he had bought the previous day and shoved them into a sports bag. He looked around for his Colt .38 and spotted Amy's purse. He opened it and found the gun. As he strapped on the holster, his eyes landed on the framed photo of Bard and Avon on the bookshelf. He tossed the photo and the purse into the bag and moved into the guest bedroom. When he had Amy's clothes packed away, he walked toward Lange.

"So, what's up?"

Lange repeated what he had related to Jack Fields about the APB turning up Avon's pickup at the Rhinecliff railroad station. "He's headed back to the city. He's gonna try to catch a flight out."

"Nah. I doubt he would try that right away. He knows he's too hot right now."

"Well, Fields did say the Feds would be watching all the New York airports."

Rizzo motioned to the living room area. "What's going to happen to all this? I gather Jake had no heirs."

"No, but his wife has a brother. He lives outside of Saratoga Springs. We'll contact him in a day or so, soon as I get Jake's funeral arrangements taken care of."

"You got the duty?"

"Who else? Oh, by the way, before you take off, let me make you a copy of those photos of Schmitt. The kids' computer does a nice job reproducing black and white."

Rizzo remained motionless, his mind turning over the events of the last few days. How in hell did a simple assignment like this turn into such a nightmare for so many? The lives of families tossed upside down by one revenge-seeking maniac.

"Luke?"

"Sorry. I was thinking how I'd enjoy killing that son-of-a-bitch."

Lange laughed.

"The photos? Yeah, I'll wait for you at the car with Amy."

Lange took a step to leave and stopped. "Hey, you asked me to check out that plate on Schmitt's rental. Turns out the car came from a Manhattan Enterprise location on the east side...Forty-fourth Street off Third Avenue."

Rizzo's eyes widened. "I know that location. Did you give that info to Fields yet?"

"No. I forgot. You know, with everything that went down here. And my deputy getting killed."

"Do me a favor. Hold off for a day. I'd like to check it out."

Lange looked at him with a questioning expression. Then he grinned.

Chapter 23

Amy suffered the long trip to the city in silence. Except for her brief expression of sadness over Jake Avon's death, she never referred to her experience in the schoolhouse workshop. Rizzo was certain she was blocking out the memory. He would never remind her—not ever. He dropped her off at the Waldorf's Park Avenue entrance, saying he would be back in two hours to pick her up for a light dinner somewhere.

He needed to return his rental to the Avis garage on the west side of Manhattan, around the corner from his small studio apartment. Before going crosstown, he would make one stop: the Enterprise garage on the east side.

Rizzo arrived and flashed his retired NYPD gold shield at the Enterprise agent. He asked to see Werner Schmitt's rental contract. The agent pulled up the page on his computer screen and Rizzo had him repeat the address listed.

"That's Bushwick, Brooklyn, isn't it?"

"Yes, sir, that's the address on the contract," the agent assured him. "He's rented from us a couple of times this week and used that same address."

"You the agent on duty when he was here?"

"Well, sir, let me see," the agent said, pulling up the signature pages of both contracts. After staring at the information for several seconds, the agent looked up. "Seems I took care of him this last time, but not the first."

Rizzo produced the two photos and slid them across to the agent. "Do you remember if this is the man who signed the contract?"

The agent studied the photos. "Lots of people been through here over the last few days, so it's fuzzy. That could be him."

"Do you remember him having an accent... German, maybe?"

The agent scratched the side of his nose, as though the gesture would help him find an answer. "No, I don't recall. But hell, most conversations with our customers are limited to replying to our questions...usually one or two-word answers."

"Thanks." Rizzo turned to leave but stopped. "By the way, did the Saugerties PD get in touch with you? The rental car this guy had was abandoned upstate, near Kingston."

The agent's puzzled expression lasted several seconds until he processed Rizzo's question. He glanced down at the computer screen, at the notes section on the contract page. "Oh, yes. I see it here. Our Kingston branch office retrieved the car today. It's in the system now."

"Thanks, buddy," Rizzo said, and headed across Manhattan to the Avis garage. Before arriving, he changed his mind. Instead of returning the car, Rizzo pulled into a space in front of his apartment, a three-story brownstone, and turned off the engine. He sat behind the wheel, trying to make up his mind. He told Amy he would have dinner with her later, but he needed to check out the Bushwick address, and soon. Schmitt could be trying to get out of the country. Once he was back in Germany, extradition would be a nightmare. The man might not have returned to Brooklyn, electing to hide out in another location, but Bushwick was a good starting point.

After a quick shower and change of clothes, he punched in the Waldorf's number on his cell phone. "Mrs. Amy

Chatsworth, please." The hotel operator connected him right away.

"Hello," her soft, tired voice answered.

"Amy, how you feeling?"

"Oh, Luke. I thought you were Avery returning my call." She let go a deep sigh. "I'm all right...exhausted but I'm calmed down now."

"You called home?"

"Yes. I have arranged for a flight tomorrow evening from JFK. I wanted him to know."

Rizzo swallowed hard. She was leaving, of course. He expected that. He had grown close to her, though he knew their relationship would go nowhere. She was a princess and he a commoner. Their situation had to end.

"Luke...are you there?"

"Oh, I'm sorry, Amy. I was thinking of something I have to do tonight. That's why I'm calling."

"No dinner?"

"I'd like to, but this is too important." Should he tell her? Her next question made that unnecessary.

"Schmitt?"

He hesitated. He didn't need to worry her.

"Luke, please be careful. Let the FBI handle him."

That would be the logical approach; however, he had never chosen to rely on others while on the Job. He was not going to start now. "I will, Amy. I will. Don't worry. Following up on a lead, that's all. If the information proves useful, I will call in the cavalry. Promise."

She fell silent. He waited.

"I'll order from room service tonight, but let's have breakfast in the morning."

"Sounds like a plan. Call you on the house phone around nine. And Amy, get some sleep."

"I'll try."

* * *

Night had fallen by the time Rizzo arrived. The street lamp at the curb of the three-story framed building splashed light on the worn doorbell pad beside the front door. Among the six names listed, none but Buchmann's in apartment 1-B was Germanic sounding. He would begin there. Using a credit card, he defeated the door lock with ease and pushed into the foyer. The dimly lit building smelled of urine and mold. He made his way across the broken tiles, past the staircase, and down toward the rear apartment, sidestepping a crawling roach. With his right hand on the butt of the Colt .38 tucked into his waistband under his jacket, he raised his left hand to knock on the flaked-paint apartment door. The voice from behind stopped him.

"Hey, mon. You lookin' for someone?"

Rizzo turned around. A large black man stood at the opened doorway of the front apartment and glared at him. Under his knitted cap, matted coils of brown, shiny hair hung down, dreadlocks of a Rastafarin. His upper torso strained the seams of his black, form-fitting mock turtle. He held a leather jacket in one hand and his door key in the other.

Rizzo slipped the .38 into the holster under his arm, covering it with his jacket, and pulled a business card from his pocket. He moved toward the man while holding his finger to his lips. The Rastafarian leaned into his opened door, reached around and produced a metal baseball bat.

"Hold it right there, mon."

"Whoa," Rizzo said, keeping his voice low. He raised the palm of one hand as a defensive sign, and waved his business card in the air with the other. He hoped the man didn't have a hair trigger and would give him a chance to explain. He slowed his approach, trying to read the Rasta's face.

"Fuck you want here?"

"Easy, friend," Rizzo whispered.

"No, you be easy, mon. Watcha doin' snooping around?"

"I'm a private detective looking for someone." Again, Rizzo extended his card. The man ignored it. Struggling to keep his voice low, Rizzo said, "Can we go outside? I'll tell you about it." Nodding toward the rear apartment, he said, "If he's in there, I don't want to alert him."

The Rastafarian motioned toward the front door with the baseball bat. Rizzo took the cue. He hurried past him and out onto the sidewalk. When he heard the lock click behind him, he looked back, surprised. The man had not followed him. Before Rizzo could move, the front door opened and the Rastafarian reappeared wearing his leather jacket. He bounded out, still holding the baseball bat.

"I thought you ditched me," Rizzo said, grinning.

"Sorry, mon, had to lock up. A dangerous fuckin' neighborhood, you know. Okay, what's this shit about?"

Again, Rizzo offered his business card, and this time the man took it. "I'm looking for a guy...a killer...of several people...so far."

The man looked down at the card then up at Rizzo and chuckled. "A killer? In that apartment? You gotta be shittin' me."

Rizzo shook his head. Did he guess wrong? Could Schmitt have given the Enterprise garage a phony address? He looked at the Rastafarian. "Why? Who lives there?"

"Hey, only a little old man, sweet as brown sugar and as harmless as a flea. You way off base on this."

Rizzo didn't know what to make of it. Schmitt had put one over on the rent-a-car agency. Now him. This was a wasted lead.

"Who's this fucker you lookin' for?"

Rizzo hesitated, reluctant to give up too much information to a stranger. "What's your name, friend?"

The Rastafarian looked at Rizzo suspiciously. "It's Jabai, mon. Jabai Saint James. But I'm called Jabba."

"Well, Jabba, the guy I'm looking for rented a car in Manhattan and gave the rental agency this building as his address."

Jabba released a soft chuckle. "Nobody here can afford to rent a car."

Rizzo glanced around. "I didn't think he lived here. Maybe staying with someone? He's from Germany. The tenant in 1-B is German. That's why I went there first."

"Otto? Hey, he ain't there anyway. In the hospital. Some fuckin' druggie mugged him the other day. Hurt him bad."

"You see him having any visitors before he got mugged?"

"No, mon. And I keep a good watch on this place."

Rizzo reached into his inside pocket, removed the two photos of Schmitt and held them out to the Rastafarian. "This is what the guy looks like."

Jabba examined the headshots without touching them. After several moments, he took one of the photos from Rizzo and studied the man's image.

Rizzo waited.

"Yeah, I see this fucker before." Jabba's facial expression contorted as though he were struggling with a bout of constipation. "Can't think where, but I seen him."

Rizzo felt a small surge of hope. "Around the neighborhood, maybe?"

Jabba remained silent, thinking. "When we have that snowstorm?"

The question's logic escaped Rizzo for a moment, but then he remembered. "Three days ago...Tuesday night. Why?"

"Yeah. That's when I see this dude."

"Here in the building?"

"No, mon, up the street. Snowing like shit. Stopped me, askin' 'bout the cop car in front. Wanted to know what's goin' down...the day Otto got mugged...when EMS took him to the hospital."

"You see where he went?"

"No, mon. In a hurry. Left him standin', gettin' soaked."

"He spoke to you? How did he sound...I mean you notice anything odd?"

Jabba screwed up his wide brow. "He sounded like Otto."

"How so?"

"Same accent, so maybe he was German too."

That was enough. Jabba had convinced him the man he saw was Schmitt. The problem was what to do about it. While he tried to decide, Jabba tossed him a question he needed to weigh carefully.

"You want to have a look in Otto's apartment? I got the key."

Rizzo glanced over his shoulder, back toward the front door. "How come you have a key?"

"Otto gave me a duplicate...case he lock himself out. Hey, old people do that a lot, you know. Besides, I kinda look after him. He got no one else."

Rizzo mulled over his options. If he let Jabba open the door with his key and they went in, Rizzo would not be guilty of breaking and entering. On the other hand, he would be putting Jabba in harm's way in the event that Schmitt was inside ready to pounce.

"Does the apartment have a window I can get a look through?"

Jabba thought a moment. "Yeah. Otto's is the second two on that side," he said, motioning with his head. "Livin' room first, then bedroom. But you need to squeeze in between buildings to get to there."

"Show me."

Six feet separated the two buildings. Two large garbage cans blocked the opening of a dirt path leading down to the rear. The street lamp in front of the building cast a broken line of dim shadows. Rizzo couldn't see beyond ten feet. He grabbed one of the garbage cans by the handles and lifted the container out of the way. Jabba dragged the second to one side. The cans were empty, but the fetid smell left from their previous contents filled Rizzo's nostrils. He controlled a retch impulse.

"Here goes nothing," he said as he stepped into the narrow pathway, stumbling, swallowing hard to avoid vomiting. Rizzo looked back at Jabba. "Keep an eye out. Okay?"

Jabba nodded.

Empty food containers and raw garbage-debris strewn along the ground made for Rizzo's unsteady steps. This path had to be a great treasure trove for the rats of Bushwick, Brooklyn.

Halfway down, he reached the two windows, Otto Buchmann's living room and bedroom. The first windowsill came to eye level. Rising on the tips of his toes, Rizzo peered through the flimsy curtains. No light or movement. He edged along to the second window. The descending path sloped toward the rear of the building and forced Rizzo to pull himself up by his fingers to the higher sill. He looked through the parted curtains. The room was dark.

"The place is empty," Rizzo said when he returned to Jabba. "Let me go in first."

"Should we knock?" Jabba asked.

Rizzo laughed. "Ya think?"

Jabba's face went serious. "No, mon. Dumb question."

"Okay, give me the key. Which way do I turn to unlock?"

Jabba had to think a moment before he answered, "To the left."

"You stay in your apartment doorway and wait."

Jabba started to object but stopped when Rizzo pulled the .38 from his waistband. "If he's in there, don't want you in the way if he starts shooting," Rizzo explained.

"Understand, mon. But how 'bout you?"

"I'm a fast ducker," Rizzo said, grinning. "But tell you what. Wait in your doorway. If he breaks for the front door, you hit him a home run with your bat."

Jabba's mouth curled up. He was a Halloween pumpkin. "Yeah, I can do that."

"I'll signal if the place is clear. You can come in then. Okay?"

"Okay, mon."

Rizzo approached Buchmann's apartment door, grateful buildings of this vintage had never provided peepholes. He knelt down at the base of the door, the .38 gripped in his right hand. Reaching up with his left, he slipped the key into the lock. He let several seconds go by before turning. When he felt the lock's bolt release, he removed the key. Looking back over his shoulder, he could see Jabba's large head peering out. Rizzo sucked in a deep swallow of air, then turned the handle. Pushing the door open, he flopped forward on his stomach across the doorway saddle. He raised the .38 to a ready position, expecting to take Schmitt's fire. Nothing. He remained on his stomach until his eyes adjusted to the little light creeping in from the hallway. The small living room slowly came into focus. Schmitt was nowhere.

Rizzo got to his feet, checked out the small kitchen on the left and darted toward the bedroom. He leaned against one side of the opened doorway, waiting, listening. No sound. No movement. He turned and pressed his chest against the wall. Reaching in and around, feeling for the light switch, he snapped it on. The room was bathed in light from a bare ceiling fixture. Again, silence. If Schmitt was hiding, Rizzo had failed to spook him.

Rizzo heard footsteps behind him. He wheeled and raised his .38. Catching sight of the shape of Jabba's colorful Rasta cap, he lowered the pistol. The big man's body filled the apartment doorway. Rizzo motioned to him to stop and back away. Jabba responded, and when he was no longer in view, Rizzo crouched low and crabbed into the bedroom, ready to return fire. Empty. The small bathroom stood empty as well. Schmitt was not in the apartment.

"It's clear," Rizzo called out.

"Sorry about that, mon. I seen lights go on. Thought everything okay."

"You almost lost a few dreadlocks, bro. I told you to stay put."

"I know. Sorry."

Rizzo looked around the living room, taking in the emptied bottle of Stolie vodka in the trash and the biscuit crumbs on the seat of the lounge chair. In the bedroom, on the unmade bed, Schmitt had left a suitcase with a pair of pants flung across the opened top. Rizzo pulled them off and tossed them aside after searching their pockets. He went through the suitcase. Finding nothing but items of clothing, he eyed a folder sticking out of a side pocket. He slid it out and broke into a smile. Schmitt's passport. *He's not going anywhere without this.*

"Jabba, I need you to help me out here," Rizzo said, tucking the passport into his jacket pocket.

"How you mean, mon?"

"This guy's coming back. When he does, he's going to know someone was in the apartment. Fucker's going ballistic when he sees his passport's missing."

"You want me to grab him...hold him for you?"

"Jesus, no. He's armed. I don't need you getting killed."

"What you want me to do, then?"

Rizzo looked into the moon-shaped face of the Rastafarian. Jabba's black, round eyes flashed an eagerness to please. This hulk of a man could break a body in half if he wanted. Schmitt would not stand a chance if he didn't have a weapon. Rizzo had no desire to test that with his new friend.

"Be a lookout for me," Rizzo told him. "That's all. I can't be back 'til mid-morning so I need you to keep watch. If this prick shows up, call me on my cell right away. Can you do that?"

Jabba flashed his pumpkin smile again. "You mean I shouldn't hit him a home run with this?" he asked, waggling the bat in the air.

"No, bro. Be my eyes. That's all."

Chapter 24

The taxi dispatcher inside the Albany-Rensselaer train depot had suggested the Red Coat Motel about six miles from the station. It was next door to a great barbecue restaurant, and the motel served a free breakfast. Schmitt told the taxi driver to take him there.

The driver, a black man with a noticeable gap between his two front teeth endowing many of his words with a sibilant sound, was a non-stop talker. During the ride, Schmitt had limited his responses to the chatty driver's conversation to one or two words. No need to emphasize his identity as a passenger with a German accent. At the motel, the driver handed Schmitt the taxi company's business card.

"Yes, sir," he whistled. "Call the dispatcher's number when ya need to go back to the station. I'll come get ya."

Schmitt had left Avon's pickup truck in the parking lot on the southbound side of the Rhinecliff train station. He felt confident the police would conclude he had jumped on the next train heading toward New York City. Instead, he boarded a northbound train, planning to hole up for a few days in the city of Albany while he figured a way to return undetected to the Bushwick, Brooklyn apartment.

He had not booked a return flight to Germany, so the Feds could search airline manifests all they wanted. His name would not appear on any of them. The name on the false passport sewn into the liner of his Tourister bag was the one he would use to purchase his return ticket. Get the phony and destroy the one with his real name.

Schmitt sat in a booth of the barbeque restaurant, his stomach knotted with hunger pains and gurgling. The server set down the full rack of ribs, and he dove in like a vulture discovering road kill. The steaming, succulent pork fell off the bone each time he picked up a rib. When he finished, he licked his fingers until most of the sticky barbecue sauce disappeared. Looking around for a clean napkin, he eyed the tiny silver packet sitting at the corner of his plate. He studied the odd container, thinking how similar it looked to a single condom wrapper.

From behind, he heard the husky female voice of his server. "Use the Handi-Wipe. That's what it's there for."

Schmitt turned his head and looked into her full-jawed face. Not unattractive, she was a powerfully built, middle-aged woman, full bosomed with big bones and strong yellow teeth. She leaned to one side, balancing a tray of dirty dishes with one hand while pinning her elbow to her hip.

"No need to lick your fingers. The wipe takes care of that."

Schmitt grinned, said thank you and tore open the packet. The alcohol felt cool on his mouth as he dabbed the sticky remnants from the corners. He seldom ate anything barbecued, but he had relished his supper.

Minutes later, the woman returned. "Coffee?"

"Yes, please."

"On vacation?" she asked casually while filling his cup.

Schmitt hesitated, thinking of how he should respond. Remembering Albany was New York State's capitol city he looked up, smiled and said, "Government business."

She set down the coffee canister. "Staying at the Red Coat?"

Schmitt nodded without thinking, but immediately regretted the admission.

The server remained standing, looking around at the surrounding half-filled tables, then back at him. "Must be lonely, traveling alone, right?"

Schmitt simply shrugged, hoping to appear non-committal and their conversation would end there.

"I'm off work at nine if you'd like company?"

The offer surprised him. What was she suggesting? An image flashed across his mind, of the English woman's curved buttocks as he stretched her out across the worktable in the schoolhouse. Aware of the pulsing beneath his fly, he was tempted. "No, no, thank you. I have an early meeting in the morning."

"Okay, no harm in asking." She cleared his table of dishes and disappeared into the kitchen.

He sat for a while, sipping his coffee, thinking about the server and her offer. He could not risk it, he told himself. Draining the coffee cup, he raised his hand when she came through the kitchen's double doors and signaled for his check. At the same instant, the front door of the restaurant opened. He looked up and went numb. Two giant-sized men in gray uniforms, Gore-Tex jackets over trousers with black stripes down the sides, and wide brim hats with a purple band, stood at the entrance. They stepped in and scanned the restaurant interior. Their eyes searched with purpose. Schmitt recognized the holstered weapons on their hips and the measured look on their faces. He slipped below the booth's high back.

A man in a white shirt and black pants pushed through the kitchen doors and rushed up to the two New York State Troopers. "Hey, guys," the restaurant manager said. "How's it going tonight?"

"Oh, there you are, Fred," the taller of the two said. "Quiet, for a change. Got a rack for us?"

"This way," the manager said, leading the two officers to a booth in the rear.

Schmitt sat up, letting go a sigh from deep within his chest. He pushed a smile at the server as she placed his check on the table. Laying a twenty-dollar bill across it, he looked up and said, "Number 121, in the back."

He hurried across the parking lot to the motel, imagining the naked form of the large woman stretched out across his bed, eager to receive him. He entered his unit, closed and locked the door. Looking around at his frugal surroundings, he examined the room for the first time. At eighty-nine dollars a night, he felt overcharged. The taxi dispatcher at the Albany train station had to be getting a kickback. He was certain of it.

He showered, letting the pulsating water on his back and shoulders relieve the tension accumulated there during the last forty-eight hours. He stood in the bathroom doorway, running the towel across his back, keeping an eye on the digital clock blinking on the nightstand. His visitor would arrive in about ten minutes. He thought about dressing but merely slipped into his trousers and left his shirt hanging in the closet.

At ten minutes after the hour, he heard the knock and peered through the small peephole. She stood alone at the door, her long coat draped over her shoulders. Schmitt opened the door and stepped back. "Hello, miss," he said.

"Are you the lonely man?" she asked, breaking into a knowing grin.

"Yes, yes, come in. What is your name?"

"I'm called Alma Sue. What's yours?"

He took the coat from her shoulders and tossed it over the back of the chair. "I'm Richard," he said, gesturing to the bed. "Do you want to be paid first?"

Alma Sue said nothing but began unbuttoning the snaps that ran down the front of her uniform. She stepped out of the garment, allowing it to fall to her feet, and stood before him with nothing but a bra and stretched-out panties covering her wide hips and strong thighs. She watched him examining her. Her skin was smooth, clear of blemishes and taut, except for the small girdle of fat ringing her middle. Her calves, like her thighs, were firm, and her overall solid build gave the impression of someone with a health club membership. "Richard," she answered, "when we're finished, I'll let you decide how much you want to give me."

Schmitt liked her answer and the confident tone she used. His eyes focused on her abundant cleavage, and he moved toward her. She received his embrace, smiling as he reached around to undo her bra's hooks. She pressed her pelvis into his hardened penis with enthusiasm. He buried his face between her breasts and then, cupping them, he licked her nipples until they hardened like two red cherries. Alma Sue reached down, undid the button on the front of his pants and pulled down the zipper. Schmitt had not bothered putting on his shorts. After she wiggled his pants down to his ankles, she took his erect penis into her hand, and with a gentle tug, edged him toward the bed. He fell across the mattress onto his back. Alma Sue slid off her panties, leaving them on the floor at the side of the bed.

"Here I come, Richard," she said, sounding like a child playing hide and seek. Alma Sue knelt down and engulfed his erection with her mouth.

* * *

Schmitt lay with his head resting on Alma Sue's stomach, his fingers laced through her long pubic hair. He was trying to remember the last time a woman had so pleasured and exhausted him in bed. That was long ago, but then as those years slipped by, so too had his opportunities. He rolled his head to one side and looked at the digital clock flashing ten-fifty-five. He needed to sleep.

"My delicious one," he whispered. "I have to rest. Perhaps you can return tomorrow when you get off work."

"I'm not scheduled to work tomorrow, but I am on duty the night after."

"Then let us plan for that, if I haven't already concluded my business here."

Alma Sue went into the bathroom, washed and dressed. Schmitt picked up the TV remote and snapped on the monitor. The local channel was airing the eleven o'clock news. Sitting on the bed, he listened with half an ear to the newscaster, his mind distracted for a few minutes by his recent sexual pleasures.

When Alma Sue emerged from the bathroom, Schmitt was standing by the door, holding out a wad of bills. The woman took the money and counted out two hundred dollars in twenties. She raised her eyebrows. Taking him behind the neck, she drew him into a long, wet kiss. When she pulled away, she said, "I guess you liked it."

"I did."

"Better than licking your fingers full of barbecue sauce?"

"More."

Before Alma Sue could reply, the words of the on-camera TV reporter caught his attention.

"...a schoolhouse in Malden, New York."

He turned to look at the TV. A photo of him filled the screen.

The announcer continued. "The shooter left two men dead. One was a local deputy sheriff sent to the location to investigate a disturbance. The second man, a Florida resident, was not identified. The police will not release more information about the shooting until the Florida man's next of kin has been contacted and the—"

Schmitt leaped for the TV remote and hit the off button before tossing the device onto the bed. A rush of panic rippled through his body. Alma Sue remained standing at the bathroom door, riveted, her mouth agape. He knew she had seen his photo and heard the announcer. Paralyzed, a combined look of confusion and fear painted her face. "That... wasn't that—?"

His right fist flew to her jaw and cut off her words. She fell backward, hit her head on the doorjamb behind her and slumped to the floor. Dazed from the punch, Alma Sue struggled to right herself but slipped onto her back, giving Schmitt enough time to grab a pillow from the bed. He charged across and landed knees first on top of Alma Sue's chest. He heard her release a whoosh of breath, and the sound of her cracking ribs filled his ears.

Straddling her torso, he jammed the pillow onto her face and pressed down with the heels of both hands, cutting off her air. Alma Sue fought him. She thrashed her arms for several seconds. Schmitt's weight on her chest and pressure on the pillow defeated her strong effort. Within minutes, her body went limp. The fight ceased. Schmitt kept the pressure on the pillow for several seconds before he released it. He checked her vital signs. She was dead. Satisfied, he tossed the pillow and stood. He looked down at the sheet-white face of his recent sex partner, her hair tossed in snarls over her forehead. Not the way he wanted this experience to end. He liked the woman. She had given him great sex. Under normal circumstances, he could visualize an ongoing relationship with her. The newscast had left him no choice.

Schmitt showered a second time. Stepping back into the room, he looked at the TV monitor with anger-filled eyes. The media's reporting of the killings did not surprise him; he expected the story would eventually be on the news shows—just not this soon. By his calculation, it cut his escape window in half. He no longer had a few days to lie low. He took his time dressing, thinking of his next move. When he had worked out his plan, he set the alarm on his watch for three o'clock and flopped down on the bed.

A moment later, he jumped up again, found his $200 under Alma Sue's cold body and stuffed it back in his pocket.

* * *

The vibrating tickle on Schmitt's wrist startled him awake before he heard the beeping alarm. He switched off the sound and sat up. Four hours of sleep. He felt refreshed.

He dressed in a hurry and slipped outside, closing the door behind him. A small light glowed above each unit's doorway. The rear parking area of the motel, pitched in darkness, gave him cover. He looked down at the lineup of parked cars in front of each unit. Was he still expert at hot-wiring ignitions? While on stealth operations in East Germany, he was quite fast at defeating any model vehicle. Many years had passed, but he was sure he had not forgotten.

He walked around each car, testing doors until he found one unlocked, a red Mustang convertible. He passed on it. Too conspicuous. The car's loud engine could alert the sleeper inside the motel unit. He continued down the line. The next door he opened was on a Toyota Camry. Perfect. He knelt down beside the passenger seat and leaned in. He finished the wiring within minutes, and the four-cylinder-engine turned over with a low rumble. Schmitt jumped in and backed out of the space. He turned toward the parking lot exit and headed out.

He encountered sparse traffic on the southbound New York State Thruway until he reached the Kingston exit around four-thirty in the morning. By this time, the blue-collar workforce of Ulster County, tired men and women heading to their workplaces, were up and running. The night's dark blanket had not completely lifted. Headlights in either direction streamed up and down the six-lane interstate like laser beams. Schmitt had another two hours ahead of him before reaching the perimeter of New York City. He would then decide where to abandon the Toyota. He knew that in any high crime area, the police would be less likely to discover a stolen car if left in a legitimate parking spot. Moreover, in a high crime area, some criminal would steal the car within the hour if he left the doors unlocked—guaranteed.

At ten past seven, Schmitt reached the upper reaches of Manhattan. He followed a route downtown and pulled to the curb under the elevated tracks of the Metro-North line. He was in Spanish Harlem at Park Avenue and 116th Street, the perfect location to unload the car. He closed the door without engaging the lock and looked back at the ignition wires dangling at the base of the steering column. He was certain the car would not be there long. He made his way along Park Avenue until he found a subway entrance. Then he disappeared underground.

Chapter 25

Schmitt waited patiently at the elevator in the hospital lobby. When the door opened, he felt his heart jump. He recognized the man in the Rasta cap standing behind two orderlies wearing green scrubs. It was the black man from Otto's apartment building.

Schmitt spun on his heel and bolted from the elevator bank, quickly pushing through the men's room door at the end of the hallway and locking it. Several minutes later, he stepped out and scanned the corridor in both directions. Satisfied the Rastafarian had gone, he returned to the elevator bank and pushed the button.

He reached Otto Buchmann's room on the fourth floor and paused at the opened doorway. He could see the old man propped up in his bed. He was alone; the second bed in the room was empty. Otto was holding a piece of toast to his mouth. When he spotted Schmitt, he pushed his breakfast tray aside. A broad grin broke across his bruised face. He held out his cast-encased left forearm and his good right arm toward his approaching visitor.

"Werner, Werner, you haf come. I am so happy to see you."

Schmitt bent down to accept the old man's fatherly embrace and kissed him on his stubbled cheek. "Otto, I am so sorry. I heard what happened when I returned last evening. I have been traveling or I would have been here sooner."

"You are busy, I know. Do not worry. You are here now." Otto pointed to the chair against the wall. "Sit, please."

Schmitt slid the chair across to the side of the bed and sat. He looked into Otto's blackened eyes and wounded face. A surge of anger shot through him as he took in the results of the savage beating the old man had suffered. These barbaric Americans. For what? A pittance...his grocery money.

Schmitt rested his arms on the edge of the bed and leaned in. "What do the doctors tell you, Otto? Your condition...is it...I mean, will you soon get well? How long will you need to stay here?" Otto reached over and stroked Schmitt's face. "A few more days. They said I had a mild concussion. They need to be sure, so lots of tests. Tiring."

"And your arm?"

"My wrist...broke. Fractured my forearm. They will heal in time, I hope. Before the good Lord takes me."

A singsong voice behind Schmitt interrupted the conversation. "Oh, Mister Buchmann, I see you're a lucky man this morning. Two visitors in an hour."

Schmitt straightened but kept his back to the voice.

Otto shot an annoyed look at the orderly standing in the doorway. "I am not yet finished with my breakfast, Chantal. Please. Come back in a while." Chantal disappeared without responding. "Always, hurry, hurry. Like they have someplace to go." Otto laughed.

Schmitt lifted Otto's hand and kissed it. He was pleased the old man kept his sense of humor. He hoped the hospital would not release him before he was well enough to care for himself. He felt guilty about leaving him, but he needed to get back to Germany.

They remained silent for several minutes before Schmitt stood. "Otto, I must go now. My flight to Munich leaves this afternoon." He leaned over the old man and embraced him.

When he pulled away, a single tear rolled down the man's cheek. "I will call you in a few days, after I return. To see how you are doing. Yes?"

"God bless you, Werner. I am sad your visit is so short, but I am happy you came. Come back again, *ja*?"

He rode the elevator down to the lobby, exited the hospital through the revolving doors and walked south.

The clerk of a sporting goods store on Wyckoff Avenue rolled up the shutters, preparing for business. Schmitt watched from across the avenue until the man finished turning on lights and was ready to receive customers.

A short time later, Schmitt exited the store wearing his new black, hooded sweatshirt and a New York Mets baseball cap. He turned up Wyckoff, walking at a slow pace as though he was looking for something. After covering several blocks, he stopped in front of a barbershop and looked through the window. A short, barrel-chested black man stood in front of his cash register, counting out bills and slapping them into slots within the register's open drawer. Schmitt entered, and the man looked up, surprised to see his first customer so early.

"Are you open?" Schmitt asked.

The man blinked. "Yes, yes, come in. Be with you in a moment."

Schmitt sat in a chair against the wall and took off his Mets cap. Taking a *Playboy* magazine from the small table next to him, he flipped open to the centerfold. He closed the magazine immediately when the barber signaled to him from the first of three chairs.

"Ready for you, my man."

Schmitt remained quiet while the barber tied on the green apron. Fingering the sparse cover of hair on top of Schmitt's head, the man leaned over and asked, "How'd you like it cut?"

"All off."

"You mean like a crewcut?"

"No. Shaved clean, please."

The barber moved in front of Schmitt and raised his eyebrows. "You sure?"

"Yes, then I'd like you to shave off my mustache."

The barber shrugged. "You're the boss, bro."

* * *

Rizzo checked his watch. Eight o'clock in the morning and his cell phone demanded his attention. He flushed the toilet and moved to the coffee table next to the unmade pullout sofa bed to grab the ringing instrument. He needed to change his ringtone. This one grated on his nerves.

The caller's number was unfamiliar. "Yeah, Rizzo here."

"Hey, mon, it's Jabba. How you be this morning?"

Rizzo's mind went on alert. Was Jabba calling to tell him Schmitt had returned to the apartment? "Talk to me, my friend," Rizzo said.

"Well, after last night, I got thinking."

"About what?"

There was a pause before Jabba answered. "About this whole shitpot deal...you know...like you chasing this spooky dude who supposed to kill lots of people."

Rizzo worried where the conversation was going. "Yeah, and so?"

"So I paid Otto a visit this morning at Wyckoff Hospital. Asked him about was there someone staying with him in his apartment. Like that. He said yes."

"Did he say who he was?"

"Yeah. The dude is the son of his old friend from Germany, here on business."

"Anything else?"

"Seems the man was born here, in this house...apartment on the second floor. Imagine that. Said he went back to Germany when he was little. Otto never saw him again."

Rizzo mulled over the information. He worried that Jabba might be having a problem accepting Schmitt as a dangerous threat. Would he get in his way if he returned to the building to set up a stakeout?

Jabba was saying something about watching TV. Rizzo almost missed it; busy thinking how to convince the Rasta the deal was legit.

"Came home from the hospital, turned on my television, watching the morning news, and there it was."

"There what was?" Rizzo asked. "What are you running on about, bro?"

"A photo of the dude...same one you showed me."

Rizzo exploded. "You saw his picture on the news?"

"Yeah, mon, the news. Channel two. Announcer guy say the man in the photo killed a bunch of people. The police hunting for him."

Rizzo expelled a mouthful of air. "God damn it!"

"What's that about, mon?"

"Nothing. Just letting go my frustrations."

"You frustrated? Why?"

"Because now the whole fucking city will be looking for him, and it's less likely he'll return to the apartment."

"That's good, isn't it?"

"Not good, my friend. I need to be the one who takes him down. Two of the people he killed were friends of mine. You understand?"

"Oh yeah, mon. Now I want to help. Okay?"

"Keep a watch on the apartment, that's how you can help. I'll be there around ten. If he shows before I do, don't try to hit him a home run. You hear? Call the police right away."

"Sure thing," Jabba replied with a chuckle.

* * *

Rizzo moved to the podium of Oscar's Brasserie in the Waldorf Astoria Hotel. The restaurant was packed with breakfast diners. He scanned the room. Before he could ask the smiling host for Amy Chatsworth's table, Rizzo spotted her at a four-top and weaved his way through a cluster of tables. He leaned over and pecked her on the cheek.

He took a seat opposite her. "Been here long?"

"Only a half-cup of coffee long. Five minutes."

He studied her brown eyes without speaking. He was surprised how clear they were, a long way from their bloodshot condition of yesterday. They telegraphed a certain wariness, and no doubt would remain so for some time. A beige cotton, long-sleeved turtleneck, the full collar folded down, hid the bruising on her neck. The long sleeves covered the marks on her wrists, and a skillful application of makeup made the raw discoloration on her cheek and the blackened area around her eye invisible.

"Did you sleep okay?" he asked.

Amy fiddled with her place setting, moving the fork, knife and spoon around like a three-card Monte dealer. She raised her eyes then lowered them, then raised them again.

"Amazing, but I did. I was too tired to do anything else."

"Get something to eat from room service?"

"Yes. Not much. I had no appetite."

Their server came to the table, exchanged a polite smile with Amy and asked, "Ready to order?" She glanced at both untouched menus. "Need more time?"

Amy tapped the menu cover. "We haven't looked yet. A few more minutes, if you don't mind."

"Take your time," the server responded with a wave of her hand. She disappeared among the chatter and din of the busy establishment.

"Did you accomplish what you set out to do last night?" Amy asked in a guarded tone.

Rizzo decided to be direct. "I did. I have a good idea where Schmitt might be going. An apartment in Brooklyn. He had been staying with an old friend of his father's. He might be going back there to pick up his passport, which I happen to have in my possession."

Amy's expression turned grim. She reached across the table. Covering his hand with hers, she said, "I really wish you wouldn't take any more risks. Can't you let Jack Fields and the FBI take over now?"

"I have, Amy," he lied, "but right now they're in the dark. They haven't a clue where to find Schmitt. Holding on to his passport at least guarantees he stays in the States."

She pulled back her hand and shot him a questioning look.

"Look, I don't want you to worry. I know what I'm doing."

Skepticism remained on her face. She picked up the menu. "Shall we order?"

After reading the restaurant's elaborate list of breakfast fare, Amy signaled to their passing server.

"What are you gonna have?" Rizzo asked, gazing at his opened menu.

"The Brasserie's famous Eggs Benedict."

"Sounds good to me."

They ate in silence. Rizzo had the feeling Amy was working herself up to discuss her departure with him. The busman cleared away the dishes, and while Amy filled their coffee cups from the carafe left on the table, Rizzo decided to open the subject.

"So, you're leaving today?"

"Yes. This evening, on British Air out of JFK."

"I'd like to take you to the—"

"It's not necessary, Luke. I have a limo picking me up at three o'clock."

Her voice was flat, her interruption curt, mystifying him. "Are you angry with me?"

She peered at him over her coffee cup. "No, silly. What makes you think that?"

"You sure?"

She paused before answering. Her mouth twisted and her brow furrowed, like someone trying to solve a crossword puzzle. "I'm not angry, Luke." She reached across again for his hand. "I guess I'm feeling guilty." A tinge of pain coated her tone.

He blinked, dazed by the admission. He looked around at nothing, hesitant to draw a hasty conclusion. "Feeling guilty about what? Leaving? Going home?"

Amy expelled a deep sigh. "Oh, Luke, I don't know. Maybe I'm worried you feel I misled you...gave you a sign about a possible future...I mean, with my behavior at the schoolhouse. I don't know what made me—"

"Amy, stop it, for Christ's sake," he shot back. "We're adults, aren't we? Isn't that what you told me?"

"Yes, but—"

"Then stop it."

They became silent, but their focus remained on each other's eyes for several seconds. Studying her, he recalled his many casual relationships and one-night stands, maneuvered purely for his own sexual gratification. He was often guilty of misleading women for his own purpose. Was Amy going through that type of guilt trip?

He leaned into the table and whispered, "Look, I never believed you thought of us as anything but two people mutually attracted to each other, sharing much-needed affection. I helped you...you helped me."

"Oh, God, I'm so relieved to hear that," Amy said. "Because last night while speaking with Avery, he dropped his stuffed shirt attitude and became the loving man I originally married. I realized I did love him, and I needed to return."

Hearing her words, Rizzo felt conflicted—a rush of disappointment and relief at the same time. The cloud over his relationship with Amy parted, her feelings out in the open, their future defined. Her sweetness and warmth, her charm, her sexiness, and her sense of humor had taken hold of him in a way he never expected. She had been right when she called him a romantic, but what was not to fall in love with?

"And he's agreed to see a doctor to be tested," she added with a note of excitement. "If he's the problem, he promised he'd be willing to adopt."

"What, a puppy?"

"No, you twit, a baby."

He caught the glowing expression on her face when she said the word, baby. Amy wanted to be a mother. He could picture her in the role. "Congratulations." He pushed back from the table and folded his arms.

Moisture muted the vivid golden color of her eyes. She reached up, brushed away the tear and forced herself to smile. "I can say," she began, "except for the last twenty-four hours, I am truly happy I came here, to spend this time with you. If circumstances had been different, maybe—"

"Hey, so am I."

Amy released a self-conscious laugh. "I'll wager you never expected the simple assignment I gave you to blossom into what happened. I certainly didn't."

Luke shrugged. "God, no. But I wish I could have prevented your father's murder."

"No one could have. You shouldn't assume any guilt. You couldn't possibly have known about Werner Schmitt."

"You're right. But I feel for you and the rest of the Bard family in New Brighton."

"I know you do. As I do," she said, lowering her eyes.

"And Jake Avon. He didn't deserve that fate."

"Well, perhaps he and my grandfather can take solace in the fact that after paying their debt in prison, they were allowed to live out their lives as they wanted to." Amy's hands formed a steeple in front of her mouth; her eyes glazed over, letting several moments go by. "I would like to have met my father."

"You'd have loved him, for sure. He was a sweet man."

The approach of the server halted their conversation. She placed the check on the corner of the table and asked, "Will there be anything else?"

"I think not. Thanks." Turning to Rizzo, she added, "And my thanks to you, Luke Rizzo."

He acknowledged her with a smile.

"Which reminds me, I believe we need to settle our bill. Why don't you post your statement after you complete your accounting? I'll get a check off straight away."

Rizzo glanced at his watch. "Okay, but I have to get going." He stood and moved around to her side of the table. Without warning, he leaned over, his face inches from her nose. "I expect to provide a dividend on your investment pretty soon. I'll call you in London when we have it."

Amy knitted her brow and looked up at him with concerned eyes. "Luke, remember. You promised. Jack Fields...the FBI. Let them—"

His mouth on hers prevented her from finishing. He was gone before she could catch her breath.

Chapter 26

"Hold on a second, Tom." Jack Fields pushed the hold button on the console and pressed the intercom. "Yes, Rachel?"

"Jack, Special Agent Brancuso on two. He says it's important."

Fields switched back to the Saugerties Police Lieutenant. "Gotta go, Tom. Thanks for the heads-up. I'll have Tony visit the Enterprise garage today, to see what info he can get off the contract. Keep you posted." The agent jumped to line two. "Ralph, what's up?"

"Hey, seems our guy was made by someone up this way."

"Schmitt?"

"Yeah, the taxi dispatcher at the Albany Metro-North station identified the bastard. One of his drivers dropped him off at a motel last night. The dispatcher spotted Schmitt's mug shot on TV this morning. He called the State Police barracks and they called us."

Fields shook his head in disbelief. "He had us convinced he was heading in our direction. The son-of-a-bitch faked us out."

"Something else," Brancuso said. "This one will frost your *cojones*. When they searched his motel room, they found a waitress from a nearby restaurant on the floor—dead. Not sure yet how she died. Troopers think asphyxiation…a pillow over her face. She had red splotches in the eyes and on her face."

"Who was she? Someone he knew?"

"A local woman. About all they could say." Brancuso let go a snicker. "I'm fucking amazed. This guy's a killing machine."

"He learned well in Germany," Fields said.

"One more thing. He skipped out on the motel early this morning without paying and boosted a Camry from the parking lot."

"So there's no telling which direction he's heading?"

"Nope. Could be Canada, for all anyone knows. We have the Camry's specs and license number. We'll email you the info. Troopers got an APB out so maybe we'll catch a break before he gets too far."

"Hope so," Fields said. "I swear, if this dirt bag slips out of the country, I'll never hear the end of it from Karl."

Brancuso chuckled. "I know how that tune goes. Remember the World Trade Center bombing in '93? We missed Mohammad Salameh. If the fucking moron hadn't tried to get back his $400 deposit on the rental van, we might have been shit-out-of luck. Stevenson never let up on me for over a year. He's the reason I put in for the transfer."

Fields let Brancuso's commentary on Karl Stevenson pass without a response.

"Listen, Ralph, you get more information on Schmitt, let me know right away. Okay?"

"You got it, Jack."

"Thanks, Ralph."

After disconnecting, Fields hit the intercom button. "Rachel, ask Tony to come in. I have a small project for him."

* * *

"This guy must be a popular person."

Condon gave the Enterprise agent a quizzical look. "Why would you say that?"

The agent handed Condon the printout. "You're the second person to ask about this customer in the last two days."

"Yeah? Who else was asking?"

"Yesterday, a cop came by wanting to know about this guy."

"A cop? NYPD?"

"That's right. Showed me his detective badge. Didn't say why he was checking on the guy. Only wanted to confirm the address on the rental form. That's all."

Could Rizzo be one-step ahead of them again? If he is, Fields will go into orbit. Especially with Rizzo identifying himself illegally as an active detective.

"When was that?" Condon asked.

"Late yesterday afternoon, end of my shift. Gave him the address on the contract. After that, he left."

Certain it was Rizzo, Condon asked anyway. "You remember what he looked like?"

"Who? The renter?"

"No." Condon snapped. He almost added, *you schmuck!* He held his tongue. "The damn cop."

"Dark, thick hair, about six feet. A nice looking guy," the agent added. "Reminded me of Dean Martin."

Condon caught the twinkle in the agent's eyes when he offered the last bit of data.

"Anything else?"

The Enterprise agent stared at him then shrugged. "You mean about the guy's looks?"

Condon clenched his teeth. The rental agent was playing with him. "No," he answered. "Did he say anything about the contract...about the renter?"

"Oh, he did show me a photo of the man. Asked if I recognized him."

"And did you?"

"I thought so, but I couldn't be sure. Then he asked me if he had a German accent. Who is this guy, a spy?"

Condon ignored the question. "Anything else?"

The agent looked down at the computer screen for several seconds. When he looked up, he wore a pleased expression. "Yes, sir. The car was abandoned somewhere upstate. The police retrieved it. The Kingston Enterprise office picked it up. It's been put back into our system."

"Oh, praise the Lord." Condon smiled and slipped out the door, happy to be gone.

Outside the rental office, Condon punched in Fields' direct dial number. "Here's what I got," he said when the agent answered. "An address on Harman Street, Bushwick, Brooklyn. Could be a phony, but that's what's listed on the rental contract."

"Okay, that's the Eighty-third Precinct. I'll notify the local precinct commander," Fields said, "so he won't get his nose out of joint. Stay put. Paul Meyers will pick you up in fifteen with the car. Call me when you get there."

Condon walked into a Starbucks at the corner of Third Avenue and ordered two containers of coffee. When the Town Car eased to the curb, Condon slipped in and handed one of the coffees to Meyers. The agent looked at the container as though he had never seen a Starbucks coffee before. "I would have preferred a Mocha Grande," he said.

"Screw you," Condon answered with a smirk. "Just drive."

"Bushwick, Brooklyn?"

"Yeah. Harman Street. You know how to get there?"

Paul Meyers, ten years younger than Condon, shot him a look of disbelief. "With my eyes closed. You forget. I was raised next door, in Ridgewood."

"That's Queens, isn't it?"

"Both. It borders Bushwick."

"What the hell do I know? I grew up in Massachusetts."

Meyers navigated the local traffic toward the Queens Midtown Tunnel. They drove in silence through the eastbound mile-and-a-quarter tube until they reached the Queens side. Crossing the Pulaski Bridge, they headed into Brooklyn.

Condon, thinking of the trail of bodies left by Werner Schmitt, asked Meyers if he had ever killed anyone in the line of duty.

After a thoughtful moment, Meyers said, "Not with the Bureau, but in Nam…a few dead gooks in the jungle. Why do you ask?"

"I was thinking. If we end up in a firefight with this guy… which I don't think we will…but if we do, and you have a clear shot, don't hesitate. Take him down."

Meyers turned off Myrtle onto Central and slowed to the curb after going four blocks to Harman Street.

Condon checked his watch. "Jesus, you made great time. You do know your way around this neck of the woods."

"I told you. Like a native."

Condon looked up at the Harman Street sign. "Which way?"

"I think it's to the right."

Condon pointed to a police car parked halfway down the block. "That must be it."

Meyers stopped behind the cruiser. They exited the Lincoln, and Condon walked to the blue-and-white's driver-side. The uniformed officer rolled down his window as Condon flipped open his ID wallet and flashed it. Ducking down to the driver's level, Condon said, "Hey, guys, thanks for the support. We need to verify if someone we're looking for is staying in this building. Shouldn't take long."

The driver nodded without turning his head. "Be right here if you need help."

"Thanks." Condon walked to the building entrance and examined the names on the occupant pad. He pushed the ringer belonging to Saint James, apartment 1-A. "Seems like a good place to start," he told Meyers, who hovered over his shoulder.

Condon waited for the buzz that would release the front door lock. When no answer came, he looked to the next name on the pad: Buchmann. He reached to press the ringer but stopped when the front door opened.

"Yeah, mon, what you want?"

Condon stepped back, bumping against Meyers. He examined the large Rastafarian filling the doorway, dreadlocks dangling from beneath his Rasta cap, and guessed he was Saint James, the occupant of 1-A. He flipped open his ID wallet.

"Special Agents Condon and Meyers, FBI. Are you Mr. Saint James?"

The Rasta hesitated, his face full of suspicion. "That's right. Jabai Saint James," he said. "Something wrong?"

Condon reached into his inside jacket pocket and removed an envelope. He extracted a photo of Werner Schmitt. "We're looking for this man. We have reason to believe he might be staying in an apartment in this building."

The man gave the photo a cursory look. "That so?"

Condon knew the answer to his next question. Law enforcement was the enemy in this neighborhood. No one volunteered information, but he asked anyway.

"Have you seen him in this building at any time or anywhere around the neighborhood?"

The Rasta shook his head. His manner came off as deliberately deadpan.

Condon looked at the name pad again. "There are six apartments. We need to speak with the other residents in the building. You know who they are, and they know you. Right?"

"That's right, mon."

"Well, how about you coming along with us? You know… to break the ice when we knock on their doors? Can you do that? You have time to help us out?"

"Sure. Don't go to work 'til later."

"What do you do?" Condon asked.

"Janitorial services...the courthouse over on Myrtle Avenue."

"Nice. Well, let's begin with the other apartment on this floor."

"Not home. Mugged a few days ago. Otto ended up in the hospital."

"Oh? I'm sorry. That would be Otto Buchmann?" he asked, pointing to the name pad.

Saint James nodded. "Old man. Been living here years."

Meyers remained at the front door while the Rastafarian accompanied Condon up the stairs. Condon was glad he thought to ask the Rasta to come along. Jabai's familiar appearance put each tenant at ease.

The woman in 2-B was at work, but after Condon questioned the remaining three occupants in the building, he was convinced Schmitt had used the address as a cover. Yet Otto Buchmann was German. That nagged him. Did he know the Stasi? He would look into that. Maybe pay Buchmann a visit in the hospital.

* * *

Schmitt reached Harman Street and Central Avenue and turned the corner. He stopped walking when he spotted a police cruiser parked in front of Otto's apartment house. He crossed to the other side of Central Avenue and yanked up the hood of his sweatshirt over his Mets cap. After tightening the drawstrings to hide his face, he walked at a fast pace up Central. His heart raced. He stopped at the entrance of a Catholic church to catch his breath and looked back over his shoulder. The police cruiser had turned the corner and was heading in his direction. Schmitt dashed up the church steps, through the door into the darkened vestibule, and past the holy water urn into the body of the church.

After a furtive look around, he slipped into a pew, sliding down the long wooden bench to the opposite end. He leaned forward, bent his head feigning prayer and listened, expecting to hear the cruiser's wailing siren. Nothing but silence. Several moments later, he sat up and scanned the surrounding pews and church interior.

An intermittent series of pillars and arches lined both sides of the church, leading up to the altar. Schmitt leaned back, his eyes taking in the half dozen parishioners scattered about, steeped in their daily devotionals. A white-robed priest moved across the elevated platform, lighting candelabras and rearranging holy objects in preparation for evening services.

Schmitt's normal breathing had returned. For the first time in a long while, he felt strangely relaxed. He fixed his attention on the ornate table with a gold crucifix sitting on top of a gold tabernacle box, then lifted his head and studied the five half-moon shaped, stained-glass windows high in the dome above the altar. He thought the church was similar to the Lutheran one of his youth.

From the corner of his eye, he caught sight of an elderly woman standing in the center aisle at the end of his pew. She was glaring at him, gesturing several times with one hand. He stared back, puzzling her meaning, until her message broke though. Reaching up, he pulled the hood and Mets cap off his head. She nodded with approval and left the church through the vestibule.

With his hood off, he felt vulnerable, worried about being recognized. His newly shaven appearance would help. He needed someplace to wait until dark so that he could slip back into Otto's apartment unseen. Could he remain in the church that long without attracting attention?

"Good evening, my son."

The voice came from the left. Schmitt jerked his head around and looked up into the face of a bearded priest dressed in street clothes. He was holding a stack of books in his arms.

"Forgive me for interrupting your meditation. I am Father Joaquin, St. Barbara's pastor. Are you new to the parish? I don't think I've seen you here before."

The priest's warm smile caught Schmitt by surprise. Swallowing hard, he felt a stab of chest pain. He realized that the last twenty-four hours had pushed his heart condition to the edge several times.

"No, Father. I am visiting a friend in the area. I was passing your beautiful church and wanted to see inside."

"Well, you're about two hours early for this evening's services. You're welcome to stay as long as you like," the pastor offered.

"Thank you, Father."

The priest remained standing at the end of the pew, looking down at Schmitt. The solemn expression on the cleric's face signaled he had more to say.

"My son, if you need a place to stay for a while, the parish supports a homeless shelter over on Wilson Avenue. The Salvation Army runs it. Go there. You'll find good food and a clean bed." Father Joaquin produced a soft smile and started toward the altar along the ambulatory.

Schmitt pulled his nitroglycerin spray from his pocket, removed the plastic cap and sprayed the back of his throat.

* * *

Rizzo sucked air into his lungs before he turned the key. He pushed open his office door and fell back against the corridor wall, remaining in that position until he was certain no danger awaited him on the other side. He released his breath and peered inside. His eyes panned to every corner of the small space. The closet door stood open, as he had left it on Monday, and the safe looked undisturbed.

He circled the room, looking for signs that Schmitt might have returned. Finding none, he sat at his desk and activated his message machine. There were seven from the past five days, mostly from sales representatives of security companies selling products and services. The seventh message, a woman's voice, caused him to sit up straight.

"Hi there, darlin', it's Flo. I hope this call doesn't scare you. Nothing wrong. I'm calling to get some information. You see…ah…my company, Avis, wants to promote me to…to supervisor, would you believe. The one catch is…now don't get nervous, darlin'. The job would be in New York at their LaGuardia operations."

Rizzo stared at the machine, smiling. The message continued.

"Since you're the only person I know from there, naturally I thought of you. Haven't accepted the job yet…besides it wouldn't be for another month anyhow. Meanwhile, maybe you know of a few nice areas near the airport where I could find a one-bedroom apartment. That's all, hon. You have my home phone. Give me a call when you can. No hurry. Speak with you later."

Rizzo erased the first six of the seven messages left on his machine. When he had the seventh one cued, he played it several times, allowing the sound of Flo's warm southern voice to wash over him like a much needed whirlpool treatment. She was coming to New York, transferred by Avis to LaGuardia. He could not stop smiling.

A rap on the locked office door brought him back to the present. He reached under his jacket for his holstered .38 and stood. Any other time, the door would be unlocked, and his response would have been a simple, "Come in." With Schmitt on the loose, Rizzo wasn't taking chances.

He moved to the side when he heard the rattle of someone trying the door. Several seconds passed before he called out, "Who's there." The answer surprised him.

"Luke Rizzo? Agent Tony Condon. I need to speak with you."

Rizzo holstered the snubbie and unlocked the door. He pulled it open and stepped back. "Come in, Tony. Sorry for the wait."

Condon was alone. Rizzo went on the alert. He had never seen Condon without Fields present.

"What's up?"

Condon ignored Rizzo's outstretched hand and walked into the room. "We got a problem, and the problem is you."

It was an easy guess that Condon had been to the Enterprise garage. The Federal agent was pissed that Rizzo had beaten him to it.

Rizzo squinted at the agent. "Me? What are you talking about?"

Condon looked around, his attention settling on the small sofa against the wall. "You want to do this standing, or should we sit down?"

Rizzo gestured toward the sofa. "Have a seat. Obviously, you got something to say. No sense standing if it's that important." He rolled out his chair from behind the desk, pushed it close to the sofa and sat down. "So, how have I become a problem?"

Condon's face was drawn and his jaw locked tight, anger in his eyes. Rizzo imagined him as a Marine drill instructor at Paris Island, prepared to tear the ass off a poor hapless recruit.

"You've overstepped your responsibilities to your client," Condon said. "You've become a liability to the Bureau. We want you to knock it off. Simple as that."

Rizzo knew what Condon referred to, and he didn't give a shit. "You mean finding Jake Avon so we could warn him? Listen, pal, if we hadn't, you think you guys would have bothered?"

Condon jumped to his feet. "God damned right we would have." He looked down at Rizzo with popped-out eyes. "Why the fuck you think we were at the Saugerties Precinct when you called, Jack? We were there to take Avon into protective custody until we could nail Schmitt. That's why, hot shot. But you let the old guy disappear." Condon remained glaring down at Rizzo, his clenched fists at his sides.

A shroud of guilt suddenly blanketed Rizzo. Condon was right. He should have involved the Feds right after he had searched the hotel registers at the Historical Society. At that point, impressing Amy Chatsworth with his sleuthing skills was more important. Jake Avon might be alive if he had alerted Fields and Condon.

Then again, maybe not.

Condon paused to take a deep breath. He sat back down. "Look, Rizzo, I understand this case is bizarre. Nobody could have guessed Werner Schmitt would be seeking revenge after fifty-eight years. But I need a few straight answers."

Rizzo was glad Condon hadn't taken a swing at him. Getting into a fistfight with an FBI agent would not have enhanced the future of his private security company.

"Okay, Tony. What is it you want to know?"

"For starters, explain your visit yesterday to Enterprise Rental in Manhattan."

"What about it?"

"Rizzo, I like you, and I'm not blowing smoke. You were a good cop. That much was clear from your NYPD dossier."

"Been checking on me, have you?"

Condon did not respond. "You delivered like a champ with your client, Amy Chatsworth. Found her father for her."

"Got him killed, don't forget."

"Okay, I get it. I know you feel responsible. And you're determined to make up for it by nailing Werner Schmitt yourself."

Rizzo kept quiet. He could guess why Condon was there, and what really bothered the Federal Bureau.

"Tell me something. How'd you find out that Schmitt rented his car from the Enterprise location? Because if Jack Fields finds out Lange fed you that info before he told us, he's going to cite the two of you for interfering with a Bureau investigation."

No way was Rizzo giving up Tom Lange. Instead, he challenged Condon. "Come on, Tony. Give me a little credit. The fucking rental car up at Jake's cabin. All I did was take down the license number. An easy find through my contacts on the NYPD. Doesn't take a rocket scientist—"

"Okay, okay. You're right. You check out the address in Bushwick?"

Rizzo couldn't hide that. "Yeah, a phony. Nobody in the building knew anything. They hadn't seen or heard of Schmitt."

Condon leaned forward, his arms on his knees as if he was going to reveal a big secret. "You speak with that guy in the ground floor apartment...1A?"

"You mean the Jamaican? Yeah, I did. Didn't know shit, but then he wouldn't say even if he knew something."

"How about the German family, first floor back?"

"Nobody home when I was there."

Condon rose and walked to the door. "Okay, we're done here. You got the message. Stand down. Do not meddle. This is a Federal matter. That's advice from a friend. Take it." Before he closed the door behind him, he added, "And don't bite my hand."

Rizzo sat quietly thinking about the agent's admonition. Had he been too pigheaded by not getting the Feds involved sooner? Could it have prevented the death of Jake Avon? He doubted it. Jake died from a bad ticker. It could have prevented the Stasi's killing of the Saugerties police officer at the schoolhouse. That incensed him. So did Amy's frightening narrow escape at the hands of Schmitt.

If only the goddamn agents had hung in there instead of bailing out when they did. Well, no use laboring the point. He had learned something on the Job a long time ago: you can't always depend on others. If you do it yourself, the job gets done right.

He glanced at the safe on the floor of the closet where he had locked away Schmitt's passport. He returned to his desk, hit the speakerphone and dialed.

"Hey, Jabba, Luke Rizzo here. Be there in a couple of hours. Wait for me."

Chapter 27

Schmitt found the homeless shelter on Wilson Avenue. Lounging street people—both male and female—propped up against the building's old, reddish stone façade, littered the sidewalk in front of the abandoned grade school. He approached the entrance warily. He might be making a mistake. He passed several of the tattered and bedraggled homeless sitting on the stained concrete. The stink of urine reached his nostrils. He held his breath until he stepped through the doorway into the lobby area.

A long table sat to the left and, behind it, a lone black woman in a Salvation Army uniform. Schmitt had read of this charity organization and had seen pictures of their uniformed officers and soldiers. This was the first time he had seen one in person. She was a large woman with skin hue that reminded him of the dark Swiss chocolate of his youth. He recognized the lieutenant bars on her collar and assumed she was the person in charge. He approached the table.

The officer looked up and exchanged smiles with him. Her white teeth lit her face like a sixty-watt bulb.

"Hello," she said. "What can I do for you?" Her tone was sincere, her smile genuine, putting Schmitt at ease.

"I would like food and a place to stay for a while. I have not eaten in two days," he lied.

The woman slid a clipboard across the table. "Can you write?"

He blinked. The question surprised him.

"You need to fill this out. Is that a problem?"

He understood immediately and shook his head. "No, I read and write English."

"Good." She handed him a ballpoint pen. "Complete the brief form and we'll get you enrolled." She motioned for him to sit in the chair near the end of the long table. "What country are you from?" she asked, while Schmitt studied the clipboard.

He looked up, frozen for a moment, but responded with the first name that popped into his head. "Austria." he said with a tightening of his voice.

"Vienna?"

"No, no. Bad Hofgastein, in the mountains," remembering the name of the ski area where he had vacationed fifteen years ago. He pictured their famous thermal baths and sighed.

The lieutenant nodded as though she knew the location. "Someday I'd like to visit your country."

Schmitt smiled. He filled in the form using a false name and inventing a last known address. He left blank the line that indicated the amount of his donation and handed her the clipboard.

She looked over the form and asked, "Do you have any money on you?"

The question stopped him. "Yes. I have fifteen dollars."

"Well, that's not enough to expect a donation. When you get on your feet again," she said, sounding cheerfully optimistic, "maybe you'll come back and make a small one to the shelter."

Schmitt bobbed his head. "Yes, I will."

She reached into a cigar box at her side and withdrew a round, plastic disk with a three-digit number imprinted on the face. "Take this, go down the hall that way," she said, pointing with her long index finger. "Keep the disk on you. It's your ID pass to the mess hall. See Pablo at the door. He'll make sure you get a meal. After you eat, he'll show you the men's dormitory and assign you a bed."

"Thank you," Schmitt said.

Before he walked away, the Lieutenant cautioned, "Doors get locked up at ten. And keep your shoes on when you go to sleep."

Schmitt stared back at her.

"Keep your money in one of them. It's not much, but you never know."

* * *

Condon sensed his partner's continued annoyance while they waited for the elevator on the twenty-third floor of 26 Federal Plaza. The doors opened and they stepped into the empty car. He pressed the button for the basement garage.

Fields turned to him. "When did Rizzo go there?"

"The Enterprise agent told me yesterday."

Fields shook his head. "Through his NYPD connections, right? That would be logical. Those guys have a tight fraternity, even with the ones on the outside, like Rizzo."

The car descended in silence and without stopping. Most of the business occupants of the building were long gone. FBI employees were always the last to leave, many remaining until late, working on current assignments.

After they moved off the elevator onto the garage floor, Fields stopped and turned. "He checked out the apartment building and tenants and found nothing there to connect with Schmitt?" Facing Condon, he waited for an answer.

Earlier, Condon had reported the visit he made to the detective's office. Fields had not reacted then. Clearly, he had given the matter a lot of thought since. Rizzo's behavior bothered him.

"That's what he claims. Not every tenant, but a few. I interviewed all but one. Not home, an old German guy in the hospital. Nobody knew anything or remembered seeing Schmitt in the building. According to the Jamaican on the first floor, a recent mugging put the old German guy in 1-B in the hospital."

"You check that out with the local precinct?"

"I did. My written report is on your desk."

"I'll look it over in the morning."

Condon nodded and started for his car. "Night, Jack."

Fields' voice stopped him. "Maybe you should speak with that German tenant in the hospital. Schmitt is German, remember."

Condon stopped and turned. "I've already thought of that, Jack. I plan to visit him in the morning."

"Oh, and another thing," Fields said. "Ask the Bushwick precinct commander if he'd have his patrol keep an eye on that building. If the old guy isn't there, he needs to alert us if they see lights on in—"

"Jack, for Christ sake. Go home. I've already done that. I'm way ahead of you."

Fields laughed. "Good. Stay there."

* * *

Using the M subway line from Manhattan, Rizzo made the trip to Bushwick, Brooklyn, in less than forty minutes. The night had a winter chill to it. He pushed his hands into the pockets of his Army surplus jacket and picked his way through the streets of Bushwick from the Myrtle Avenue station. In the '40s, '50s and early '60s, the neighborhood had seen a more prosperous time. He could see signs of resurgence, but real change was at least a decade away before Bushwick could reclaim its position as a "nice place to live."

Rizzo pressed the bell to Jabba's apartment and waited. Jabba opened the front door. His face beamed from ear to ear. Rizzo had seen the Rasta smile before, but the gold tooth on the right side of Jabba's mouth jumped out at him like a spotlight.

"Hey, bro, close your mouth. You're blinding me."

Jabba stepped back. "Funny, mon. That tooth's my annuity. 'Spect gold to skyrocket in five years, ya know."

Rizzo slipped by and stopped at Jabba's opened apartment door. "You ready to do a little stakeout?"

"Come in," Jabba said. "Got something interesting to tell you."

Rizzo entered the small living area and looked around at the sparse furnishings. A round pedestal table with two bentwood chairs nestled against the street-facing window. The Rasta's entertainment center consisted of a thirty-six inch Sony TV on a rickety TV stand. A large, patched beanbag chair sat on the floor in front it. A small table with a lamp to one side of the entryway was loaded with magazines and a few paperbacks tucked between a pair of bookends. The Rasta's baseball bat leaned against the wall on the opposite side of the door. Jabba lived a cautious but uncomplicated life.

"How long you been here in this place?" Rizzo asked.

"Ten years. Why?"

Rizzo laughed. "You need a few more sticks of furniture, bro. Where do you expect all your guests to sit?"

"Don't get a lot of guests, mon. How many chairs you need?"

"Heard the Feds visited you today."

"Yeah. Told them nothing 'cept about Otto. Checked out the other apartments. Same."

Rizzo gestured toward the window. "That's where you keep watch on this place?"

"When I'm home."

Rizzo moved to the table, took off his jacket and sat down. The Venetian blind over the window had several broken slats. From his position, Rizzo could monitor anyone entering or leaving the building. At the same time, anyone outside the window would have little trouble seeing in while it was still daylight. Not the perfect situation for a stakeout.

Jabba sat in the second chair and leaned into the table on his elbows. He had picked up on Rizzo's concern.

"Gonna have to wait 'til dark, right?"

"Yeah, bro, real dark. That's what our killer's going to do."

Rizzo reached over and spread apart several slats. The white halogen street lamp at the curb bathed the sidewalk and building entrance in its glow. Rizzo squinted through the blind.

"With the lights out in here, wouldn't matter if they're opened or closed."

"I got a feelin' he gonna come tonight."

Rizzo twisted toward Jabba. "How's that?"

"I say, I think he's gonna come tonight."

"Why? You saw him today?"

"I didn't, but one of my guys thinks he did," Jabba said with an expression that gave Rizzo another shot at the gold. "Earlier today, a man checks in the homeless shelter over on Wilson. This friend sees him go in. He knows everyone in that shelter. Anybody new, he would spot."

"How the hell did your friend know him? I mean, how would he recognize Werner Schmitt, the killer?"

"Hey, they have TV over there…at the shelter. He saw the dude on the news, like I did. Only problem is, the man he saw at the shelter don't have a mustache. Had on a Mets ballcap and a black sweatshirt."

"So how the hell did he make the connection?"

"Said his features exactly like the guy on TV. He could tell."

Rizzo stared at the Rasta, trying to decide if he believed him.

"Look, this guy used to draw faces…you know…in charcoal…at street fairs…for ten bucks. Made a good livin' that way, once. He's good, but there ain't no street fairs no more…least not around here."

"And he thinks the guy is Schmitt…even without a mustache?"

"Like I say, he studied the man's features. Came by here all excited. Wanted to know should he go to the police."

"Does he know I'm looking for him?"

Jabba hesitated. He flashed his toothy grin again. "Yeah, but he don't know who you are. I told him someone…besides the police…wanted to find him. So to keep his trap shut."

"Bro, I hope he listens to you."

"He will. I trust him." He tilted his head and nodded, as though needing to emphasize his sincerity.

Rizzo looked at the Rasta and studied his expression. Jabba's dreadlocks had cascaded over the right side of his face, partially covering that eye. The result gave him a menacing effect. Rizzo remembered the Rastafarian practice of wearing dreadlocks put off many of his former NYPD brethren. The image was foreign to them, always guarded where Rastafarians were concerned. For sure, none had ever met Jabba.

"You trust me, bro?" Rizzo asked.

"Yeah, I do. I know good people when I see 'em."

Rizzo thought about the turn of events that led him here. Providence had surely put the Rasta into the picture. Jabba was good people, too. Rizzo was certain if the situation with Schmitt ended the right way, he would have his new friend to thank.

"He gonna call when the man leaves the shelter," Jabba said.

"Who?"

"My friend. Night guard gonna let him use the phone in the office."

"Then we better lay out how this should go down."

"I'm ready," Jabba said.

Chapter 28

The lights in the large dormitory room dimmed. Schmitt closed his eyes, but never intended to sleep. The school building's old heating system pumped steam through the floor vents, creating a sauna-like atmosphere. Perspiration trickled from his underarms. The fact that he was fully clothed wasn't helping. The Beretta tucked into his waistband under his sweatshirt jabbed him in the ribs, but he dared not remove it. He needed to stay alert and heed the Salvation Army lieutenant's warning about protecting his valuables.

None of the homeless he had passed earlier on the sidewalk had remained outside the building. They occupied most of the beds, and a nasal symphony of snorting and snoring filled the pungent air like a series of cloudbursts. He held his watch to his face. Six minutes before they would lock the doors to anyone not yet in the building. He planned to stay put until well into the night. Getting out through the doors would not be a problem.

"Hey, old man, you gotta be hotter than hell in that shirt."

Startled, Schmitt's hand slipped under the sweatshirt and onto the Beretta's grip. He turned up on his elbow and looked at the man in the next bed.

"Take off your shirt, stuff it under your ass, you worried 'bout somebody filching it."

Schmitt hesitated. He had no desire to encourage a conversation with this total stranger. "I am fine," he snapped.

"Shit, it's gotta be eighty degrees in here."

Schmitt ignored him and rolled to his other side. The homeless man got the message. He offered no further comment.

With his eyes closed again, Schmitt drifted into thoughts of what he needed to accomplish. His angina condition troubled him. He worried his spray would run out before he could make it back to Germany. That would put him at serious risk of a heart attack. Moreover, if he had any chance of getting out of the country, he had to get back into Otto's apartment. He needed the backup passport supporting his present shaved appearance.

He would remain in the shelter until early morning, when he could slip out without being seen. After leaving Otto's apartment, he would need to find a car he could hot wire for his transportation to JFK. He knew the usual density of vehicles at the airport's long-term parking lot would swallow up the car and allow it to go unnoticed for hours.

"Your first time here?"

Schmitt turned and glared through the dim light at the homeless man in the next bed. He worried the vagrant could become a problem. "Please! I am trying to sleep."

The man rolled the other way and muttered over his shoulder, "Fuck you."

Schmitt fixed his eyes on the beams at the ceiling. A blanket of drowsiness covered him as he fought the urge to drift off. The heat in the dormitory made it hard to stay awake. He hoped the street person next to him did not have that problem.

Forty-five minutes later, Schmitt welcomed the snorting sounds coming from his neighbor. He had another two and a half hours before he would make his move.

The image of poor Otto in the hospital room crept into his thoughts. He was glad he had visited his father's old friend yesterday, knowing he would never see him again. Otto would be long gone before he could come back to the States, if ever. Before leaving the apartment, he would have to remember to return the old man's Beretta to the drawer in the night table.

* * *

The only illumination came from the small *ON* light of the Mister Coffee sitting on the counter in the Pullman kitchen. Jabba moved to the table at the window with the coffee carafe and poured a third refill into Rizzo's cup.

"No more for me," Rizzo said. He pushed the cup away. "I'm wired enough."

"You want to snooze?" Jabba asked, pulling out the second chair. "I'll wake you when my friend calls."

Rizzo looked at his watch. Not quite midnight. "Thanks. I don't think that would be smart. Besides, that bean bag chair doesn't look too comfortable."

Jabba motioned toward the bedroom. "Hey, mon, use my bed."

"No, I'm okay. Thanks. I'll just sit here."

Rizzo thought about the endless stakeouts he had endured during the years on the Job. The hours staring through binoculars into apartment windows, freezing on cold city nights in darkened hallways, waiting for a drug suspect to emerge from a tenement in Spanish Harlem, or sitting in his Mustang Cobra on steamy mornings watching a drug deal go down on the opposite corner, not his favorite part of the Job. The pain of all that boredom and discomfort evaporated quickly once he made a collar. Nothing in his everyday life satisfied him more than the thrill of the hunt and the capture of a drug dealer. He missed that.

"You don't have to work tonight?" Rizzo asked, remembering Jabba had a night job with a cleaning crew at the local courthouse.

"Nah. Phoned in sick after you called."

"Sorry to lose you a day's pay. I'll make good when this is over. Okay?"

"That be okay, but I make two-hundred an hour." He laughed and slapped his large palm on the tabletop. "Can you afford that?"

"That's more than Bob Marley made doing concerts."

"You never heard me sing."

"You ever see Marley perform?"

"Yeah. Lots. Last time about twelve years ago, before he died. A concert in Kingston. You like reggae?"

"Not really. I'm more into John Coltrane, Miles Davis and Dave Brubeck. You know that form of jazz?"

"Yeah, of course."

Jabba fell silent. Rizzo could see the outline of the Rasta's tangled hair in the slivers of light coming through the blinds. He had his head locked in the direction of the phone with a finger twisting one of the curls in a nervous tell.

"What's the matter, bro? You worried about something?"

"What? No...no. I mean, I was thinking maybe my friend fucked up...let on to the dude he was watching him."

Jabba was getting edgy.

"You think he should be here by now? It's not yet midnight."

"Yeah, well—"

Rizzo reached over and pulled the cord, raising the blinds half way. "Lots of people still on the street. Relax. He won't make his move until later. Less chance of being seen."

"Probably right, mon."

"Tell you what, bro. No point in risking it. I'll go into the old man's apartment and wait there. Keep the lights off here, and move back from the window so you can't be seen from the outside." Rizzo stood and took his jacket from the back of the chair. "When your friend calls, ring me on my cell. If he doesn't call, and you spot the bad guy approaching the front entrance, dial my cell, two rings then hang up."

* * *

With the exception of periodic bathroom visits by several of the homeless, the hours of Schmitt's restlessness had passed undisturbed by any of the residents. At two-thirty, he sat up and swung his feet to the floor. His neighbor remained asleep along with the rest of the dormitory. Schmitt slipped into the hallway and turned toward the building's double front doors.

The next challenge was the guard station halfway down. As he approached the room, he could see the partially opened door. He listened and heard a light snore. Gliding past, he reached the front doors.

He examined the security bar. To open the door, he needed to press down. The release, wired to a security system, would activate the alarm. He hesitated, but realizing he had no choice, he pushed down. Silence.

* * *

Hearing footsteps nearing the door made Rizzo's neck hair stiffen. He moved quickly through Otto's darkened living room and into the bedroom. He pressed his shoulder to the wall on one side of the doorway and listened. Jabba had not given him a warning call. He wondered what happened.

A key slid into the door lock. Its metallic resonance had the effect of a rifle bolt sliding into position. A long stretch of silence. Rizzo's throat tightened. He strained to hear the snap of the lock. The silence continued. Had something spooked the Stasi? He took a firmer grip on the .38. and peered around the door edge.

The apartment door flew open. Werner Schmitt's outline filled the space, backlit by the hallway's overhead light fixtures. His weapon gripped with both hands, he held it at chest level prepared to fire.

"I got your back, mon." The voice came from Jabba's doorway.

Schmitt spun and fired at Jabba. The bullet skimmed the hallway wall before it found the exposed Jabba. The Rasta fell forward to the floor with a loud thump.

"Police. Freeze, motherfucker!" Rizzo yelled before he dove behind the sofa.

Schmitt turned and got off two more shots into the darkened apartment. Both bullets disappeared into the wall behind Rizzo. Schmitt broke for the front door, but stopped in front of Jabba's fallen body. Going down to his knees, he placed the gun at the base of the Rasta's skull and called out to Rizzo. "Your friend is breathing. Don't be foolish unless you would like to see him die right now."

Rizzo crawled across the floor to the side of the door and sneaked a look into the hallway. He made out the two figures, Jabba face down, and Schmitt crouching to the side of the Rasta's big body.

Rizzo brought up his .38 with both hands and pushed the gun out in front of his face. He took aim at Schmitt but Jabba's big frame was in his sightline. With his chest pressed against the floor, Rizzo found it difficult to breathe normally. His extended arms began to cramp. No way could he take the shot and risk hitting Jabba.

"Leave him now," Rizzo shouted. "I'll let you go."

He waited for Schmitt's reply. The only sound he heard was Jabba releasing a loud moan.

"I will kill him if you don't do as I say."

Rizzo raised his chin from the floor.

"Leave now. I'll wait ten minutes before I call for help." He heard the pleading tone in his voice and hated it.

"Yes, exactly, but not before you bring out my suitcase. I do not leave without it."

"Where is it?" Rizzo asked, hoping the question appeared innocent. The bag was on the bed where he had left it two days ago.

Schmitt sounded anxious. He needed the passport locked away in Rizzo's office safe. The suitcase would be a harmless tradeoff for Jabba's life.

"In the bedroom. Get it now."

Rizzo rolled onto his side and stood. He felt his way through the dark to the bedroom and found the case on the bed. He closed the lid and hurried back. Standing to one side, he called out, "I have it."

"Good. Now, one more thing," Schmitt announced. "Place your weapon inside."

The demand was a kick to his stomach. Why didn't he expect that? He remembered he hadn't fired back at Schmitt. Maybe he could convince the Stasi he was unarmed.

"I don't have a gun," he yelled.

"You are lying. You are police. Put your weapon inside the case. Push it out into the hallway and close the door. Do it or you will lose your friend."

The son-of-a-bitch. If he did that, they'd both be dead. Frantic, Rizzo looked around the room and spotted the pair of bookends on the table to the side of the door—seated monkeys dressed in Moroccan attire wearing a fez, each with a book in his lap. In the dim light, maybe one of them could pass for a gun. He would try it.

Staying back out of view, Rizzo slid the reopened suitcase into the doorway. He held out one of the bookends, gripping the object as he would a weapon.

"Here's my Colt .45. I'm putting it in the bag."

Before he could close the case, the wail of sirens announced the arrival of police cruisers.

Schmitt turned to the foot of the stairs. He looked back at the downed Rastafarian and raised his weapon.

Rizzo jumped to his feet. "Hold your fire, or I'll blow your fucking head off."

Schmitt pulled back his arm and, throwing a quick glance toward Rizzo, raced up the stairs.

Rizzo bounded after him, taking the steps two at a time. He reached the mid-landing of the first flight and stopped at the top step before he took the turn. Catching his breath, he pressed against the wall, listening to the silence. He hadn't heard Schmitt climbing to the third level yet. He pictured him at the top of the stairs waiting for him to move around the landing, into the clear.

Rizzo grew impatient. Schmitt hadn't made a sound. He inched forward, and before his foot reached the first step, Schmitt fired. Several shots pinged off the marble-tile wall above Rizzo's head. A shower of dust landed in his hair as he went to his knees. He leaned around the banister corner, pointing his .38 up the stairs at an unseen Schmitt. He could hear the man's rapid steps as he took off for the third floor.

* * *

Jabba managed to lift his chest inches off the floor. His eyes were open. When he turned his head away from the wall, he found himself staring at the shoes of a uniformed police officer.

"Central, I got one down, possible gun shot," he heard the officer yell into his radio.

"I'm okay, mon. My shoulder…caught one there, but I'm okay." Jabba struggled onto his back and looked up.

"Who are you? What's your name?" the officer asked.

"Jabai Saint James. I live here. This apartment," Jabba nodded toward his opened doorway. He strained to get the words out. His breathing came in quick gulps. "Fucker you want up those stairs."

Two more uniforms showed up in the hallway, guns drawn. "Whadda we got?" the one wearing sergeant stripes asked.

"This one's been hit. Says he lives here. Says the shooter went up the stairs."

"Call for a bus and additional units, Hank. Stay with him until EMS gets here. Luis, you're with me. Let's go up."

Before the officers could move toward the stairway and start up, Jabba screamed, "Wait!"

The three officers froze, looked down at the Rastafarian and then at each other.

"There's a P.I. chasing this fucker…up those stairs." Jabba closed his eyes, feeling a sudden rush of pain to his shoulder.

He sucked in a supply of air like a diver about to knife through the water. "Shooter's a killer you guys been lookin' for. Don't hit the damn P.I. by mistake."

"What's the P.I.'s name?" the sergeant asked.

"Rizzo."

"Luke Rizzo?"

"Yeah. That's him."

"Hank, get EMS on the double." Motioning toward the staircase with his 9 mm Glock, he said, "Okay, Luis, let's go."

"He's a good guy," Jabba whispered before he passed out.

* * *

Condon rolled over to check out the lighted face of the clock on the bedstand. His wife sat up looking dazed. Three-twelve was an ungodly hour for Fields to call, but it had happened before, though he couldn't remember when and why. "Yeah, Jack, I'm awake."

"The Bushwick Eighty-third Precinct just got bombarded with calls reporting gunfire at that Rastafarian's apartment house. Ten minutes ago. My gut tells me that SOB, Schmitt, is involved. How fast can you get there?"

"Five minutes to dress and maybe twenty minutes to make the trip."

"Forest Hills isn't that far away, and at this time in the morning, you shouldn't hit any traffic. It'll take me longer from Manhattan. Get there as soon as you can. There'll be plenty of backup from the local police. They're already in position."

* * *

Rizzo reached the second floor, crouched at the top step and peered down the hallway. He could only imagine what the occupants of the building were thinking as they huddled within their small apartments, frightened by the sound of gunfire. He prayed no one would be foolish enough to open a door.

He moved to the foot of the stairs leading to the third level and listened. The quick steps he heard from above had a metallic ring. Schmitt had ascended the iron staircase leading to the roof doorway.

Rizzo mounted the stairs, sliding crouched along the wall, out of view. Schmitt had yet to exit onto the roof. The man would need to push the release bar, and Rizzo would hear the door opening. He was sure Schmitt waited at the top, hoping to take another shot at him.

Rizzo knew the Stasi had nowhere to go once he went through the door. After that, the pursuit became a standoff—unless Schmitt could fly. Rizzo would be an easy target if he followed.

Hurried footsteps pounded the stairs below, followed by a breathless warning cry. "Rizzo, Rizzo, NYPD. Back off, dammit. We've got this."

Hearing the shout, Schmitt hurtled himself through the roof door and out onto the tarred surface. Rizzo stood and darted toward the metal staircase, taking the ten steps in five jumps. He reached the door just before it closed. Holding it for a moment with his free hand, he pushed back all the way as he dropped down to his knees. Schmitt had dashed across the roof, dodging air vents, pipes and clotheslines. He was heading toward the rear, to the ladder leading to the fire escape at the third floor. Before reaching the edge, Schmitt whirled. He fired at the approaching Rizzo. The shot went wide. Rizzo raised his .38 and squatted into a shooting position, keeping a low target.

"Get the fuck out of the way. We got him."

The voice reached Rizzo before he could pull the trigger. He lowered his arm and moved to the side of the roof. The two police officers sprinted past.

Before they could get close, Schmitt turned and raced toward the side of the roof that paralleled the next building. He reached the edge at full speed. Without breaking stride, he leaped. His lead-leg foot landed on the top of the low cement ledge. His second leg thrust forward like an Olympic athlete in the long jump. He flew outward, his arms wildly flailing the air. The six-foot distance between roofs might well have been miles.

Schmitt's toes scraped the side of the opposite building just below the roof ledge. His momentum carried his chest and head forward, pounding them into the side of the structure. He bounced off the house like a pinball and landed among the rubble in the alleyway three stories below.

Rizzo had moved to that side of the building after the police called him off and watched Schmitt's mad sprint and leap, witnessing the Stasi's fatal plunge from a front-row seat.

He slid to the tarred surface of the roof, leaned back against the ledge and closed his eyes.

The events of the past two weeks worked their way through his mind like scenes from a bad dream. Every murder, every narrow escape amazed him—how the Stasi, a man well beyond his professional prime, became a lethal threat, a destroyer of innocent lives, all under the noses of those pursuing him. The final chapter of Schmitt's life came none too soon.

"You son-of-a-bitch, Rizzo, what the hell you doing chasing killers? You're supposed to be finding deadbeat husbands who owe alimony."

He looked up at the approaching officer, puzzled, until Sergeant Jimmy Burke pushed up into his face.

"Jesus, Burke. You at the eighty-third now?"

Burke reached down and took Rizzo's proffered hand. "Yeah, a promotion from the South Bronx. After you left for your cushy private-eye life, it wasn't fun anymore."

Burke's radio interrupted. "Sarge, two Feds down here. You need to speak to them."

"Right. Tell them to wait."

Rizzo stood and grabbed Burke's arm. "Listen, Jimmy. I'm not here. Cover for me or they'll have my ass."

"Huh? What's that supposed to mean?"

"I was ordered to stop chasing this guy," Rizzo said, nodding his head toward the edge of the roof. "I'm in deep shit if the Feds find out I didn't listen."

"Rizzo, you still trying to save the world alone?" Burke smiled like a lottery winner. "Okay, pal, but you're gonna owe me big time. Stay here. I'll get rid of them. One of my guys'll be back up when the coast is clear."

"Oh, and the Rasta who got shot?"

"Alive," Burke said. "Called EMS. Should be over at Wyckoff Hospital by now."

"Jimmy, some way to get word to him before the Feds get there, that I wasn't here? Just your squad. Okay?"

"You gettin' pushy, but I'll take care of it with the officer taking his deposition."

"Thanks, Jimmy." Rizzo looked down over the edge of the roof. Turning back, he added, "Almost a nice collar. Should get you back to the lovely South Bronx. Ya think?"

Burke released a loud guffaw and headed toward the doorway. "Later, hot shot. You can explain what went down here when you buy me dinner at The Palm."

"You got it, pal."

Burke and his partner disappeared through the door. Rizzo walked to the building's front side and looked down on Harman Street. Flashing white and red strobes from four police cruisers lit the area and the alleyway between the buildings. Rizzo could see sleepy faces gawking out of nearby apartment windows, occupants all-to-familiar with the sight of a police action in progress.

They had cordoned off the street to local traffic. Rizzo spotted the two Feds' cars double-parked at the front entrance. The call from the eighty-third probably roused Fields and Condon out of their beds. They had arrived from their homes separately. He hoped they wouldn't be there long.

The early morning chill sent him shivering. He was grateful his Army jacket was lined. Exhausted, he looked around for a place to sit. He found none that offered some comfort. Instead, he walked to one side of the roof doorway, put his back against the structure and slowly slid to the surface. Facing east, at least he could watch the sunrise if his wait became a long one.

Rizzo brought his knees up and hugged himself, closing his eyes to rest. A moment later, he popped them open when a thought jumped out at him. Something Jabba said.

That Otto Buchmann told him Werner Schmitt had been born in this Bushwick apartment house. A smile crept across his face. Born here…died here. How's that for irony?

* * *

Rizzo checked his watch as he walked from the elevator to the nurses' station in the middle of the floor. It was a few minutes past seven. Flashing his shield, he said to the nurse behind the counter, "Jabba Saint James, which room?"

She looked down at her monitor. "I don't think the doctor has approved visitors yet."

"It's okay. Only be a few minutes. I need to get some names. Be out of the way fast."

The nurse hesitated, but when Rizzo showered her with his Dean Martin smile, she said, "Three thirty-one, last room on the right. He's heavily sedated, probably asleep."

"Thanks, won't be long."

It was a single room so he wouldn't be overheard. The Rasta had his eyelids shut tight, and his broad chest heaved slowly and rhythmically. The intravenous drip hung at the head of the bed and fed steadily through the tube attached to his forearm.

Rizzo pushed a chair close to the bed and sat down. He looked into the face of the man who had taken a bullet trying to help him, and fought back tears. Reaching over to cradle Jabba's hand, he noticed the scrape on his flat nose. Rizzo guessed he must have done it when he hit the floor face down. He wished he could speak with the attending doctor to get the lowdown on Jabba's condition. He would be certain to do that on a return visit. Right now, he needed to get out of Brooklyn before someone ID'ed him.

Jabba's lids fluttered open as though sensing someone's presence. "That you, mon?"

"Hey, yeah, my brother. How you doin'?"

An easy smile played at the corners of Jabba's mouth. "We get the motha?"

"He got himself. Tried to fly like a Jamaican Booby bird."

"That good?"

"Better than good."

The Rasta's eyes fluttered again and then closed. Rizzo stood and pushed his chair away. "Listen, bro. I want you to know I'm here for you...now and in the future. You get some sleep. I'll be back to check on you real soon."

"Okay, mon," Jabba said in a broken whisper.

Chapter 29

"I made the call yesterday afternoon," Fields said. "She sounded genuinely surprised when I told her what happened." Fields pointed to Condon's end of the booth. "Pass me the ketchup, will you?"

Condon put down his sandwich and wiped his chin with a napkin. "Rizzo hadn't told her yet?" he said, sliding the Heinz Big Mouth bottle towards Fields.

"Appears that way."

Condon regarded Fields with amused uncertainty. "Do you think he doesn't know?"

Fields doused his chopped steak with the red condiment, did an overkill with the pepper mill and looked up. Smiling, he said, "Not for a fucking moment."

"Me neither, although I'd like to believe he listened to my warning."

Fields eyed his partner with skepticism. "He knows. We can't prove it, but he knows. The bastard was there when it happened."

"Not according to the report by the responding officers."

"Fiction...pure NYPD fiction."

"Why do you say that?"

"First off, the door to Buchmann's apartment was open. Second, how do you account for the slugs they removed from the wall in the apartment? They were from Schmitt's Beretta. They found the gun in the alleyway next to his body. Who was he shooting at? The old German? He was still in the hospital." Fields raised a fork full of mashed potatoes to his mouth.

Condon waited until Fields finished swallowing.

"And why was Schmitt's suitcase in the doorway to the apartment?"

"That's the reason he went back there," Condon suggested.

"Exactly. He needed it. He'd sewn his fucking phony passport into the bag's lining, for Christ's sake." Fields gulped down the remainder of his coffee and looked at Condon with an indignant expression. "I'll give you odds Rizzo knew about that."

Condon agreed with a nod. "I can't figure how the hell that bookend got into the suitcase. They checked it out. Nothing. Just a bookend."

Fields chortled. "I can't even guess. We're going to remain in the dark about that unless Rizzo decides to tell us."

"You let that captain know…the one in New Brighton?"

"Did that yesterday. Said he'd fill in the Bard family."

The agents finished eating. Condon motioned to the passing waiter and laid a credit card on the table.

"I got this," Fields said. "You bought yesterday."

Condon slid the card back into his wallet without comment.

Fields handed his card to the waiter. "I understand the old man is out of the hospital. Back in his apartment."

"Should I visit him, see how much he knows?"

"At this point, to what end?"

Fields was eager to close the book on Werner Schmitt. Condon didn't push the issue. "And the Jamaican? How'd he make out?"

"Not too serious. The bullet glanced off the wall before hitting his shoulder area. Never penetrated any major blood vessels, although it did nick his lung. They're keeping him a few days to make sure it doesn't collapse. Could have been a lot worse."

"Yeah, like dead. He could have been number six. Lucky for him Schmitt couldn't shoot straight."

The waiter returned with his receipt and Fields signed it. He looked over at Condon. "Ready?"

During their stroll back to Federal Plaza, Condon asked, "Do you think Rizzo would have made a good agent with the Bureau?" The question brought his partner up short.

Fields answered with a tinge of exasperation. "Rizzo was a good cop. A good detective too. However, I don't think his M.O. would go over very well with Karl. What do you think?"

"He's a tenacious son-of-a-bitch, I'll give him that. No, he wouldn't last long with the Bureau. Too bad, though."

Fields chuckled. "Get that look off your face."

* * *

The phone rang several times before Rizzo could unlock the door. By the time he got to his desk, whoever called had become impatient and hung up. Caller ID listed Amy Chatsworth's number in London. He set down the container of coffee and checked his watch. London time was early afternoon. He reached down for the small stack of mail on the desk and fanned through the envelopes, eyeing each one with little interest. Included were the latest utility bill, a direct mail solicitation from an alarm company, his current bank statement and this month's credit card bill from American Express. That one concerned him.

The return address on the final envelope in his hand leaped out at him. His former client was double-teaming with telephone and written communication. He sat at his desk and tore open the envelope. It contained a short handwritten note and a check.

Dear Luke: I received a phone call a few days ago from FBI Agent Jack Fields. He reported that Werner Schmitt had died attempting to escape capture by the New York City

Police Department. Seems he fell from the roof of a building in Brooklyn while being pursued. Jack was short on detail; however, reading between the lines, I could sense he held the opinion that you were somehow involved. My dear Luke, if you were not, I would be the most shocked person on the face of the earth. My dividend, you said that morning at breakfast. I am eternally grateful to you and your efforts, despite ignoring my warning to leave it to the federal authorities. You are truly my Sir Lancelot.

I received your invoice for ten days of security service billed at seven hundred and fifty dollars per day. For some reason you failed to include your out-of-pocket expenses. I took the liberty of increasing the amount shown on the invoice (with Avery's concurrence) as an expression of my heartfelt appreciation for your performance, risk-taking on my behalf, and kind treatment of this damsel in distress during the most trying day of my life. Please stay safe and in touch.

Amy.

The check had fallen face down on the desk. Rizzo pinched it with two fingers and flipped it over. His eyes widened as he examined the amount scripted in Amy's hand. He was certain she had made an error until he caught the five digits in the check's right hand corner. He took in a deep breath and leaned back in his chair, both palms gripping the padded arms as if to prevent him from toppling out. Amy had made out the check for twenty-five-thousand dollars.

Luke dialed her London number and waited.

"Hello, Luke."

"Amy. Sorry I missed your call."

"That's all right," she said. "I guessed it might be a bit too early to reach you at the office."

"No, I heard the phone. I was juggling a Starbucks and my key. I couldn't get the door opened fast enough. I meant to call you earlier this week and give you the news. I see Fields beat me to it."

"You received my note, did you?"

"And the check. Amy, have you lost your mind? You only overpaid me by a hundred and seventy-five percent."

"Some of that covers your expenses."

The matter-of-fact tone of her voice launched him into a fit of laughter. "Oh Lord, am I going to miss your dry English sense of humor."

"Well, if you call occasionally, I'll be happy to share it with you."

"I will. And thanks, Amy. Your generosity is exceeded only by your beauty."

"See, you are a sweet man. A sappy romantic, but a sweet man. Bye, Luke."

"Bye, Amy."

Rizzo leaned back and put his feet up on the desk. He glanced back at the twenty-five-thousand dollar check. He shook his head and puffed his cheeks each time he opened and closed his eyes. The largest payday of his life had him feeling lightheaded. He'd share some of this windfall with the Rasta. Several seconds later, the giddy feeling faded. He sat up and reached for the phone.

He hoped Matt would answer, but instead his ex-wife picked up.

"Terri, hi. How are you?" He felt his throat constricting. He hadn't spoken with the woman since that day in divorce court.

"Fine, Luke. You doing okay?" Terri's voice was polite, not warm.

"Doin' great, thanks. Just finished a major job that kept me hopping for almost two weeks. Catching my breath, finally." He was certain his words sounded as if he was bragging. He was, and he didn't care. "Hey, I was thinking. If Matt has no plans tonight, I could meet him in the city. Have dinner with him, if it's okay with you. You know, maybe try to repair our father-son relationship a little."

Terri paused before answering. Rizzo suspected she would give him a hard time. Instead, her reply was surprisingly agreeable. "That sounds like a terrific idea. He's not here right now. Down at the Y playing basketball this morning. He'll be back at noon. Let me have him call you on your cell. I'm sure he'll want to do it."

* * *

He had selected Patsy's, an Italian restaurant in Manhattan's Murray Hill section that specialized in brick-oven pizza — Matt's favorite. In the past, they would come here for dinner before taking in a Ranger game at the Garden.

Rizzo waited in front of the restaurant. When he spotted Matt crossing Third Avenue, walking with the confidence of someone who knew his way around, Rizzo's heartbeat quickened. Matt reached him, and they hugged without speaking.

Once the host had them seated, Rizzo asked, "How was the subway ride?" No response. Matt had fixed his attention on the large open brick ovens in the rear, watching the white-aproned chefs moving about like animated puppets, inspecting or removing their baked creations.

"Matt?"

"Huh." He looked up. "Oh, sorry, Dad. I did okay. Messed up a little when I came up at Grand Central, but I figured it out."

In the past, when they would come to this restaurant, Rizzo would travel with him on the subway ride into Manhattan from Queens. Today, for the first time, Matt made the trip alone. At fifteen, Matt was more than capable of navigating the city and the subway system without his help.

Matt wore a Jets sweatshirt under his lined ski jacket. His dark, thick hair, combed back behind his ears, almost reached his collar. Rizzo observed a thin trace of facial hair under his nose, not heavy enough to require shaving, but soon. When he spoke, his deep, robust voice no longer sounded like that of a teenager. He was growing up fast.

Rizzo took the hard cover menu from the young server and set it down in front of him. Matt opened his to the tri-fold interior, and studied each panel of listed entrées as though he were looking for something other than pizza. Patsy's offered a wide assortment of tasty Italian fare, but Rizzo knew his son would select a large mushroom and sausage pizza.

"Hey, Matt, take off your jacket. You'll be more comfortable."

Matt raised his eyes. "In a minute."

"What did you think about the Series?"

Matt replied without moving his head. "Mets shouldda won. I hate the Yankees."

Rizzo laughed. "Games were close, even if it didn't go past five. Their relievers were too tough. Won the Series for them, especially that Mariano Rivera."

Matt stood, removed his jacket and hung it over the back of his chair. He sat down and continued his scrutiny of the menu.

Rizzo changed the subject. "My last assignment, you know where it took me? Beaver Falls, Pennsylvania, Joe Namath's hometown."

Matt's chin shot up. "Was he there?"

"God, no. Left years ago when he went to college. But a man I met there had seen Joe play football in high school."

"Really? I read he was a star even then."

"That's what Frank Bard told me."

The voice of the server interrupted. Standing at the table's edge, she asked, "Are you ready to order?"

Rizzo smiled. "I think so. Matt, the usual?"

Matt folded his menu and handed it to the server. "Think I'll have—"

Rizzo waited, watching his son's studied expression. Was Matt going to surprise him by ordering something other than pizza?

After seconds of indecision, Matt squeezed out a stream of air from between his lips. "...a large mushroom and sausage pizza, and a cherry Coke, please."

Rizzo grinned. Nothing's changed. "I'll have the same," he told her, "but make mine a medium. And a regular Coke for me."

The server departed with their order. Rizzo looked around. The popular eatery was filling up fast. He remembered the last time he and Matt were here, close to two years ago. They stopped at the restaurant for an early dinner before taking in a Ranger game. Matt had just entered his first year of high school and was anxiously looking forward to trying out for their freshman baseball squad. He made the team that first year and had a strong season. Now he was hoping to earn a spot on the varsity this spring.

"How are things at home?" Rizzo asked with a slight hesitation. He hoped Terri had moved beyond badmouthing him to Matt.

"Okay...I guess. Mom's working full time, and me being in school, I don't see her that much."

"You keeping up your grades?"

"Oh yeah. I have to if I want to play varsity ball. They're pretty strict about that."

"That's good. You might have a shot at a scholarship to some college...like Fordham. They have one of the best baseball programs in the city."

"Man, that would be great." Matt's voice became animated. "You think—?"

"You never know. Keep your nose in the books. No letting up. "

Rizzo remained silent for a while, awaiting the delivery of their order. He saw Matt looking at him with curiosity. The next moment, Matt revealed what was bothering him.

"Hey, Dad, how come you ordered a Coke just now? Didn't you used to always have a couple of Buds?"

Rizzo had forgotten to tell him about joining AA, that it had been over a year since taking the pledge. Coming through these past two weeks, with all the tension and anger, without being tempted was proof enough he'd made the crossing. Time to share it.

"Don't drink anymore...alcohol, that is. Joined AA over a year ago. Haven't touched a drop since." He studied his son's face for a reaction. A smile formed. He took Matt's hand. "It screwed up our lives once, didn't it? I won't let it happen again."

Matt stared at him. Tears appeared in his eyes, and his face flushed. He stood, came to Rizzo's side of the table and wrapped his arms around his father's shoulders. He pressed his lips to Rizzo's cheek and kissed him with a surprising ferocity. When he pulled away, he whispered "God, Dad, I missed you."

"I missed you, too, Matt. Let's not ever go back."

* * *

Sunday afternoon, the American Airlines terminal at LaGuardia Airport was experiencing its usual busy time with arriving and departing travelers. The lighted board indicated Flo's flight had arrived from Pittsburgh ten minutes ago. Gate six.

When he spotted Flo among the crowd passing the security checkpoints, Rizzo hoisted a placard over his head. He had lettered the card's message with a thick, black Sharpie. *Looking for my Avis Angel.*

As Flo neared him, she caught sight of the card. He watched her face light up. The butterflies in his stomach made him feel like a kid on his first date.

With a rolling carry-on behind her, she took small, quick steps until she stopped in front of him, released the handle, eyed the card, and raised her arms. "Darlin', I'm here."

Her kiss was slow and passion-filled — an instant reminder of how much he had enjoyed this part of their lovemaking.

Someone's rolling suitcase creased the back of his heel. He looked around and realized they were blocking the path of other arrivals. Rizzo pulled back and looked into her sweet southern eyes. "We should move before I devour you right here."

"Now that would be embarrassing," she said, and released her embrace.

"Flight okay?" he asked, leading her out the terminal door.

"Smooth. Right on time, departure and arrival."

They crossed the footbridge to the parking garage. "I have a few places lined up not too far from here. One in Bayside and two others in Forest Hills."

"Are we going there now?"

With a glint in his eyes and a smile turned up at both ends of his mouth, he said, "No. We'll check them out tomorrow. Today, we check out each other."

Walking through the garage, Rizzo kept peeking at Flo's profile as though he wanted to be certain he had the right woman. She bounced with a confident step, giving off an aura of excitement. Was he projecting his own feelings? He was prepared to accept both possibilities.

Rizzo tossed her carry-on onto the back seat of the rental car. Before backing out of the parking spot, he leaned over and kissed her cheek. "I apologize," he said. "I rented this from Hertz. Their garage is down the street from my office."

Flo giggled. "Traitor."

—End—

We hope you have enjoyed Howard Giordano's novel, *The Second Target*. If you have not had the chance to read his first thriller, *Tracking Terror*, it is available through

www.bluewaterpress.com/target

as well as other online bookstore retailers.